THIS SIDE OF DARK

Evil is darkest in the shadows.

THIS SIDE of DARK

CAREN HAHN

This Side of Dark by Caren Hahn

Published by Seventy-Second Press

www.carenhahn.com

Hardcover ISBN-13: 978-1-958609-07-1

Paperback ISBN-13: 978-1-958609-06-4

Cover design by Andrew Hahn.

Cover image from Deposit Photos.

Edited by Polished Copy Editing Service.

Printed in the USA

For Christina, a true light in the dark.

BOOKS BY CAREN HAHN

Find all of Caren Hahn's work on Amazon.com

CONTEMPORARY SUSPENSE:

This Side of Dark

What Comes After

THE OWL CREEK SERIES

Smoke over Owl Creek

Hunt at Owl Creek

ROMANTIC FANTASY:

THE WALLKEEPER TRILOGY

Burden of Power

Pain of Betrayal

Gleam of Crown

THE HATCHED TRILOGY

Hatched: Dragon Farmer

Hatched: Dragon Defender

Hatched: Dragon Speaker

Visit carenhahn.com to receive a free copy of *Charmed: Tales from Quarantine and Other Short Fiction*.

TREATMENT OF SENSITIVE TOPICS

While I aim to tell stories which can be enjoyed by a wide audience, *This Side of Dark* contains sensitive topics that may be unsettling for some. Compared to mainstream portrayals, *This Side of Dark* is low on graphic description and high on emotional resonance, but out of respect for any readers who may have experienced similar trauma in their lives, you may find a low-spoiler list of some of the more triggering subjects on my website at https://carenhahn.com/books/dark-trigger-warnings. (See QR code below for a quick link).

As an author, I've attempted to treat these subjects sensitively, compassionately, and without gratuitous indulgence. But only you as a reader can determine if you wish to join me on this journey.

THIS SIDE OF DARK

CAREN HAHN

DECEMBER 14

FRIDAY

1 DAY AFTER DISAPPEARANCE

GRACE

THE GRAVEL PILE looms in the dark like a living thing.

Watching.

Waiting.

Grace's hands tighten on the wheel as she pulls her car into the parking lot of the First Hope Church, the headlights swiping over the pile. Evan said the gravel had been dumped over the summer and was waiting to be spread until Deacon Thomas's cousin could borrow a bobcat from work. But it's December now and still the gravel crowds out the back end of the parking lot where dirt encroaches on grass and grass gives way to the pine needles and ferns of the thick rainforest understory.

Grace parks near the entrance to the church and shuts off her headlights. She tells herself she's waiting for her eyes to adjust, but the truth is, she doesn't like the dark.

Leaving the safety of her car gives her the same stomach-squeezing feeling she felt as a teenager when swimming with friends in a local lake in Northern California. The deep water was so dark that sunlight broke into separate rays and disappeared a few yards beneath the surface. The feeling of her legs dangling above all that darkness made her heart race, and she sought the safety of the boat, refusing to join her friends splashing in the water.

Looking toward the woods bordering the church property gives her that same feeling now, like something unknown lurks just out of reach, something that can see her even though she can't see it.

Grace doesn't like to be alone at the church, yet here she is again, no more than eight hours since she left. The building itself is relatively uninspiring. It sits as a squat rectangle in seventies-era brick that gives way to thin windows in amber-colored glass on either side of a large white cross. The structure's one ambition is a steeply-pitched roof over the sanctuary creating a high vaulted ceiling in the worship space.

Grace reaches for her purse and steps out of the car, pulling her coat tighter against the chilly mist drifting in from the ocean. She resists looking back at the gravel pile as she hurries to the front door. A breeze lifts the ends of her hair and works its way under her scarf to the bare skin of her neck.

The scarf was a gift from River. She recently took up knitting, and Grace was the lucky recipient of the first project River deemed worth sharing.

"I know how you like the blue-greys," she said hesitantly, but with a gleam in her golden brown eyes that told Grace giving the gift meant as much as it did for Grace to receive it.

Grace didn't know what to say. The tissue paper rasped like dry leaves under her fingers as she pulled it out of the gift bag, revealing the bundle of soft knitting that offered itself to her touch like a cat seeking affection.

"Don't think this act of domesticity gets you off the hook. I'm still counting the days until you come back to Jiu-Jitsu class."

River smirked. "You know I'll kick your butt as soon as I lose this baby weight."

"I'm counting on it."

Now Grace burrows her chin deeper in the scarf as she unlocks the door. The key Evan gave her is always a bit tetchy, and it takes two tries to turn. When it surrenders at last, Grace pulls the door open and is greeted with the cool dry air of worship. It still smells faintly of the new industrial carpet that was recently installed and decades of potluck dinners, funeral luncheons, and holiday pie socials.

Grace bypasses the light switch. Being alone with the lights on makes her feel like she's in a fishbowl. Anyone could be watching outside and she would never know.

She doesn't attend First Hope Church as a congregant, but she's seen it radiating light and joy and warmth when full of a community worshipping together. Now, in the early hours of the morning with dawn still more than an hour away, it's far too empty and restless.

She slips through the heavy double doors into the sanctuary. Only then, safely away from windows, does she turn on the lights.

Immediately, the tension in her stomach eases. Though the church doesn't look like much from the outside, the sanctuary is where the people of Ellis Cove really show their devotion. New benches were installed with the recent remodel, featuring padded seats set against wood in a dark mahogany stain. The rostrum wall—though dating back to original construction and too geometric for Grace's taste—is hand-carved and matches the altar and pulpit as a complete set. Faux evergreen garland hangs in perfect symmetry along the low wall, softening its geometric lines.

Grace's eyes seek out the artificial tree she set up the previous night. In the drafty room, it looks small and insignificant, but she knows lights will brighten the space with holiday cheer. The PTO moms will be coming with another tree later today to place in the foyer, but Grace feels compelled to finish decorating this one herself.

The storage tote she left last night is still sitting where she left it. So commonplace, it takes her aback. It almost begs her to pretend that nothing out of the ordinary happened last night. But as she opens the lid and begins taking out red balls—shatterproof, a clever word for plastic—she can almost feel the crunch of the gravel beneath her feet. Hear the sound of footsteps that aren't her own.

This won't do.

Grace reaches for her earbuds and selects some calming music on her phone. Not Christmas music. Not when every working day is filled with teaching festive tunes to elementary school children. For now, she turns on a collection of new age mood music to help her relax and get her mind off thoughts of last night.

The decorations go quickly. Red balls sprinkled with glitter. White angels with feathers as soft as baby's breath. Crosses tipped with gold sequins. It's all a bit garish up close, but when Grace steps back and surveys her work, the effect is lovely.

When her fingers brush something sharp, she yanks her hand back as if she's been bitten. The star tree topper is made of metal painted white and gold. She pulls it out and thoughtfully examines the detailed grooves and stamped design that won't even be visible once it tops the tree.

Something makes her turn, she isn't sure what. Did she hear a noise under the strains of *Book of Days*? When the door cracks open at the end of the hall, for a brief second all she sees is darkness. Someone is waiting in the shadows, watching her.

Her pulse calms as Evan steps into the room, his smile brilliant against his rich brown skin.

"I thought I saw lights on," he says. "Should have guessed it was you. Anything I can do to help?"

Grace drops the star back into the tote. She hasn't yet used her voice that morning and it comes out scratchy and weak. She clears her throat and starts again.

"I'm about finished up, but thanks. I wanted to wrap up a few things before school this morning."

"It's looking real nice," he says, his eyes following the lines of the garland.

"Thanks. The PTO will be in today to work on the foyer. I told them no Santas," Grace says before he can ask.

"I appreciate it." When Evan smiles, a single dimple on his chin is just visible under his close beard. His puffy jacket is unzipped over a simple button shirt and jeans. He's taller than Grace and seems taller still with his hair abounding in tight coils. Cut close on the sides, the style is an appealing mixture of both the restrained and the unruly that Grace finds irresistible.

Grace remembers the pastor where she attended church as a little girl dressing the part even on weekdays. But Evan prefers a casual style that Grace likes. It fits his temperament and makes him seem ready to pick up a game of football on the church lawn as quickly as he'd hold someone's hand through a faith crisis.

Her cheeks warm thinking about last night. What might have happened if he hadn't answered his phone?

"How did things go last night? After you left," she amends, in case he's thinking of the moments before the phone call.

He shifts his insulated tumbler to his other hand. "All right. Crisis averted. Hearts healed. World saved."

"Typical."

"Well, I don't want to brag..." His dark eyes are bright with humor. "Sorry I had to abandon you. I hope you weren't here too late. I looked for your car when I came back, but you'd already gone."

Grace feels a twist in her chest. He came back to check on her? What if... "I left a little after you did." She stifles a yawn.

"Hey, do you know where Diana went after decorating yesterday?"

Grace looks at him sharply. "No, why?"

"Nora called early this morning. She said Diana didn't come home last night and wondered if I knew where she was. She sounded pretty worried."

Grace's morning coffee churns unpleasantly in her stomach. "If she were really worried about Diana, she would have kicked Leo out years ago."

"He's...probably not the best father figure those kids could have. But I'm not sure Nora was doing that much better on her own. And he even comes to church with them sometimes."

"Have they checked with Diana's friends?"

"I don't know. Nora said she wasn't home by the time she got home from work last night. You don't know if Diana had plans to go anywhere else?"

"Not that she mentioned. But I wouldn't expect her to tell me if she did."

"Hopefully it's nothing and she just spent the night at a friend's house."

"Hopefully." But the change in conversation casts a pall over the room and Grace reaches for her bag. "Well, I'd better head in to work."

"We're still on for tonight right?"

Right. Grace forces a smile. "Of course. I'm looking forward to it."

She senses Evan's eyes on her and wonders what he sees. She hasn't slept, not really. But she tended to her appearance as best she could, trying to disguise the fact that her eyes burn with grit and she feels like she's moving through molasses.

It doesn't matter how she feels. Today is Friday and she's facing hour after hour of elementary students ramped up with excitement for the weekend.

It's going to be a long day.

RIVER

THE CUSHION MAKES a soft sigh as River sits. It was thoughtful of Grace to bring in her padded piano bench from home. River's tailbone will still ache before the day is over, but the cushion delays the inevitable for a while.

Her belly bulges and the baby kicks softly as she settles into place. She loves that feeling, even when it's sometimes hard to breathe. He's a strong one, and growing right on schedule. Who would have thought River could create something so wonderful and...normal?

Such a relief, even when he pushes so hard against her ribs that she can see his foot sticking out. She pushes gently against it until he moves again, bringing a roller-coaster feeling as her insides shift. She doesn't know if the baby is a boy or not—she and Todd have decided to keep it a surprise—but she's been writing down the heartbeat at every doctor's appointment and it usually falls in the male range.

"How are you feeling today?" Grace asks as she enters the classroom, her gray-blue eyes taking in River's baggy sweatshirt and mussed hair. Dark circles shadow Grace's lower lids like she had a rough night too.

River shrugs. People never really expect you to answer honestly. They just want you to say something polite and move on. Not Grace. She knows too much and won't be put off by a shrug.

But River doesn't want to talk about it. It's only five minutes before the fourth graders are due in Grace's classroom.

"I'm feeling better than yesterday. Sorry I couldn't be there to help decorate the church."

"It's all right, we managed."

"It looks good on you," River says, then begins warming up with a snappy *Rockin' Around the Christmas Tree.*

Grace hesitates.

"The scarf."

Grace's expression clears and she fingers the yarn. "Thanks. I have an in with the manufacturer. If you'd like, I'll introduce you. She's very elitist, though. Doesn't take commissions from just anyone."

River snorts a short laugh.

The unmistakable sound of two dozen pairs of sneakers and dress flats echoes from down the hall, announcing the first class of the day. Grace affects a cheery smile as the fourth grade aide ushers in the nine- and ten-year-olds.

River plays a jaunty rendition of *Jingle Bells* while the kids settle into their seats, pushing and shuffling to get near whoever is their favorite that day. When she finishes the final chord, the buzzing chatter doesn't stop.

"Boy, you all are in a mood today," Grace says, raising

her voice above theirs. "Do you have some extra Christmas excitement?"

"It's not that, Ms. Miller," one of the kids pipes up.

Connor, River thinks his name is, eyeing the boy in a brown striped sweater. She has a hard time learning their names from behind the piano.

Connor has pink spots in his cheeks as he delivers his news. "Danny Beck's sister ran away yesterday."

River's stomach surges with something ugly and cold.

Diana.

"Why do you say that?" Grace asks sharply.

"Everyone's saying so."

Grace's expression grows grim. Her eyes scan the room. "Where is Danny today? Is he absent?"

"Yes." Several voices answer together.

"Why do you think he's not here?"

The students shrug and look at each other. A girl with French braids tied off in peppermint-striped scrunchies raises her hand.

"I guess he's too worried about his sister to come to school today."

"Do you feel bad for him? Do you want to help?"

Most of the class nods. Some of the kids look at the floor.

"The best thing you can do to help is not spread rumors about Diana. I'm sure everyone is working hard to find her and we don't want to make their job harder by sharing made-up stories." Grace fingers the pendant hanging around her neck, winding the chain around her finger. She lets her words settle in the room, then moves to her music stand.

With a more gentle tone, she says, "Does anyone have

any favorite Christmas carols they'd like to sing before we work on our songs for the concert?"

River starts. Her mind was wandering to Diana. Kids aren't the most credible sources of information, but she wishes Grace had let them talk a little more. Unease snakes through her chest, making it harder to breathe. She reaches for a songbook of carols and her hands tremble, turning the pages to find *Frosty, the Snowman*.

Poor Diana. She reminds River of an early spring crocus, daring to push herself out into the world where she is more likely to get stepped on than noticed. Diana loves to feel River's baby kicking. River doesn't let the other kids touch her belly. Their hands are so possessive, so demanding. But Diana had been so hopeful and hesitant, so afraid to do it wrong, and River saw herself in her eyes. So she placed Diana's hand on the hard spot stretching against her skin.

"You feel that?"

Diana's brown eyes shone. "Is that it?"

"Push on it and see."

Diana pushed gently and the baby rolled over, pulling away.

Diana laughed. "I felt it! I felt it move!"

Since then, Diana frequently stayed after choir rehearsal a few extra minutes to try and feel the baby. River recognized the aching need in the poor girl to be wanted. How could she say no?

After a couple of warm-up songs, the tension in the room ebbs a little and Grace moves on to the concert selections. The smoothness of the keys under River's fingers is soothing, helping to keep the anxiety at bay. Like rubbing a polished stone.

Learning to play the piano was a life saver for her. Grandma Billie had laughed in her nasty way when River asked for permission to take lessons from Mr. Holland after school. But she must have caught her in a good mood because Grandma Billie signed the form and from that moment, changed her life. River still doesn't understand why, but she is grateful for it every day.

She watches her hands moving over the keys, her long sleeves pulling back from her wrists. She wants to tug them back down, to cover the pale scars that indict her. Show her weakness. But she'll have to wait until the song ends.

Mr. Holland had seen the other scars too, the ones further up her arms. She hadn't liked his questions, and coming up with fresh lies kept her on edge around him. But it was worth it to be near the piano. It was like learning a foreign language, only far easier and more interesting than the German she took her sophomore and junior years of high school. She felt like she was learning to break a secret code. What was once foreign and indecipherable could be transformed from black marks on a page to an infinite variety of expression that carried her away. Mr. Holland said she had a gift. When she advanced enough to move on to the Romantics, she often felt transported in a way that let her get outside of her head and leave the pain behind.

Playing Christmas carols for singing fourth graders doesn't have the same effect, but she likes the bright voices and sentimental tunes. Sometimes it feels like something out of a movie, these children with their full stomachs and store-bought clothes celebrating tinsel and bells and all the trappings of the season. How can this be her life? She didn't do anything to earn it.

She takes a shuddering breath against the tightening in her chest, hearing Grandma Billie's voice in her head.

"You little slut. Your mother was the worst kind of whore, running off and leaving you like you're nothing but trash. You're going to grow up to be just like her. Worthless trash."

River's hands falter and she tries to refocus on the music. Why does Grandma Billie's voice seem so loud today? It's been getting more insistent lately, and now, with worry of Diana creeping into her mind, it's hard to hear anything else.

The fourth graders end with *In the Bleak Midwinter,* and Grace sighs appreciatively.

"Well done today, ladies and gentlemen. Enjoy your weekend and be kind to each other!"

Chairs knock against each other as the children tussle their way to the door.

"You spoil me," Grace says, coming to lean an elbow against the piano. "I forget to tell you what I need because you do such a good job anticipating before I ask."

River stands and stretches her back, feeling the increased circulation warm her legs. "What have you heard about Diana?"

Grace's expression of concern hardens into something else. Anger?

"Just that she didn't go home after decorating last night. Apparently the rumor mill can't wait to get started. Poor Danny."

"Poor Diana. At that age, I doubt she ran away."

Grace shivers. "Let's hope she turns up somewhere safe, then. I'm going to the break room to refill. You coming?"

"No, I'm trying to cut back for the baby."

Grace is almost to the door when River remembers. "Isn't tonight the big date?"

Grace looks slightly panicked but smiles through it, tucking a lock of hair behind her ears. "Not so loud. Yes, it's tonight."

River grins. "I called it. I saw the way he looked at you on Sunday. Are you going to start coming to our church then?"

"No! That would be weird."

"Nothing weird about it," River scoffs. "Even if you ignore the fact that he's hot and you're super into him, Evan's great at teaching. His sermons really make the Bible come alive."

"Yeah, I enjoyed his sermon on Sunday. But my mom went to Community Baptist. It reminds me of her, even if I do have to drive all the way to Coos Bay."

"I see." It's partly true. River accepts as an intellectual fact that lots of people have fond memories of their mothers, but she doesn't know what it actually feels like. "Well, if you change your mind, half of Ellis Cove goes to First Hope. You'd know a lot of people."

Grace wrinkles her nose. "Because I need my dating life to be more public than it already is?"

"You didn't really think people wouldn't talk after you sang together, did you?"

"He asked me to! It wasn't…a thing." Grace blushes, her skin flaming to the roots of her brown hair.

"Well, you made beautiful music together," River says suggestively, "for all the town to hear."

"Stop it!" Grace laughs and grabs her thermos. "You're ridiculous. I'm getting coffee."

After Grace leaves, River glances out the window that looks onto the parking lot and spies her car. The old gray Taurus is an eyesore, with a blue rear door that Todd found at a scrapyard but couldn't afford to get painted to match.

The sight of a fresh scrape on the front bumper and broken turning light fills her with shame. She probably shouldn't have driven here. But Grace didn't say anything about the car. With so much going on, maybe she won't notice.

GRACE

THE WELCOMING AROMA of coffee greets Grace before she even enters the break room. Red and gold tinsel garland hangs over the doorframe, fluttering slightly as she passes. The garish trim is also draped across the windows, a cheery contrast to the misty gray day outside where a lone seagull waddles through the staff parking lot.

The school secretary, Nicole, is bent low and searching through the first aid cupboard. Her eyes brighten as she sees Grace.

"Just the person I wanted to see. Marilyn is looking for you."

"You on nurse duty today?" Grace asks as she reaches for the coffee pot. She's settled into the rhythm of performance that her workday requires, but exhaustion lurks at the corners of her mind.

"Robin's out today and Perry Santiago lost a tooth at recess." Nicole withdraws a small ice pack and closes the door with satisfaction. She leaves through the side door that connects the break room to the administration office, snapping gloves on as she goes.

"Grace is in the break room," she calls, and Grace imagines Nicole ducking her head into Marilyn's office as she passes.

Grace leans against the counter and breathes for a moment. The break room doubles as a work room, with heavy rolls of colored butcher paper mounted to a large rack against one wall and stacks of construction paper and die cuts shelved nearby. Two round tables and chairs sit near a small kitchenette on the opposite wall.

Grace remembers as a child passing the teacher break room of her own elementary school and sneaking glances into the forbidden space. Even though she can't remember ever being strictly told to stay out of it, she knew—they all knew—that there was something special about it. It wasn't for kids. It was a place where adults called each other by their first names and laughed freely at confusing jokes.

She wonders now if any of her teachers felt like an outsider when they were first starting out. Tolerated, even welcomed. But not fully accepted. Not yet. Or maybe that's a unique experience for teachers in small towns. Ellis Cove has little industry and few opportunities for economic growth. It's the kind of place where people stay because they were born and raised here. Where after twenty years of living and working in a community a person can still be considered a newcomer.

Marilyn appears in the break room doorway, her lined face serious. As principal, she always has a kindly manner, but now she looks almost stern. Grace wonders for a moment if she's going to get in trouble.

"Grace," Marilyn says quietly. "There's a police officer in my office who wants to speak with you. Diana Beck is missing."

The feeling of dread that's been hanging over Grace all morning finally settles into shape.

"Is it serious? You know things at their house—"

"Police are taking things seriously, yes," Marilyn says, her mouth tight.

"Well, that's something." Grace glances at the clock above the door. "I have a class coming in just a few minutes."

"I'll talk to River and ask her to cover for you."

Grace follows Marilyn into the office waiting area. A little boy with wide eyes is sitting on a chair holding a wet cloth to his mouth. It's tinged with blood and Grace shies away at the sight. Mouth wounds have never been easy for her. Back when she and Max were together, she warned him that if they ever had kids, he would be on Tooth Fairy duty.

Waiting in Marilyn's office is a uniformed police officer who smells heavily of aftershave. His radio crackles as Grace enters and he turns it down before reaching forward and offering a hand.

"I'm Artie Williams. You must be Ms. Miller?" His blue eyes are keen.

"Millar," she corrects, placing the emphasis on the last syllable. She reaches for his hand as his radio crackles again. "How can I help you?"

"If you need anything, I'll be just outside," Marilyn says, closing the door as she leaves. The blinds on the door are pulled up and look out toward Nicole's desk. Two large windows invite filtered gray light from outside, but Grace still feels enclosed. The strong musky scent of aftershave fills the space between them.

"I'd like to ask you a few questions about yesterday," Officer Williams begins. "I understand that Diana Beck attended an after school choir rehearsal, is that right?"

"Yes. Sort of. She's part of our chamber choir, but we weren't rehearsing yesterday. We were decorating the church to prepare for the concert next week."

"Do you usually meet after school?"

"No." Grace pauses as Officer Williams scratches some notes on a notepad. "We usually practice during lunch, but the students were excited to help decorate after school. And I was happy for the help."

"Did anything seem unusual about Diana yesterday? Anything seem to be troubling her?"

Grace falters, her stomach curling on itself. Officer Williams senses it and looks up, his expression probing. For as kind as his voice is, Grace knows his job isn't to give her the benefit of the doubt.

"Officer, I don't really know how to answer that question. The truth is that Diana's normal *is* troubled. I get the sense that school is an escape for her. She asked me if we could always have choir practice after school because it gave her somewhere safe to go."

One eyebrow rises in response to this and the officer scribbles hastily on his pad. "She said that? Somewhere safe?"

Grace tries to remember. "Not those exact words. But she did say she wished we could have practice every day. And I knew what she meant."

"Has she ever told you about abuse or violence in the home?"

Grace frowns. She doesn't want to unload everything on this officer, but there is no simple way of answering his question. She takes a deep breath. "Have you ever worked with children? They don't come right out and share their secrets. But I wasn't born yesterday. As the music teacher, every child in this school comes through my classroom during the year. I know the signs. Malnourished, rarely washed, hungry for affection."

Officer Williams continues to write without looking up. "Have you ever seen bruises or any suspicious wounds?"

Frustration burns like the smell of his aftershave in the back of her throat. "No. Not like that. But sometimes on hot days Diana will come to school in a sweatshirt and long pants while everyone else is in shorts. It could just be that she doesn't have clean clothes to wear. Or it could be that shorts and a tank top will show things she's trying to hide. Then there was a time recently when she showed me a letter her mom wrote. She was so proud of it, like it was something to be cherished. But it was full of name-calling and shame. If that's the kind of letter that's worth saving, how is she normally treated?"

The officer grunts. He finishes writing and meets Grace's eyes. She resists the urge to look away. "Have you ever reported your suspicions to authorities?"

Guilt wells up in her throat. "I...I was going to. I started taking notes about things I noticed a couple of weeks ago so I had something to report besides a hunch. I didn't want to overreact just because they're poor. I don't know for sure what goes on in that home. But I know Diana isn't happy."

"Do you think she might have run away?"

"At eleven? I don't know. Maybe. If she did, I suspect it was with good reason." The room is too warm and Grace longs for fresh air, worrying that she's said too much, injected her own biases instead of just answering the officer's questions.

He reaches for her hand again. "Thank you, Ms Millar. I appreciate your time."

Relieved, Grace moves to the door and stops. Her fingers wander to her necklace. "Do you have any idea where she is?"

The officer's expression is hard to read. "Her brother reports that she never came home last night. Which means you could be the last person who saw her before she disappeared."

"She left the church hours before I did. Sorry I can't be of more help."

Exiting the office, Grace takes a deep breath to clear her lungs of the taste of aftershave. Marilyn waits near Nicole's desk, but she isn't alone. Matthew Knight, Diana's fifth grade teacher, stands next to her. Their conversation trails off as soon as Grace appears.

"Am I next?" Matthew asks. He's a short man with a slight build who wears a goatee to disguise his receding chin. Grace doesn't know him well, but she's heard enough complaints from her students to know he isn't well liked. She's also had enough experience with ten-year-olds to know that their opinions aren't always fair and unprejudiced.

Marilyn nods. "It shouldn't take long. They're talking to everyone who saw Diana yesterday to find out if she made any plans after school. Besides decorating," she adds, with a nod to Grace.

Matthew runs a hand over his thinning hair. “Better get it over with, I guess.”

Nicole watches him go and smirks. “He looks more nervous than you did, Grace. Poor guy.”

Grace manages a wan smile. “There’s nothing to be nervous about. They’re just trying to find her so anything I can do to help, I’m happy to do it.”

“Of course,” Marilyn says. “That’s how we all feel. Poor thing. I hope they find her soon.”

Nicole and Grace murmur their assent, but Grace can’t help glancing at the bald spot on the back of Matthew’s head and wondering what he’s so nervous about.

EVAN

THE RICKETY SCREEN door slams behind Evan as he steps into the little house, sidestepping an eager German Shepherd who easily outweighs the child holding her back. The dog lunges for Evan, leaping up with an excited bark.

"Stay down, Sadie!" Danny cries.

"Shut-up, Sadie!" Nora shouts from the table. She sits on a vinyl-backed chair that looks like it came from a hotel chain dining room. "Danny, take her out!"

Evan lets the dog sniff him and resists the urge to wipe off the slime her nose leaves on the back of his hand. "Hello there, pup. Hi, Danny."

"Hi," Danny grunts, straining against Sadie's collar until she finally lets him lead her away.

"Stupid dog," Nora growls, cigarette smoke leaking through her teeth. "Sorry about that."

"She's a beautiful animal," Evan replies.

He steps over a sunken place in the kitchen floor to join her at the small table that sits only a few paces from the door. A large tv is mounted on the opposite wall in the living room where it can be viewed from anywhere in the two rooms. A small Christmas tree sits in one corner, but what Evan first thought were presents turns out to be paper grocery sacks filled with empty beer cans. Probably waiting to be returned to the store in exchange for a few coins. The shag living room carpet is barely visible under piles of clothes and trash, and the smell of fresh cigarette smoke doesn't quite overpower the musky odors of damp and mold emanating from the walls around him.

A tattered fleece blanket hangs over the kitchen window, blocking out the light of the clear afternoon. The tiny kitchen is illuminated by a single fluorescent tube above the sink, showing counters stacked so high with dirty dishes and discarded boxes from freezer meals that Evan wonders how Leo even found the coffee maker, let alone managed to find a clean mug to pour a fresh cup.

The poverty doesn't bother him. Many people in Ellis Cove struggle to make ends meet, and there's no shame in that. But the clutter and filth, that tells him it isn't just money trouble. It's evidence of long hours spent accumulating overtime, a general despondency when the Becks have free time, and a certain absence of feeling like they deserve better. What is it about the human spirit that, when fighting for survival, fails to do the simple things to care for what they already have?

Nora looks up at Evan with bloodshot eyes and takes a shaky drag on her cigarette.

Watching her blow out the smoke, Evan breathes a silent prayer. *Oh Lord Jesus, help me not to screw this up.*

"How are you holding up?" he asks.

Nora grunts. "I'm still here, ain't I? Keep sitting here hoping she'll walk through that door any minute. Every time Sadie barks, I think maybe it's Diana coming up the hill."

"Have you heard anything from the police?"

"Nothing useful," Leo grumbles. He's a thickset man whose flannel shirt hangs open to reveal a grubby t-shirt stretched over a potbelly. "These cops ain't even looking that hard. Keep wasting their time grilling us instead of getting out there and finding her."

"I'm sure that's a normal part of the investigative process. Gotta find out what her regular routine is, right?"

Nora shoots Leo a dark look. "They talk to us like they're suspicious of everything. Like we're the ones who done something wrong. I keep telling them they need to be out there looking for her, but they aren't listening. If we knew where she was, why would we call them in the first place?"

They haven't invited Evan to sit, but he scoots over a pile of laundry from the nearest chair and sits anyway, perched on the edge, his left leg braced to keep him balanced.

"Do they have any leads at all?"

"Not that they're saying," Leo says. "Keeping it all real close to the chest."

"Sitting on their butts is more like it. I'll bet if this were the Anderson girl or one of the Vances that they'd have found her by now. But no one cares about anyone in this town unless you have money. Anything can happen to your kids and they won't do nothing. It's discrimination or laziness—"

"—or both—" Leo interjects.

"—and I've half a mind to sue the whole department," Nora announces self-importantly. She ticks off the offenses on her fingers. "Negligence. Discrimination. Child endangerment. My mom has a lawyer she says I can talk to once I've built up my case."

Maybe it's time to change the subject.

"Some folks from the church are asking about bringing meals to help out. Would you be okay with that?"

Nora looks around the filthy room with a baleful eye. "I don't want no do-gooders coming in here and judging me."

"No one will come if you don't want them to. I could deliver the meals myself if you want. But no one's gonna judge you. They only want to help."

Nora presses her lips together. "I suppose if you bring them yourself, that would be all right. Or my mom. I don't want no one else coming here like a bunch of vultures."

"Your mom lives here in town?"

"Yeah. She works at Fred Meyer. Been calling me every two hours on her breaks asking if we heard anything. She usually takes the kids in the summer when I'm on days." Nora chokes up and she tugs at the drawstring on her stained hoodie. "Look, I know I'm not the best mom. I don't got a nice job that lets me be home with my kids all day like some moms. But it's the best I can do."

"No one's blaming you," Evan says, but he feels guilty remembering his earlier conversation with Grace. "No one has a right," he amends.

Nora's voice is muffled as she scrubs her face with a sleeve. “If she did run away, I swear I’ll whip her sorry butt when she comes back for putting me through this.” She doesn’t sound angry, though. She sounds desperate.

“Is that what you think happened, then? That she ran away?”

“No.” Danny is so quiet, Evan didn’t realized he’d returned. He stands at the edge of the living room where the matted carpet gives way to chipped linoleum. “She wouldn’t have done that.”

Nora glowers at Danny. “Where’s Sadie?”

“She wanted to stay outside.”

“Then get back out there with her.”

“But it’s cold.” Danny’s gaze flits to his mom as if taking a risk. His hair is chopped unevenly in a way that Evan can only describe like a mullet gone wrong—if it were possible for a mullet to go right. His fair complexion suggests his hair would be a light blond if it were clean, instead of the stringy brown Evan has always seen it. He chews at a fingernail self-consciously.

“Daniel Joseph, get out there and watch that dog! For cryin’ out loud, can’t you just do what you’re told for once?”

Danny slinks away, not looking at Evan.

Nora puffs angrily on her cigarette. “He’s getting to be as bad as Diana. She’s had a real chip on her shoulder these days.”

“Do he and Diana get along? Does he have any idea where she could be?””

“They’re thick as thieves, the two of them. Police asked him, but he didn’t tell them nothing,” Nora says.

Knock it off with the questions. You're reminding them of the police, Evan chides himself. *That's not why you're here.*

"If Danny thinks of anything, I'm sure he'll tell them. I brought my Bible in case you wanted to read some verses together. Any favorites you have? Or I could share some of mine if you'd like."

Leo looks down at his phone and Nora stubbs out her cigarette. "I don't think I could stand it right now, thanks anyway. Unless you have some verses that will tell me where my daughter is."

"Not in those terms, no. But there are plenty of verses that talk about our Lord Jesus healing broken hearts and soothing suffering souls."

"If it's all the same to you, it don't feel like Sunday right now."

Evan smiles to show he isn't offended. "That's understandable. Know there's lots of good people in town praying for Diana to come home safe. There's not much we can do, but we can do that." It sounds inadequate even to his own ears.

"I don't get why nobody seen her," Leo says. "It's like she just poof! Disappeared into the night air. But somebody had to see her leave the church. Seen where she went. This town is small, but it ain't a ghost town." The way he says it sounds like it's a well-rehearsed complaint.

"I'll bet some people don't even know she's gone missing." Evan is struck with an idea and seizes it. "But you know what might help? How would you feel about holding a candlelight vigil? Something the whole community can attend. We can talk about Diana and share the tip line where they can call police to report anything they've seen. I'm sure we could get KCBY to run a story on it."

At the mention of the Coos Bay news station, Nora's mouth hangs open. "You think so?"

"Absolutely. The more people who are keeping their eyes out for her, the better."

"What do you think?" she asks Leo, but it's clear from her excitement that she's already made up her mind.

"Reporters are worse than cops," Leo grumbles. "I don't want them coming anywhere near us."

"But if they put the story on TV, then everyone will hear about it. People all over the county will be looking for her."

"You don't have to decide right away, but think about it. I can talk to the school and see about holding it there. It doesn't have to be a church thing," Evan adds for Leo's benefit.

This softens Leo and the conversation turns to details about what a vigil might look like. By the time Evan prepares to leave, his throat is raw from the cigarette smoke. But when he asks if they can pray together, Nora agrees. She clasps Evan's hands across the table, then snaps at Leo to join them.

"It's all right," Evan insists. "Only if you want to."

But Nora glares until Leo begrudgingly adds his own meaty hand to the pile. Evan doesn't know if it's a resistance to religion or him personally. Being a Black pastor in a White town gives him some notoriety and he knows some of the older members view him more like a mascot than one of their own. But men like Leo he suspects would never feel comfortable with the change.

He bows his head and offers a prayer aloud. It's easy to get too wordy in his vocal prayers. He feels the pull as it tries to run away from him, but with the weight of Leo's hand on his, he keeps it brief.

Walking to his car a few minutes later, Evan offers a silent prayer of his own, calling down all the blessings he wanted to ask for but kept locked inside. Blessings for Diana to be safe wherever she is. Blessings for Danny to know what it means to be loved. Blessings for Nora and Leo to heal from whatever pain makes them so stingy with their hearts.

NOVEMBER 27

TUESDAY

2 WEEKS BEFORE DISAPPEARANCE

GRACE

"I'VE GAINED OVER FIFTY POUNDS," River confessed as she hefted her bag onto her lap. The pale purple tote was embellished with a design of a single bird and cherry blossoms. But the pattern was printed on, not embroidered, and the corner of one of the branches was flaking off. She pulled out a small bag of carrots, taking advantage of a few minutes of calm before the chamber choir came in during their lunch recess. "If I get any bigger I won't be able to fit into my clothes, and I don't want to buy more with less than three months left."

Grace rested her elbows on her desk, unsure what to say. River's initial pregnancy glow had given way to a swelling in her face, neck, hands...everywhere. Her short black hair was still fastidiously styled when she showed up at the school each morning, but there was a weariness in her eyes. A wariness too. River was slight of frame, so her baby bump showed early. Now, six months into her pregnancy, her back arched to accommodate her growing stomach.

"I think you wear it well," Grace announced generously.

River ignored the compliment, crunching down on a carrot stick. "I told Todd he's going to have to get a Wide Load sign to put around my neck."

"Complete with a beeping alert when you're backing up?"

River snickered.

"Don't worry about it," Grace said. "You look fantastic. And I'm sure a little Jiu-Jitsu after the baby comes will help you bounce right back."

"Are you still going?"

"Not right now during concert season. But I plan to get back into it after the holidays. You've got me hooked."

"Mmm…I miss it," River said wistfully. "I also miss being able to bend over and see my feet."

Grace glanced at River's ankles bulging wide over her low boots. "What does your doctor say?"

"She's not too worried yet. But I have my glucose test next week and have been reading up on gestational diabetes just in case." River leaned back on the piano bench to stretch her back and the wooden joints creaked.

"Do you want me to bring in my bench from home? It's got a nice, thick cushion."

River laughed, showing a row of teeth that seemed too small for her mouth. "What's wrong? You tired of hearing the squeaking accompaniment?"

"Not at all! It's the least I can do. You're giving up your time to help me out, I can at least give you a padded bench."

River had initially only been hired to accompany the

chamber choir, Ellis Cove Elementary's audition group who competed in festivals around the state. But it was late November, and that meant Christmas program time. River had volunteered to help this year, and Grace was amazed at the difference it made to not have to be behind the piano while trying to teach groups of timid children how to follow her directing cues.

The legs of the bench scraped noisily against the industrial tile floor as River pushed it back to stand. "I've just got to get my circulation back. I can feel the blood pooling in my feet the longer I sit there."

"Sounds like Todd needs to give you a good foot rub tonight."

"Right." River snorted. "Todd has a thing with feet. He wouldn't touch mine if I paid him."

"Really?"

"Yeah. He's really grossed out by feet. Especially now."

Something in her voice made Grace wonder. Had she just imagined it or was there a tension there? Grace didn't know Todd well, but River always spoke warmly of him. He was handsome in a rugged sort of way, even if he did dress like he'd come straight off a construction job every time Grace saw him. Which was probably true, actually. What was he, a roofer? Grace couldn't remember.

The door opened and Marilyn entered wearing a loose, flowing pant suit. Her red hair didn't show a bit of gray and Grace suspected she colored it. Grace hadn't yet turned thirty and had already found a few strands of her own.

"Oh good, I was hoping to catch you on your break."

Marilyn paused and spoke deliberately, as if considering her words carefully. "I have some bad news for you both. Last night the school board voted to cancel the Christmas concert. They've decided it's too much of a conflict of church and state."

The words didn't connect right away and Grace found herself staring at Marilyn, trying to make sense of what she'd said.

"It started with Mary Ann Olsen, obviously," Marilyn said apologetically. "I can't imagine anyone else on the board caring. But she's always pushing her liberal agenda, and used fear over what happened in Warrington last year to convince them to go along with it. You never know when someone's going to get offended and decide to take it to the courts."

Grace waited, expecting some modifier to follow. "So, do they want us to call it a holiday concert instead? Or a winter celebration?"

"No. They don't think it should be held at all. The school shouldn't be sponsoring a gathering that could be seen as overtly religious."

"You're kidding me. Did you tell them most of the songs aren't religious? Or that I incorporate music from around the world to highlight different cultures? Jewish, Hindu, they aren't even all Christian."

Marilyn shook her head. "If we had more time, maybe we could get them to come around. But I argued up and down with the chair and they'd rather be safe than sorry."

Grace leaned back as if bracing herself against a wave. "I can't believe it. We've spent weeks on these songs. It's going to break the kids' hearts."

"Not just them," River added. "This is the biggest holiday event in the whole town."

Marilyn's voice took on the I'm-the-leader quality she always used when she had to enforce something unwelcome. "It's fine if you continue to teach the songs. But the school can't sponsor a religious-themed concert. At least, not this year. I suspect that when the community hears about it, there will be such a backlash that they'll be open to reconsidering next year."

Grace's disbelief gave way to frustration. It had been hard enough coming to Ellis Cove two years earlier and stepping into the shoes of a long time music teacher who'd built a robust program over a forty year career. The labor-intensive Christmas concert had left Grace feeling shell-shocked her first year. But it had been Mrs. Peterson's baby and was one of those traditions the community valued. Canceling it felt like a personal failure.

"You know people will think it's my fault. They'll think it was my idea."

The bell chimed announcing the beginning of lunch recess. The chamber choir students would be coming in soon. Marilyn glanced at the clock.

"I'll send out an email to parents and make it clear that this was the board's decision."

"Can you wait on that?" River asked.

Grace and Marilyn looked at her.

"What if it wasn't a school activity at all? What if it was voluntary and held off-campus? A community event, not a school event."

Marilyn wiped her reading glasses on her sleeve. "That could work if the board approved it. Do you think you'd get a hundred families to show up for an optional activity?"

River grinned. "Trust me. They'll come. Especially if it's sticking it to Mary Ann Olsen."

Marilyn's eyes glinted. "Tell you what, if you can find someone willing to host it and work with what you've already got planned, I'll take it to the superintendent. The board can't stop you from doing it on your own time. And if I happen to show up to help with the rest of the teaching staff—all volunteers, of course—what can they say?"

As she opened the door to leave, the rambunctious energy of students going out to the playground filled the hallway. Grace stood and shifted a few chairs back into alignment, knocked out of place by the unruly second graders who'd been her last class of the morning.

"I'll bet we could do it at First Hope," River said, joining her. "It's a nice, big space and Evan's always looking for opportunities for community engagement."

"Evan's your pastor?" The chamber choir was scheduled to perform at First Hope the following week, but Grace had only been in contact with the secretary, a cheery woman named Barb whose emails glittered with enthusiasm.

"Yes. I could ask him this Sunday if you want."

The door opened and Diana Beck came in, slightly breathless as if she'd run to get there.

"Hi Ms. Vincent, Ms. Miller." Few elementary students pronounced Grace's last name correctly. She'd been teaching long enough that it didn't bother her anymore, and she was pleasantly surprised when one got it right.

"Hello, Diana!" Grace greeted in return.

Diana's ill-fitting jeans were stained and Grace was pretty sure she'd worn the camo unicorn shirt the day before. One shoe was coming apart at the sole and a dingy sock peeked out. It didn't help that Diana was entering that awkward time of adolescence when showers were becoming a necessity. While the girls in her class were wearing deodorant and trading social currency about who had started menstruating—using code words as if Grace didn't know what they were talking about—Diana seemed completely oblivious to personal hygiene, widening the social gap between her and her peers.

Not that Ellis Cove was particularly affluent. The coastal town lacked the long stretches of sandy beach that drew tourists to its neighbors to the north and south. The harbor was small and unable to accommodate large ships, so as the heavily forested hills were logged, the lumber was trucked to Coos Bay to the north which boasted the largest harbor in the state.

As the other students filed in, Grace noticed Diana showing a piece of paper to River. River nodded appreciatively, but when she glanced at Grace, her eyes were pained. Curious, Grace raised an eyebrow. River shook her head slightly. They'd talk about it after the students left.

The chamber choir was made up of twenty-four students, six singing each part. None of the boys could hit the bass notes yet, so Grace usually stuck with arrangements that had split soprano and alto parts. Occasionally she bypassed the SSAA arrangements for SAT and wrote a second alto or tenor part herself.

They were practicing an arrangement of *The Coventry Carol,* and Grace grinned in appreciation as they followed her dynamic gestures. They'd learned a lot since September, when it took so much effort to follow the notes on the staff they couldn't pull their eyes from the music. Her goal in the early days had just been getting them to look at her. Now they were able to respond to dynamics, though she had to exaggerate the changes for them to follow.

Diana clutched the folded paper all through the rehearsal, fingering it in a way that reminded Grace of Max's mother and her rosary beads. Just as the accompaniment swelled, something in the notes tripped.

Grace ignored it, knowing River would recover without too much trouble. But then there was another wrong note and another, as if River's fingers were lost on the keyboard.

The piano stopped. A few kids chuckled and Grace smiled, waiting for River's apology, maybe a joke. But River was silent.

Grace glanced over at the piano. River was looking down at her hands, and something about her posture looked troubled. Grace's smile fell. She glanced at the clock.

"Well done, ladies and gentleman. I'm going to let you go a few minutes early today. If you brought your permission slips for our concert this Friday, put them on my desk. Otherwise, don't forget to get them signed tonight!"

Students scattered for the pile of backpacks near the door. A few students clustered around Grace's desk, jostling to place the salmon-colored forms in a pile.

"Miss Miller," a sixth grader said, brushing away a long strand of hair that had escaped her braid. She was one of the few experienced choir members, having joined last year as a fifth grader. "When are we going to audition for the descant solo?"

"Next week, Savannah. After our performance for the senior citizens. Not inside, boys," she warned two boys wrestling over a beanie.

"Ms. Miller!"

Grace turned and found Diana behind her, holding out a sheet of notebook paper.

"Look what my mom wrote." Diana's freckled cheeks were lined with pink and her eyes were bright.

Grace took the paper and glanced it over, one eye on the scuffling boys. "Gentlemen, take it outside."

It was a letter addressed to Diana. Immediately Grace felt like an intruder into Diana's private life and wanted to return it. But Diana was watching her expectantly so she made a show of reading it. At first she meant to skim, but as she did she grew increasingly appalled and couldn't help slowing down to read it more carefully.

Diana,

I'm sorry I got so mad tonight. I was so tired from work and you know how Leo gets when I work late. I wish you kids would do something for yourselves once in a while instead of expecting him to do it all. It's not that hard to heat up a frozen pizza, the directions are right on the box. And I just couldn't take it tonight after putting up with a whole shift of whiny teenagers who spend more time on their phones than they do picking up a broom.

But don't think I don't love you. Of course I love you. I'm not one of those moms who say it all the time, but you'd have to be an idiot not to know it. Look at everything I do for you. Why would I do it all if I didn't love you? Try paying attention to something besides yourself once in a while. If you had any idea how hard I work for you kids, you'd work harder to help Leo more when I'm gone.

Grace cringed, but couldn't tear her eyes away. It was a full page of insults and passive aggressive jabs. She felt Diana watching her and kept her smile fixed in place, hoping Diana wouldn't sense her shock. What must Diana's life be like that she thought this was a letter of warm affection?

Grace finished the letter and handed it back to Diana.

"Wasn't that nice?" Diana's eyes shone.

"Very nice," Grace lied, thinking to herself that she wished she could shake the woman who'd written it.

"It was waiting on the table this morning. She must've written it last night while I was sleeping. I'm going to put it somewhere special where I can keep it forever."

"That's a good idea. I liked to keep special notes from my mom too. I still have some of them, in fact." Grace wasn't sure where the box was that held sentimental mementos from her childhood. Her garage had become the repository after her mom died, and she still hadn't found the gumption to sort through it all. Her brother

Greg had offered to fly out from Texas to help, but it was too easy for both of them to keep pushing it off.

Diana was the last to leave, and as soon as she was gone, Grace turned to River. The younger woman was bending awkwardly to pick up some sheet music that had fallen to the floor, her stomach pressing against her legs and her heavy bag threatening to slip from her shoulder.

"Here, I'll get that." Grace jumped forward to grab the music. "Are you sure you're okay?"

River wouldn't look her in the eye. "I'm okay. But I think I'd better go home."

"Sure. Of course. I'll be fine this afternoon. Whatever you need." Grace waited for an explanation about why she'd struggled on *The Coventry Carol,* but River didn't say more. She stuffed the sheet music into a folder and slipped it into her bag.

Grace looked for something to draw her out. "Can you believe that letter from Diana's mother?"

River's expression darkened. "Poor thing. I hope she finds a good therapist someday. She's gonna need it."

Grace watched River carefully as she reached for her jacket and keys. Her dark eyes were sad and distant. Something was definitely bothering her. After she left, Grace wondered if she realized that she hadn't said goodbye.

RIVER

RIVER SLAMMED the car door shut with her hip and felt a tug. Looking down in dismay, she saw her skirt had been caught when she'd bumped her hip against the door. How had that happened? This was one of the few skirts she could still wear with her growing belly.

Balancing a potted poinsettia in one arm and a sack of groceries in the other, she leaned over to open the door.

"Mrs. Vincent! I can help you!" a little voice cried from outside the carport. Diana stood on the sidewalk, her hair damp from the mist and curling around her forehead in perfect little ringlets.

"Thanks, Diana. This hasn't been my day. I'm not usually this clumsy."

Diana opened the door and River's skirt hem came free. She'd have to inspect it later for holes.

"Is this where you live?" Diana asked, looking up the steps of the mobile home hopefully. The siding was collecting a layer of grime and mold. A cedar fence divided their carport from the trailer next door, weathered gray from the harsh coastal wind. A solitary wind chime tinkled faintly near the back door.

"Yeah. Thanks for your help."

"Can I...do you think I could come inside?" Diana asked. "I can help you with the groceries."

River didn't want Diana to linger, to look at her with such a hopeful expression. She didn't want to have to come up with an excuse for her to go away, and she couldn't bring herself to say the words, *You'd better go home now*.

River, of all people, couldn't send her home.

But Diana shouldn't be there. River liked her privacy and didn't have visitors. Oblivious, Diana ran up the stairs and grabbed the screen door, pulling it open with a loud protest.

Letting her help would make her feel important.

"Here, hold the poinsettia and I'll open the door."

Diana held the plant, her fingers crinkling the red cellophane. "It's so soft," she murmured, and pinched a petal until it snapped off.

River didn't tell her not to touch it, even though now the flower petals looked imbalanced.

She worked her key into the lock and held the door open so Diana could go in. Suddenly River was aware of the shoes by the back door, the newspaper sitting on the floor where Todd had left it last night, dirty dishes in the sink, and a soiled towel left out on the counter. But Diana didn't seem to notice. She looked around in wonder, taking in the light colored paneling and the thin carpet as if it were a house out of a magazine.

She wandered to the small Christmas tree in the corner by the TV. It always seemed like a waste to River to put up an artificial tree when there were two Christmas tree farms just outside of town, and lots selling live trees on nearly every street corner. But Todd was allergic so their little artificial tree would have to do. River had never had a tree as a child, so even a cheap artificial one felt like a luxury.

"Where will the baby sleep?" Diana asked.

Something flickered in River's chest. The house might be messy, but the nursery was her special joy.

"The baby's room isn't finished yet," she answered, "but it will be soon."

"Can I see it? Do you have a crib in there?"

It was one thing to let Diana come into the house and set a plant down on the table. But to walk past the living room and down the hallway to the bedroom? That was serious.

But River didn't know how to tell her no. And she didn't think Diana would hurt anything. So she led her down the hallway to the first bedroom door, past the unfinished bathroom with its torn up linoleum.

"We're still working on the bathroom," she said apologetically, but Diana didn't even seem to notice.

River opened the door to the nursery and flipped on the light switch. The room was flooded with light, making the pale blue walls almost glow. River had nailed up chair rail and painted it white, and a white crib sat in the corner. Beside it sat a small dresser they'd found second-hand in Coos Bay and a used changing table that River planned to paint.

Diana caught her breath. "Wow. Your baby is so lucky."

She ran a hand over the rail of the crib and pulled open the top drawer of the dresser, revealing little onesies, diapers, and flannel receiving blankets.

She cocked her head at River. "Is it a boy or a girl?"

"We don't know. I tried to pick colors that could go either way."

Diana nodded in approval. "I like this color of blue. Do you have any baby toys yet?"

"A few, but it's going to be a while before the baby needs toys." River was careful to call it "the baby" and not "he" when she talked about it. But in her heart, she knew she was becoming more and more attached to the idea of it being a boy. That would make a lot of things easier.

There was a scratching sound like a key in the lock at the front door.

"Okay, Diana, I think it's about time for you to go home," River said, hating herself for the words.

Todd stopped midway from hanging up his jacket as they walked out into the hallway.

"Well, hello. Who are you?"

"This is Diana, one of the students in our choir. She was helping me bring in a few things from the car."

"I like your nursery," Diana said, looking around the little trailer wistfully. The dirty dishes and thin carpet faded away as River saw the house through the girl's eyes. It was the same thing Bess saw. A family. A family who loved each other and had enough food to eat and a comfortable couch to sit on.

"It's almost dark," Todd said. "Don't you think you

ought to be going home?" He sounded tired. Must have had a tough day. He was paid per square foot, so when given a roofing job with dormer widows or complicated architectural details, Todd could spend a whole day and barely make fifty bucks.

River felt a stab of shame for not having dinner ready yet. She'd taken too long at the grocery store. Suddenly the poinsettia seemed like such a silly purchase. She should have hurried and come straight home.

"Bye, Mrs. Vincent. Thanks for letting me see your baby's room."

"I'll see you tomorrow, Diana," River said, fighting the urge to rush to the kitchen and whip up a quick grilled cheese sandwich.

What would Erica say? *Don't put words in Todd's mouth. Don't assume he's thinking things he hasn't said. Look at the evidence.*

Diana moved past Todd to the door and River tried not to blurt out an apology as soon as it closed behind her.

"I had to pick up some things at the store. I haven't started dinner yet."

"That's okay," Todd said, moving to the kitchen and opening the fridge. He pulled out a can of beer and cracked it open. "I'm not all that hungry."

River looked for a sign that he was lying, but he seemed tired, not angry. She breathed a little bit easier. She threw a frozen lasagna into the oven and mixed up a salad.

"Are you bringing work home with you now?" Todd called from the couch.

River poked her head around the wall. "What?"

"The girl. What was that all about?"

"Oh. Diana. She was just helping me bring in groceries. It won't happen again." Remembering, River looked down at her skirt hem, relieved when she saw only a small puncture. She pulled on the fibers to hide the flaw.

Todd's beer can clinked as it fell into the bag of cans by the back door. River started. She hadn't seen Todd come into the kitchen. His eyes were bloodshot but also looked concerned.

"You don't have to ask me for permission, you know."

River ducked her head, focusing on cutting cucumbers. Nice, even slices.

"I'm your husband, not your boss. Or your dad."

River flinched at the word. "Sorry."

"This wasn't a therapy day, was it?"

River shook her head. "Erica's out of town until next week."

She wished she had an appointment sooner. Next week seemed so far away and River had almost lost it during rehearsal that day. It was the letter that had set her off. River could hear Grandma Billie's voice in her head as if she were right there in the same room. What would Erica have said about it?

She looked at Todd and realized he'd been talking.

"Sorry, what did you say?"

Todd sighed and ran a hand through his hair. It was getting long. River would need to cut it soon. "I don't know, River. Maybe all that therapy is just making it worse. Things weren't this bad before you started seeing her."

Anxiety flared in her chest. *That's why I'm seeing her*

now. Because things have gotten so bad. But she kept her objections to herself. She reached for the plastic salad tongs in the utensil pitcher on the counter. It had a big crack down the side of the ceramic.

"I'm fine." *Stay calm. Be strong. Don't make things worse.*

The oven chimed and River busied herself dishing the food onto two plates and setting it on the table.

"Oh come on. Come sit in here and eat with me."

River looked into Todd's brown eyes. Behind his beard, she saw the inviting smile that she could never say no to. Not since three years ago when they'd met on the jetty in Bandon. She and her roommate, Sarah, were visiting Sarah's family in the late summer before school started again in the fall.

River had assumed the Pacific Ocean would be like the Atlantic, warm with wide stretches of hot sandy beaches. But the sun hadn't shone for the whole week they were there, and they'd bundled up against the cold with sweatshirts and jackets. That hadn't stopped them from enjoying the sights though, braving the cold wind to build bonfires on the beach and eating hot dogs gritty with sand.

"It's the heat," Sarah had explained. "The hotter it is inland, the colder it is here. But sometimes the reverse is true as well. In December we get some of our best weather."

It wasn't what River had expected, but they'd gone to escape the Arizona heat, and that's exactly what they'd gotten. Standing on the jetty, the waves had swelled around them, crashing against the giant rocks and raining overhead.

Todd had seen her shivering and offered his sweatshirt before sharing a cautionary tale of the number of people every year who get swept off jetties and pulled out to sea. He'd suggested that they get fish and chips downtown. Sarah had been interested in Todd initially, but it was clear that he only had eyes for River. By the time the week had ended, River was struggling to smooth things over with her friend, while trying to figure out if a long-distance relationship had any hope.

"What's that smile for?"

"I was just thinking about the first time we met. Never guessed I'd find myself living here with you and getting ready to have a baby. It seems like a dream sometimes."

His eyes sparkled. "As long as it's not a nightmare."

River grabbed her plate obediently and followed him to the couch. But her smile faded. She didn't like eating in the living room. She wasn't allowed to eat in the living room. It was likely she would drop something on the floor.

If she spilled her food, Grandma Billie—

No. Grandma Billie wasn't there. River blinked to clear her head. She pushed her food around on the plate, but wasn't very hungry anymore. Todd flipped through the local stations on the TV, clearing his plate without seeming to notice that she was barely touching hers.

When he was done, she took it from him and slid it under her own. She wanted to snuggle against Todd on the couch, but the dishes in the sink were calling to her. So she pulled herself to her feet and waddled into the kitchen.

"Do you need help?" Todd offered.

"It's all right," But she thought about how he used to

not have to ask. He used to get up and do dishes with her when they were first married. Sometimes he would even tell her to sit down and not move while he did them instead. Maybe when the baby came, he would do that again.

BESS

MOTHER'S DAY

IT'S RAINING. Or it was raining. Wasn't it? I can't tell. I hear water dribbling down the rain gutter outside, but I can't see out the window because there's a big cabinet blocking it. It's missing a door and has a microwave sitting on the countertop. But I'm not allowed to use it. If I want a burrito from the freezer, I have to let it sit and warm up on its own. If I run the microwave, She'll hear me.

Sometimes when She takes a nap during the day, She's happier when She wakes up. She smiles and says something with a laugh like, "Guess you didn't burn the place down this time."

Sometimes She isn't happy. Sometimes She smacks me on the back of the head with a rolled up newspaper and says that I made too much noise for Her to get any sleep, even though I sat in silence and could hear Her snoring.

It was Her own snoring that woke Her, anyway. She choked and it turned into a cough and the next thing I knew, She was sitting up, gasping and reaching for her newspaper.

In my hands is a flower from school, made of yellow tissue paper and glued to pink construction paper, with green tissue paper twisted to look like leaves. I tucked it in my shirt on the walk home from the bus so the rain wouldn't ruin it.

Now it shakes a little as I watch her sleeping. Shakes like it's afraid She'll wake up. Trembling with both excitement and fear. It's Mother's Day on Sunday and we got to make a card for our mothers. Mama hasn't come back yet, so Mrs. Pitt said I could give my flower to Her instead.

The other kids wrote a poem on the inside of the card.

It was supposed to begin,

Roses are red,
Violets are blue.

Then each kid was supposed to come up with something nice to say about their moms.

Something like,

Honey is sweet,
And so are you.

Or

Roses are red,
Violets are blue.
When I want to feel happy
I think of you.

I'd stared at the boy who wrote that one until he glared at me and shifted his elbow so I couldn't see his card anymore. I don't know why he was mad. I was just trying to figure out if he meant it.

I wondered what She would think if I wrote that. Would She give me a hug and kiss me on the forehead the way I saw moms greet their kids when they picked them up after school?

I'd thought and thought for a long time about what to write. When recess came, my card was still blank. Mrs. Pitt made me stay inside so I could finish it. When she saw me staring out the window, she made a small sighing sound and sat beside me, making suggestions. But none of her ideas fit. I wanted my poem to be special, to make Her smile in a nice way instead of in that mean way She has.

I wanted it to tell the truth. And I wanted the truth to be beautiful.

Roses are red,
Violets are blue.
I miss my Mama
So I'm glad I have you.

Now I sit in the corner between the cabinet and the wall, waiting for Her to wake up. She sits in her brown chair, the one I'm not allowed to sit in. I did once when She was in the kitchen talking on the phone. It felt as soft and comfortable as it looked, fitting around my body like a marshmallow. It was so soft I forgot to listen for Her footsteps. When She saw me, She grabbed me by the hair and pulled me out, throwing me to the floor and kicking me, all while still talking on the phone. The whole time, Her voice didn't change, except for short gasps of effort breaking up Her sentences. She didn't even sound angry.

Now I only sit in the chair when She's out of the house. At a doctor's appointment or having lunch with a friend when I know She'll be gone a long time. It's one of those rules I've made for myself.

Her rule is "Don't Sit in My Chair."

My rule is "Only Sit in Her Chair When She'll Be Gone a Long Time and Make Sure You Don't Turn the TV Up Too Loud So You Can Hear Her Park the Car and Have Time to Turn Off the TV and Move to the Couch Before She Opens the Door."

Sometimes Her rules change. Sometimes Her rule is, "Get Your Own Food and Don't Bother Me." Other times it's, "Stay Out of the Food You Selfish Fat Pig." So I eat as much as I can at school just in case I won't get anything at home.

Weekends are hard, because there's no school. Sometimes my stomach hurts so bad I can't think about anything else. My rule when that happens is, "Pretend to Get a Drink of Water and Stuff a Piece of Bread into Your Pocket While the Water's Running." Bread squishes down really small and doesn't make noise like the refrigerator or freezer. I like it when we have bread.

She's waking up now. I can hear Her grunting and scratching herself.

The flower in my hand wobbles heavily on its stem. It was like magic the way Mrs. Pitt bunched up the tissue paper on one end so it formed a group of petals on the other. I wanted to make a whole garden of them. I wish I knew Mama's favorite colors so I could make a bouquet of flowers for her. Then maybe she would come back. She would beam at me and tell me how beautiful the flowers are and how much she loves me.

I wonder if She knows Mama's favorite color.

I don't remember very well what Mama looks like. I remember her warmth as I sat next to her on the couch in our old house before. I remember looking at a book with a train that had a face on it while she read the words and I looked at the pictures.

It had to be Mama because She's never read me a story.

But I can't remember Mama's voice. And when I try to remember her face it looks too much like a woman on Her favorite TV show. I try and try, but no matter what I do the memory of her real face won't come back. Once I asked Daddy if he had a picture of her and he just swore at me and said he hoped he never saw her lying, cheating face again as long as he lived.

The sharp scent of cigarette smoke fills the room.

"What's that you've got?" Her voice is rough as She blows out a cloud of smoke. She's seen me in my corner.

I stop just out of arm's length of the chair and stretch out my hand with the card in it.

"Happy Mother's Day," I say quietly.

She takes the card. Gives it one glance. Tosses it on the round table next to Her chair.

She picks up the TV remote and mutters, "Good thing I'm not your mother. I'd kill myself if I'd given birth to you. You're like a rat with your pointy nose and beady eyes. It's no wonder your own mom ran off and left you."

Suddenly I worry that I wrote the wrong thing on the

card. Maybe I should have just stuck with "honey is sweet." I wonder if I can take the card back when She isn't looking.

But, as if She can read my thoughts, She stops flipping through channels and reaches for the card.

She reads the poem quietly to herself. She sucks on her cigarette so the end glows. Her eyes squint at me behind her glasses.

"What's this supposed to mean? You think I'm not a good enough mother to you, is that it? You want your own mom back?"

I shake my head. Yes, all those things were true, but that wasn't why I'd written the poem. I'd been trying to tell her that I was glad She took care of me after Mama left.

She leans forward and taps Her cigarette in the tray on the little table next to Her chair. "Let me tell you something about your mom. She was a selfish little whore who didn't care a bit about you. Oh, having a baby was fun when it was something cute to show off. But once you got big enough to get boring, she ran off with some boyfriend and never looked back. Not that I can blame her. I wouldn't take you either if not for the goodness of my heart. You're a fat pig eating me out of house and home and you'll grow up to be a slut like her some day."

I try not to listen to her words as I watch her mouth moving. I try to think instead about me as a baby and Mama being proud of me. Wanting to show me off. Were we happy then?

I don't realize my mouth has formed words until She grabs my wrist and pulls me closer.

"What did you say? Speak up if you've got something to say. Don't mumble like some retard."

I want to turn my head away from the stink on her breath but I know it'll only make it worse. "What was Mama's favorite color?" I ask before I can stop myself.

She smiles and Her teeth are brown with black around the edges. It's not a nice smile. She holds Her cigarette in front of Her like She's holding a card in a game and considering whether or not to play it.

"You wanna know what her favorite color is? Let me show you."

She reaches for my sleeve and pulls it up so fast the Mother's Day card falls to the floor at my feet. Ash sprinkles like gray snow on the gentle petals as she grinds the cigarette into my arm.

DECEMBER 14

FRIDAY

1 DAY AFTER DISAPPEARANCE

GRACE

THE SKY overhead is a vibrant blue as Grace leaves the school after work. Puffy white clouds billow from the west, their bases tinged with gray. A seagull shrieks overhead and Grace frowns at the fresh stain of bird poop on the windshield of her black Camry.

A police cruiser sits near the front entrance. Was Officer Williams talking to everyone in the school? It makes sense. If Diana planned to run away, she might have confided in someone. Lunch workers, teachers, aides, librarians, they all knew Diana.

Suddenly Grace feels ashamed. How many of those adults knew things weren't right at the Beck home? Grace has never reported suspicions of abuse before and was too afraid of doing it wrong, afraid the authorities would think she was overreacting without real evidence besides a feeling deep in her gut that it wasn't just poverty and hunger that gave Diana the haunted look in her eyes. Keeping a list of specific concerns seemed like the responsible thing to do at the time.

Now, though, with Diana missing and police prowling the school, her plan to keep a list feels cowardly. Had Grace called the hotline two weeks ago, Diana might be safe today.

Grace tosses her work bag in the back seat of her car and slides in behind the wheel just as her phone rings. It's an unfamiliar number, and she feels the same little jolt she always does when someone calls from out-of-state.

"Hello?"

The pause grows long.

"Hello, is this Mrs. Miller?" The voice has a strong New England accent and Grace's hope sours.

"Yes?"

"Hi, how are you doing today, ma'am?"

Grace pulls the phone away and clicks it off. Just a telemarketer. She shouldn't be disappointed. She hasn't heard from her sister in almost a year. But still, she always hopes.

Last time Jess called, she was excited about a new job and a fresh start. Grace had allowed herself to hope for the first time in years. But then Jess went radio silent. Again. Which could only mean she'd fallen off the wagon and was too ashamed to tell Grace.

Grace had persisted until an annoyed stranger had answered and explained that he'd had the phone number for two months and was tired of getting phone calls for Jessica Millar who had clearly screwed up her life to have so many creditors and small claims levied against her.

As Grace runs her wipers with generous fluid—smearing the bird droppings across the windshield—a familiar tightness pains her chest. The same feeling that always comes when she thinks about Jess. It's worse now that Mom is gone. Even though Grace was always the one Jess called when she needed help, while Mom was alive at least Grace had someone else to guide her. Someone else who loved Jess and would do anything to help her.

Not that Greg doesn't love her too, but there's a ten-year gap between him and Jess so they've never been close. He would get angry when he found out their mother had given Jess money or paid her rent. Grace figures the less he knows, the better.

Grace tries to push these thoughts away as she drives down Main Street past the pharmacy with its plastic lighthouse that the kids in town like to climb, and the bakery with the huge undersea mural that fills the northern wall. Holiday lights outline windows and matching fir wreaths hang from every shop door.

There's a newer shopping plaza outside of town complete with a dollar store which frequently saves Grace a trip to Coos Bay. But the old town area leading to the harbor has a quaint feeling to it that only comes with age and personality, with its gift shop, sweet shop, and even a barber shop complete with vintage, striped pole. Only half a dozen blocks long, it doesn't qualify much as downtown, but it's still the heart of Ellis Cove life.

Grace started coming to the southern Oregon Coast after her mom retired to Coos Bay six years earlier. She liked the wild, rocky coastline and beaches that were never crowded. So unlike the long beaches in the Seaside area up north where Portlanders go to escape the city.

Grace's first teaching job was in Beaverton, and she'd enjoyed her time taking advantage of Portland's vibrant art scene and unique hipster-lumberjack culture. But when her mom had a stroke three years earlier, Grace left it all and never looked back.

Almost. She took the cat.

A giant ship's anchor sits mounted to a plinth in front of a wide stretch of lawn that constitutes Ellis Cove's single park, with a playground and pavilion tucked away from the road and nestled under the trees. Turning at the park, Grace's gaze wanders over to two kids crawling up the slide.

A man watches them nearby. At his feet rests a large backpack, like the kind backpacking tourists wear when they pass through in the summer months. But he doesn't look like a tourist. He wears jeans and a faded jacket, his greasy hair beneath his stocking cap curling at his shoulders. Bearded as he is, it's hard to see his face as Grace passes. She fights the urge to warn the children playing nearby.

Just because he looks transient doesn't make him a threat.

The road grows steeper as she moves away from the harbor. She brakes for a dog crossing the street toward the trailer park where River lives. A lifebuoy hangs from the sign post announcing Harbor Lights. It's a cozy name, but the trailers are old and the tiny yards are more full of trash than anything else. Easily overlooked, Grace drove past it for months when she first moved here before realizing it was there.

The further she climbs up the hill, the tidier the yards get. Some of the homes are painted bright colors of blue and even purple, as if thumbing their nose at the persistent gray of the coastal climate.

Grace owns a little house on Maple Street, one of the main roads that runs the full length of the town instead of being broken up by dead end streets as with so many of the other neighborhoods. It's considered a busy road by Ellis Cove standards, but is quiet compared to what Grace was used to in the city. She slows to wait for a teenager in a hoodie passing on a longboard before pulling into her driveway.

The cedar shake siding on her house has faded to a silvery gray, but the snug windows were recently replaced and the roof is only a few years old. Grace was happy to find such a nice option so close to the school. Even in a small town like Ellis Cove, real estate prices are ridiculously inflated compared with the rest of the state.

Nothing like California, though, which is why Grace's mom moved there when she retired from her job as an ER nurse in Sacramento.

"This way, I'll be closer to you and still have enough money to travel to Texas and visit Greg's family," she explained. Neither of them mentioned Jess. At the time, neither of them had known where she was.

The smell of wood smoke greets Grace as she steps out of her car. She has a wood fireplace herself, but rarely uses it since she has central heat that doesn't pollute the air or require chopping down trees. But for many other residents, wood is their sole heat source and a film of smoke is a constant during the winter months. Grace always finds it cozy, even as she feels guilty enjoying something that increases the town's carbon footprint.

But today she doesn't worry about that. She needs cozy after pushing herself to get through the long day.

"Hello, Grace!"

Her next door neighbor, Sonya, is on her knees tearing out the grass creeping onto her stone path.

"Hey, Sonya. Gorgeous day, isn't it?"

Sonya leans back on her heels and tilts her face appreciatively toward the sky. The sun is dipping in the west, sending bold rays of light through the evergreen trees and the faint haze of smoke. "I was planning on going to Coos Bay for some Christmas shopping today—my pension check came—but I had to take advantage of the break in the rain."

Grace murmurs appreciatively as she grabs her bag.

"Did you hear about that girl who went missing?" Sonya pushes to her feet and wipes her dirty gloves together as if that might make a difference in the amount of mud caked into the fibers.

"Yes." Grace shoulders her bag and leans against her car. "It's a horrible thing to happen."

"Especially this close to Christmas. Poor Nora. She's had more than her fair share of hard times. This has got to be killing her."

"I don't really know her," Grace says, hoping for a quick end to the conversation. Sonya is generous and has helped Grace navigate the history and politics of Ellis Cove more than once. But she can go on forever when she gets started on a story.

"That's right, you wouldn't. Nora's brother was shot and killed in a hunting accident when he was, oh, I don't know. Twelve? Thirteen? Nora was in high school. Her parents split up over it. She's had a rough time. Dropped out of school and quit softball. She'd hoped to get a scholarship and play in college. Married Michael Beck, but we all knew that wasn't gonna last. If I remember right, I think her mom took the kids for a while. I'm not sure when they came back. Kids need their mom, I suppose."

Grace shrugs. She doesn't want to say anything bad about Nora, especially now, but it's hard to believe any kid needs mothering like that.

Instead, she says noncommittally, "That's too bad."

"I heard on the scanner that the police were looking out on the dump road today. Someone thinks they saw Diana out there on her bike this morning."

"Oh." Grace hadn't heard this bit of news.

"You look pretty tired. You feeling okay?"

Grace blinks and straightens her spine. "I had a late night decorating the church for the Christmas concert."

"Ah, I heard about that. What a load of butt-crap, pardon my French. That concert has been a part of Ellis Cove's Christmas season for as long as most people in this town can remember. Then you get a couple of liberals on the school board and suddenly we can teach about condoms but can't sing Christmas carols."

Grace fights a smile. "They aren't teaching about condoms in the elementary school. And I'm still teaching the students a mix of traditional Christmas carols while expanding their cultural awareness. It's going to be a great concert."

Sonya wrinkles her nose. "You sound like one of those PC people."

Grace can almost hear the derisive word *millenials* churning in Sonya's head.

"The concert will be really lovely, I promise. You should come. It's Tuesday at the First Hope Church."

"First Hope? Why didn't you hold it at Unified Community? They've got a lot more room."

"I know the pastor at First Hope, so that seemed easiest on such short notice. But that's good to know for next year."

"That's Mr. Sheppard's church, right? Such a neat man. He sure loves working with the kids. My granddaughter is part of his youth group and she adores him. He never misses a night and is always available anytime they need him. Really hands on."

A white pickup truck pulls up to the curb at the end of Grace's driveway. A heavily-bearded man in a denim shirt leans forward to shout through the passenger-side window.

"Your wipers came in today, Sonya. I haven't had a chance to call yet, but anytime you want to bring in the Honda, I'll put them on for you."

Sonya turns abruptly and slaps her gloves against her pant leg. "How about now? I'll open the garage for you."

Grace seizes the chance to make a quick exit, shaking her head over a mechanic making house calls. That would never have happened in Sacramento or Portland. But Ellis Cove is something else.

By the time she unlocks the door, Milton is sitting in the middle of the entry, waiting for her. His throat rumbles in a low purr as he winds himself around her ankles.

"You're not going to like this but I'm leaving again." She gently nudges the cat away so she doesn't step on his tail as she drops her work bag to the floor.

Milton is the last sign of Max in her life. Bringing him with her prompted the fight that made her decide she wasn't going back. Max had brought him home from a shelter one day as a surprise for her. At least, that was how she remembered it. But when it was time for her to leave, Max insisted that Milton had been his all along.

The fight was pointless because Max's new apartment didn't allow cats, but neither of them knew it at the time and the angry words that flew between them said more about the neglect in their relationship than ownership of the cat.

Grace met Max in Beaverton where he was head of IT for the school district. She'd been required to attend a district-wide training on a new software system, but since very little applied to her as a music teacher, she amused herself watching Max instead. The way he flushed a little whenever someone asked him a direct question. His dark eyes that brightened when he got excited. He was handsome and intelligent, and since she was new to the school, it was an easy excuse to introduce herself.

Looking back, she realizes they probably moved too fast, but at the time it was hard to imagine that the thrilling wave of attraction and devotion wouldn't last when romantic walks and candlelit evenings were replaced by morning breath and a video game compulsion that tied up Max's weekends and left Grace feeling like she might as well be single. When her mom's health crisis upended Grace's life and she suddenly faced the prospect of moving to the Oregon coast to care for her, there was no question of whether Max would go with her. He started shopping for apartments the same day.

"The space will be good for us both," Max said the morning after the fight about the cat. "Help us decide what we really want."

The next time Grace heard from him was a text a

couple of weeks later asking if she'd canceled the utilities when she left because he had an outstanding bill in his name.

It stung to realize how little she meant to him after almost two years together, that navigating an unpaid bill was the only time he missed her.

She'd thrown herself into caring for her mom, arranging hospice and administering the details of her estate after she passed. The small home was outdated and worth very little, but the oceanfront property on a cliff overlooking the Pacific had realtors calling even before the memorial service. Her mother had only lived there a few years, expecting to enjoy a long retirement in the town of Coos Bay. To Grace, the house represented her mom's last disappointment after a lifetime full of them.

So she sold it.

But instead of returning to the Portland area, or looking for work in her native California, she bought a little house in Ellis Cove where she'd been hired as the new music teacher. Someday she might be ready to go back to the city, but for now she's content to envelop herself in the safety of small town life.

Except she's never realized how sinister small town life can be.

Thinking of the Becks and wondering how they're holding together, she goes to the bedroom where a soft black sweater with a deep v-neck lies expectantly on her bed. She doesn't remember laying it out before she left for work, but it's all a blur in the haze of a sleepless night and early morning. Milton jumps lightly onto the bed and bats at the sweater's cuff.

"Knock it off or you'll have to go out," Grace warns. Why is she thinking about Max tonight? Is it because she's about to go on her first official date since they broke up? Sonya has tried to set her up with her nephew a few times, but Grace always manages to slip out of that one before it can stick.

Evan is different. He excites her in a way no one has for a long time and for all the right reasons. She isn't necessarily looking for the thrill of new romance, but feels it all the same.

More importantly, though, Evan feels safe. Like she can trust him with her broken pieces and he'll be gentle. At her age, with the milestone birthday of thirty looming next spring, that's more attractive than ever.

But now she regrets agreeing to the date. The thought of spending the evening turning on the charm and trying to impress Evan makes her want to curl up in a heap on her bed. She feels like the taffy hanging in the front window of the sweet shop downtown, being pulled long and thin on a turning metal hook. All soft and stretched out. Not quite collapsing into a heap, but getting dangerously close with each pass.

RIVER

RIVER LOOKS at the wall of yarn and feels like she's looking at a display of modern art with the array of colors and hues. She's never been to a fancy gallery to see any famous artwork for herself, of course. She fought to put herself through college and saved every last scrap she could, donating plasma when she ran short on groceries and walking instead of buying a car. There was no time or money to travel, except for the occasional road trip with Sarah where they split gas money, ate snacks from mini marts, and slept in the car.

River has always dreamed of seeing New York City and riding a subway, but with every passing year it seems less and less likely that she'll ever get there. Todd's work as a roofer is hard to count on in the winter months, and with a baby coming things will only get tighter.

Which is fine. More than fine, even.

River's life now seems like a fairy tale. Todd doesn't drink or do drugs and he goes to church with her most Sundays. He only complains a little bit about work, and not enough that she worries he'll quit his job and pack up in the middle of the night, driving away from their life with little more than a suitcase. Quietly, so as to not alert the neighbors.

Todd didn't go to college and doesn't have any grand aspirations, but that's okay with her. It's his kindness and desire to take care of her that she fell for.

At least, she thinks she did. Lately, it's been hard to remember.

That's why knitting is such an escape. Erica suggested it as a way for her to relax in times when she was feeling anxious. She loves the way the soft yarn pulls in her fingers, and the creative power of being able to take one thing and turn it into something else is deeply satisfying.

Todd teases her about turning into an old lady, but he doesn't understand. His grandma was a sweet woman who baked cookies and organized fundraisers for the local VFW hall. How remarkable to think that grandmas were boring. Kind. Cliche.

Another woman turns down the aisle with her rattling cart and smiles politely when she sees River. River steps out of her way and pretends to be interested in the thick blanket yarn. She doesn't know how long she's been standing there. Maybe it's time to pick something and go. She's been practicing with scarves and wants to make a small blanket for the baby. That's right. That's why she's here.

Her baby. The thought both thrills her and terrifies her. The chat groups and online blogs she reads indicate that most first time moms feel the same way. But she wonders if any of them fear actually harming their child.

River has never hurt another person in her life, but what if that changes after the baby comes?

Or worse, what if she changes her mind? What if she decides it's too hard and she doesn't want to be a mom?

It's easy enough to shrug off her fears as first-time jitters, but River knows it's more than that. Her nightmares have increased lately because of Diana. She feels a kinship with the girl that worries her.

Something about her need speaks to River on a deep level. She knows that need. And now, approaching the twenty-four hour mark of when Diana disappeared, she can't shake the feeling that Diana hasn't run away. That something much worse has happened.

"Do you know what you're having?"

River starts.

The other customer is resting her forearms on the grocery cart, a long sweater with fine detail draping over her wrists. River wonders if she made it herself and feels ashamed at her own novice skills.

"No. We want it to be a surprise."

"How exciting! That must make it hard to choose then."

River shrugs. She doesn't like pink anyway, so it's not that hard.

"A nice yellow could go either way," the other woman suggests helpfully.

"Sure." River reaches toward the yellow and fingers the strands.

Yellow reminds her of the rug in Grandma Billie's house. One of her favorite pastimes was looking for patterns in the weave. Grandma Billie said toys were a waste of money and time. It was bad enough that her mother saddled her with the ungrateful brat. She didn't have to get comfortable like she'd be staying.

Don't you dare cry about it either. Your mom didn't cry when she left, did she?

River puts the yarn back. She feels warm and sticky, like it's a hot summer day, even though it's December. She reaches instead for the teal.

Her mother had a shirt this color. It comes to her suddenly, and with it, the memory that it was ruined somehow. Stained. River wonders if her mom ever had a nice thing in her life.

She remembers once when her mom took her to a secondhand store to buy a pair of shoes. River felt so special, going into a store like she mattered. The smell was so strong that River still feels a sense of nostalgia any time she enters a Goodwill.

She fell in love with a pair of glittering gold flats that were practically brand new. But they were too small and her mom had set them aside for a pair of stained boys' sneakers that were only half the cost. That's when River realized that just because she mattered enough to go into a store didn't mean she mattered enough to have money spent on her.

No.

Just because her mom wasn't able to buy frivolous shoes doesn't mean she didn't want to.

River tries to separate her feelings of the event from the facts. She doesn't know what her mom did for work before she left. She knows that Grandma Billie said she was lazy and useless, but River doesn't remember her acting lazy.

Not the way Gene did. Gene left beer bottles and

newspapers and condoms scattered all over the house and neither he nor Grandma Billie would clean up after him or his friends. It was always River who had to do it so that she didn't grow up to be fat and lazy like her mom.

Always River who paid for the sins of her mother.

River understands why her mom wanted to leave. She spent her own childhood wishing she could be anywhere but there in that little house on Vine Street. Why should her mom have felt any different? Why shouldn't she have taken the chance when it finally came—in the form of a job or a man, River doesn't know—even if it meant leaving River behind?

River isn't angry. No one else wanted her. Not Grandma Billie. Not even Gene. Why would her mom be any different? What's the use in being angry?

Erica thinks getting angry at her mother might help. She might be better able to let go of the guilt that she drove her away if she can get angry about being left in the first place. Erica thinks it's unhealthy for River to nurse the hope that her mom left because she had a good reason and something prevented her from taking River with her. Erica wants her to face the ugly truth about being abandoned so she can mourn it and move on.

For years, River expected her mom to come back and spent every birthday thinking that would be the day. That would be the day when a car she didn't recognize would pull up to the curb and Mama would get out of the driver's side, the ends of her red hair dancing in the breeze, a wide grin as she lifted her sunglasses and called Bess's name. Bess would come running and Mama would sweep her up into her arms, laughing and hugging her and never letting go.

River hates birthdays.

"Don't forget to pick up your raffle tickets for the VFW's Christmas quilt hanging in the window. Half off with a purchase of fifty dollars or more."

The announcement comes over the speaker and drags River away from her memories.

How long has she been standing there staring at the ball of teal yarn? Her face warms and she grabs three more skeins. At the checkout counter she's met with a small poster of Diana taped to the register. It's a simple color photo copy with the words, "Have you seen me?" in bold type across the top. A picture of Diana with her arm around a large dog fills the page. Her smile is hesitant, as if she's afraid of relaxing into the feeling.

"Sad about that girl, isn't it?" the clerk asks as River hands over the yarn.

"They still haven't found her, then?"

"Not a trace, from what I've heard. I heard they were searching the woods for her today. Someone thinks they saw her riding her bike outside of town."

"I hope they find her soon."

The woman murmurs in assent. "This is nice yarn. What are you going to make with it?"

As the conversation turns to River's pregnancy and the baby blanket, her mind drifts. She never owned a bicycle as a kid, but she watched some of the other children in town on theirs. They looked so free; the wind blowing in their faces, their legs pumping, standing sometimes to get more leverage and pick up speed. It all seemed a glorious miracle to River. What would it be like to have that kind of freedom? She'd imagined herself with a backpack on her back, riding far away from St. Morris and their little Florida town.

Now, looking back, she wonders if she could have gotten away even if she had the chance.

Had Diana?

NOVEMBER 29

THURSDAY

2 WEEKS BEFORE DISAPPEARANCE

GRACE

THE GREEN HOUSE sagged on the hillside as if it were preparing to give up its last breath. A wide covered porch leaned precariously on concrete blocks, and one window was boarded up with plywood. Most of the roof was covered by a brown tarp that drooped with puddles of rainwater. The part that wasn't protected by the tarp sat under a layer of moss so thick, it was hard to see the shingles beneath.

Moss and lichen left the porch steps slick under Grace's boots as she stepped up to the front door. How had the little house escaped being condemned by the city?

It hadn't been easy finding the address. Although it sat near city limits, the road wound up a forested hill and shielded the house from below. There were lots of little lanes branching off the main road with no posted house numbers, so it wasn't until her GPS alerted her that she realized she'd driven past it.

Noise like a TV sitcom drifted out of the house, and

she thought she heard the faint sound of someone crying. The smell of damp rot filled her nose and Grace eyed the rickety screen door doubtfully. Instead, she knocked on the door jamb.

A dog barked, and Grace wished for the pepper spray she kept in her purse.

"Danny!" a man shouted from inside. "Go get the door!" He let out a stream of expletives that made Grace wonder if he knew she could hear every word.

The door opened to reveal a long snout with snapping jaws. Grace stepped back, but the dog didn't break through the screen. Instead, a boy pushed the dog away and planted himself in the gap of the door between Grace and the threatening teeth.

Danny Beck was fair and freckled like his sister. He looked so thin that Grace thought one exuberant hug might crush him. But the haunted look in his eyes suggested he wasn't in danger of that kind of affection. His eyes were red and Grace wondered if he was the one she'd heard crying.

"Hello, Daniel. Is your mom home?"

The scent of cigarette smoke and body odor poured out the door. Grace shifted so she could catch a fresh breeze.

"She's at work."

"Who is it, Danny?" the man called again.

Grace peered through the screen door, trying to see the owner of the voice. A vague shape suggested the back of an easy chair.

"I'm Grace Millar from the school," she called, directing her voice to the chair. "I teach music. I wanted to talk to Diana's mom about an opportunity for our chamber choir that's happening tomorrow and—"

"Nora's at work. You'll have to come back later." The chair squeaked under his weight, but the man didn't move.

"Do you know when she'll be home?" Grace asked. She smiled at Danny, trying not to let her annoyance show.

"What do I know? She comes home when she wants to come home. Can you blame her? Leaving me here to watch her two brats, she could be halfway to Vegas for all I know."

Danny blushed at the scorn in the man's voice. He shivered in the cold, and the air coming through the screen door didn't feel any warmer than the air at Grace's back. A tall woodpile sat against the side of the house, but Grace couldn't detect any warmth of fire or smell any wood smoke. She wanted to leave this place of cold darkness, and immediately felt ashamed considering that Diana and Danny called it home.

"Can you at least tell me if the number I have for her is correct? I've left several messages but she hasn't responded."

With a heavy sigh, the bulk in the chair finally shifted and rose. The man came to the door, a cigarette in one hand and a remote in the other. He wasn't very tall, but he was broad-shouldered and stocky in the way of someone who had once been muscular but was now mostly sedentary. He looked Grace over with a keen look of distrust.

"Who did you say you are again?" His tone warned

that she'd better have a good reason for getting him out of his chair.

She forced a wide smile. "Grace Millar. And you are…?"

"Leo. What do you need with Nora?"

"I'm the music teacher at the school. Diana is in our chamber choir and we're performing for the senior citizens tomorrow at the First Hope Church. It's during school hours and requires a parent or guardian signature."

She held out the permission slip, hoping this man could sign it. At this point she didn't even care if he had a legal right. She just wanted to get back to the warmth of her car.

He barely glanced at it. "You'll need Nora for that. I'm not their dad."

Grace bit back a frustrated retort and kept her voice calm. "Here's the number the school has on file. Is this the best way to get a hold of Nora?" Clearly not, since Grace had been trying for a week with no success.

"Yeah, that's her cell. I'll tell her you stopped by." He turned away.

"Is Diana here?" Grace called to his retreating back. "Can I talk to her?" If she gave the form directly to Diana, it might be more likely to find its way into Nora's hands. She was sure this man would toss it as soon as she left.

"Suit yourself. Diana!" His shout was so loud, Grace jumped.

She smiled sheepishly at Daniel. He didn't smile back.

Diana emerged from a back bedroom. When she saw Grace, her face lit up.

"Hi Miss Miller. What are you doing here?"

"I still don't have a permission slip for tomorrow, so I was hoping to catch your mom at home."

"I thought today was the last day to turn them in."

"If you bring it tomorrow, it's not too late. I just need it before you get on the bus. Here's another form in case you need it."

Diana pushed open the screen door to take the form and Grace noticed the linoleum in front of the door was stripped to the bare subfloor with dark spots that looked like rot. The dog lunged and Grace yelped, but Diana grabbed its collar and tugged.

"Danny! Take Sadie. I'm trying to talk to Miss Miller."

Danny grabbed the excited dog and tried to pull her away from the door, but this just made her bark louder.

Leo bellowed from the chair, "Shut up you little turd!" A water bottle flew toward them both, hitting Danny on the back as he wrestled the dog down the hall.

Grace was seized with a sudden desire to grab Danny and Diana and get them away from the rotting house and angry man.

Diana looked embarrassed, and Grace tried to keep her face neutral. She pitched her voice low so Leo couldn't hear her over the TV.

"Is there anything I can do for you, Diana? Any way I can help?"

"Well, I was wondering…I meant to ask you today, but…do you think I have a chance for the solo?"

It's not what Grace had in mind, and she tried to cover her surprise with an enthusiastic, "Well, sure! Are you thinking of auditioning?"

Diana's cheeks pinked. "I wasn't sure. I don't want to try if you don't think I have a chance."

Grace thought of Savannah and Layla who both had the confidence to make their solos shine. Diana wouldn't have been her first choice with her thin voice that lacked warmth. But with this age group, part of Grace's joy came from working with any willing singer to give them a chance in the spotlight. Stretching like that gave them confidence. Helped them battle their fears. If Diana was willing to take up her sword and shield in that battle, Grace would be honored to be a part of it.

"I would love to see you audition. Right now we only have the one solo, and it may not be a good fit for everyone. But I promise we'll have more coming as we prepare for the music festival in the spring. The more practice you get auditioning, the less scary it will be."

"Thanks, Miss Miller." Diana's eyes shone.

"Are you gonna close that door or leave it open all night?" Leo barked.

"I'm just about finished, thank you. Have a good evening, Diana, and I'll see you tomorrow."

As the door shut behind her, Grace breathed the fresh air deeply. Mist was forming along the ground as early twilight descended. She exhaled, her breath streaming out in a long cloud, trying to shake off the clinging stench of the house.

Her phone rang as she got in the car. She hurried and started the engine so the call came through the car's audio. She didn't feel comfortable lingering after Leo had so clearly wanted her to leave.

"Hi Grace, how's your evening going?" Marilyn didn't call Grace after hours for kicks. Grace immediately tensed. Had she forgotten to submit the paperwork for the bus tomorrow?

"It's fine. Just wrapping up some things for tomorrow's performance."

"I wish I could make it. This chamber choir is such a fantastic idea. Giving these kids a chance to act as ambassadors for the school. At such a young age, that kind of experience will be unforgettable."

"I agree." The validation felt nice. The chamber choir was a new program Grace had introduced last year, and—as with all things new—it was taking time to catch on. It was an audition choir consisting of fifth and sixth graders who gave up their lunch recess every day to practice. In the first year she'd only had twelve students. This year, the number had doubled.

"How can I help you, Marilyn?"

"Well, I just wanted you to know that I've talked to Roger about your idea to turn the concert into a community event."

"Yeah?" It was River's idea, but Grace didn't correct her, anxious to hear what the superintendent had said. She shifted into second to ease down the steep hill. The road wasn't paved, and deep ruts jarred her in spite of creeping along at a snail's pace.

"He says that as long as you don't mention the concert in class or in your lesson plans, you're welcome to move forward. The board doesn't even need to be involved because it's not a school event."

Grace mulled this over. It would be extra work, but not impossible. "I can do that. Can we get the word out through normal channels? I see fliers going home all the time for private cheer camps and swim lessons, that sort of thing. And how about the PTO? They usually help a lot with logistics."

Marilyn's voice held a smile. "I've already talked to them and they're on board. Not officially as the PTO, of course. Just a private group of parents facilitating a community celebration."

"That's fantastic." Grace stopped at the bottom of the hill and waited to turn onto the main road. "Thank you, Marilyn. That's great news. First Hope says we can hold it there, so I'll work out the details with their secretary."

"Wonderful. It's all settled then. Sorry to put you through this yo-yo, but I appreciate your flexibility, Grace."

"Of course. Things like this matter to the students more than we know." Grace's left eye twitched and she pressed a thumb against it to keep it still. She could handle the extra stress. It was worth it. "Marilyn, I have a question for you before I let you go."

"Yes?"

"I stopped at Diana and Danny Beck's house to drop off a permission slip for tomorrow. It wasn't...it doesn't seem like a very safe place. How do I know...when do you think authorities should get involved? I've done the abuse training, of course, but it always seems more clear-cut than this. How do I know if I should call or not?"

"Hmm. You said this was the Becks?" It sounded like Marilyn was talking around a pen cap and Grace pictured her writing down what she'd said. "In general, it's best to call if you suspect any sort of abuse or neglect. But with the level of poverty in this town, there are a lot of good people who are doing the best they can to get by."

"It's more than that. Diana showed me a letter from her mom on Tuesday that was pretty...disturbing."

"Disturbing in what way?"

"Well, *I* was disturbed by it. But there wasn't anything criminal about it. It wasn't very...loving, I guess. More like her mom was annoyed with her all the time." Putting it into words made her feel like she was overreacting. Embarrassed, Grace added, "It's more of a feeling than anything I've actually seen. I don't want to ignore warning signs, but I also don't want to get them in trouble over nothing."

"It's not our place to decide whether or not it's nothing," Marilyn said firmly. "But if it makes you feel better, I've reached out about providing support services to the family in the past, so they do have options. If you're worried there's more going on, call the hotline. And be as specific as possible. Dates, if you have them. Let them decide whether or not it's worth looking into."

"Okay, I'll do that." Grace made a mental note to start a list as soon as she got home. If she watched for a few weeks and wrote down specifics that concerned her, then she would have something more tangible to report. And a few weeks shouldn't make that big of a difference, should it?

RIVER

RIVER COUNTED out the pills into the pill box. It was ridiculous how many meds she was taking these days. And none of them seemed to be helping. None of them stopped the nightmares.

Flashbacks? Hallucinations?

All of the above?

It wasn't so bad when Todd was with her, but when he was gone during the day or sleeping at night, she couldn't seem to rest her mind. She heard things. The wind outside battering the trailer home's siding. Someone's trash can rolling down the street. Grandma Billie reaching for her belt.

River grabbed the countertop and breathed in through her nose, closing her eyes and focusing on the air filling her lungs. She opened her eyes and looked at the bottles of medication lined up on the bathroom counter. How easy it would be to dump them in the trash. Flush them down the toilet. Nothing was getting better, and now she was stuck taking them every day because to stop abruptly could cause a seizure.

It was cold in the bathroom. The floor had been ripped up, and a draft seeped in from under the tub. Drywall along one wall had been removed to the studs, and the bare innards were ugly and rough, threatening splinters if she got too close. It was their only bathroom and Todd had promised to finish it before Christmas, but that was less than four weeks away and there was still so much to do. If River knew how to repair drywall and lay flooring, she would have finished it herself. But as it was, she couldn't even paint when the drywall was finished. She didn't want to risk the fumes hurting the baby.

She didn't like the look of the bare studs. It made her feel like she was living in an unfinished house. Unfinished like the basement room Gene had called her special bedroom. A room he built special, for a princess.

River started the water in the shower and let it run until steam filled the air. Then she stripped and climbed over the side of the tub. With her swollen belly, her center of gravity felt off all the time and she had to be careful not to slip.

The hot water beating against her body should have been relaxing, but the sound of the shower dampened all other noise. She strained to hear over the running water. What if Todd came home and she didn't hear him? What if someone called? What if there was a fire? Or a burglar?

She knew her fears were unfounded, and she tried to ground herself in the soothing feeling of the hot water coursing down her back. The sharp tingle of her cold limbs as they warmed up. Water trickling over her shoulders and down her belly.

Gentle and light.

Until the water became black ants swarming over her, thousands of them. Writhing in a dark mass, they crawled through her hair and spilled down her back. Piling over each other and tickling her skin.

River screamed and grabbed the shower curtain, tearing down the rod in her panic. She jumped out of the shower, nearly slipping over the edge of the tub as she reached for her towel. Panting, she rubbed her body. Rubbing off the ants.

She whimpered in panic, her breathing loud and fast. She scrubbed until she was dry and looked in the mirror, terrified she would see them in her hair, crawling out of her ears.

Her damp face looked back at her through the condensation on the glass. Her hair dripped down her forehead, but there were no ants.

The shower curtain lay in a heap next to the tub, and the water was still running. Steam filled the tub so it was hard to see, but River stepped closer. Made herself look.

The water ran clear. The tub was clean.

But she'd felt them. She'd seen them. Ants. Swarms of ants.

River closed her eyes and saw them spilling out of the wall over her head. She snapped her eyes open again. She couldn't remember that now. Maybe next week when she met with Erica in therapy. It would be safer in her room with the plants and the water feature trickling quietly in the corner.

But the memory wouldn't stay away. The mass of black ants pouring out of the wall and onto her felt so real. Nausea swelled in her stomach, tingling the back of her throat. River leaned over the tub and vomited. She trembled as she rinsed it down the drain, shut off the shower tap, and shakily wrapped herself in a towel. Todd would be home soon. She needed to start dinner.

But the ants, they were everywhere.

There'd been a colony living in the bathroom wall. The bulge had swelled until Gene cut into the drywall to see what the problem was. Bess had been standing beneath with a bucket when they spilled out. She'd screamed. Dropped the bucket. Ants had poured over her instead.

Gene had laughed.

Grandma Billie had made her clean them all up with her hands.

Bess wouldn't use the bathroom with the door closed again.

When Grandma Billie figured out why, she turned the handle around so she could lock Bess inside whenever she wanted. No beating hurt Bess as much as being locked away in that room.

River lay on her bed, curled in a ball, trying to keep Bess at bay. She didn't want to relive it again. She didn't want to go back to that house on Vine Street.

That bathroom where she was locked up.

The basement room Gene made special for her. But not really for her. For *them*. The men who called her *Princess*.

"Hey, baby, what's the matter? You feeling sick?"

Pressure on her head made her flinch. Todd was there, kneeling at her side, his brows drawn together with concern.

River blinked. She wasn't in the bathroom at

Grandma Billie's. She wasn't in the basement room with the pink bedspread. She was lying on her bed in the trailer and Todd was there.

She nodded. It was easier than trying to explain.

"You're freezing cold. Here, let's get you dressed."

Todd helped her stand and took off the wet towel. The cold air made her shiver. He looked her over and she wished for the towel back. He ran a hand down her back and she recoiled, thinking of the ants. She stepped away and grabbed clothes from the dresser.

"Sorry," he said. "You're just so beautiful."

River didn't feel beautiful. She felt worn and filthy and vulgar.

"How was work?" she asked, changing the subject. She pulled a sweatshirt over her head and looked at the clock, disgusted with how much time she'd lost. She moved sluggishly, still feeling off.

"Good. I got a nice run on that duplex over on Fourth. It'll be a quick job." He dumped the change from his pocket on the dresser with his wallet and keys. "I'll need the car tomorrow. Josh can't drive."

"That's fine. It's the concert for the old folks home, so if you can drop me off at the school I'll be there most of the day anyway."

Todd sat on the bed to pull off his boots. "If this job at the school is getting to be too much—" he began, but River stopped him.

"It's fine. I haven't felt great lately, but it'll be fine."

"It's the holidays, isn't it?"

River shot him a look, surprised.

"You were like this last year too. I thought it was just

because we'd moved, but it's not that, is it? It's because of her."

River didn't have to ask who he meant. "I guess. Probably. I've never really liked the holidays, but you could be right."

As much as River had loved school as a child—because it got her out of the house for almost eight hours a day—the time from mid-October to January was brutal. While all the other kids talked about Halloween costumes and trick-or-treating and visiting grandparents for Thanksgiving and what they wanted to get for Christmas, River had gone home each day to Grandma Billie. Grandma Billie treated each holiday like a retailer conspiracy designed to get her to waste her money on a worthless, ungrateful slut.

The last day of school before Christmas break was full of treats and parties and gifts. River had dreaded the gift exchange because she never had anything to share. Somehow there were always enough gifts for all the kids, and it was only years later that she realized the teachers must have come prepared with extras. But she didn't know it then, so she spent the whole time with her face hot and the blood rushing in her ears, sure that someone would realize there weren't enough gifts to share and everyone would know it was her fault.

She did like the treats, though. Parents brought in snacks and popcorn balls and other goodies, and River ate as much as she could, knowing that it was the only candy she would get that Christmas. When the other kids left to go home, excited because their holiday was beginning, she trailed sadness, knowing that hers was behind.

School starting again after the break was bittersweet.

Finally, she could leave home and return to her one safe place. But all the other kids were full of talk about what they'd done over the break. Traveling to relatives or going to amusement parks or playing video games all night. No one ever asked her what she got for Christmas. Maybe they could tell because she wasn't showing up with new jewelry or shiny shoes with white laces.

Into her mind flashed an image of Diana, her toes poking through the torn sole of her shoe. Her sudden interest in her backpack when other kids talked about their holiday plans. Was this why the memories were getting so much worse? Was it because River was spending every day at a school during the hardest time of year?

River let Todd hold her and tried to make herself lean into him. She knew his feelings would be hurt that she'd rejected his earlier advance. She thought about trying to explain what she was feeling. Could she tell him about the ants? Could she explain that every touch made her feel like something was crawling on her? But then she'd have to speak the words. She'd have to say them out loud, which took more courage than she had.

"Do you think you could work on finishing the bathroom tonight?"

She felt Todd's sigh.

"I was hoping to relax and watch the game. I'm too tired to jump into that project."

"I know, but it's not getting done." *And it's triggering bad memories.* "Is there anything I can do to help it go faster?"

Todd snorted and pulled away. "You? I'm not going to have my pregnant wife on her hands and knees working on a remodel project. Besides, what if you hallucinate or something while you're running a drill or a saw? No way. Just leave it to me. I'll take care of it. You need to take care of yourself. And the baby."

I am *thinking about myself*, River thought.

But that made her feel selfish. She hardly made any money working for the school. Todd was the one who paid their monthly rent and put food on the table. The least she could do was not complain when it took him a long time to finish a project.

"Come on. Let me get you something warm to drink. That'll warm you right up." He grabbed her stomach with both hands and shook it gently. "Right, little Sorrel?"

"Sorrel?"

"I heard it on the radio today. What do you think?"

River grimaced as she followed him down the hall toward the kitchen. "Girl or boy?"

"Either. But I was thinking girl."

"I don't even know what that is."

"It's some kind of plant."

River wrinkled her nose.

"Okay, fine. So you don't like Sorrel. How about Elizabeth?"

River started. She was glad Todd's back was turned. "I've never liked the name Elizabeth. I like Miriam, though."

"Hmm...sounds a bit old fashioned."

"More old fashioned than Elizabeth?"

Todd reached for a mug and the box of tea. "What kind?"

She picked out a caffeine free peppermint and resisted the urge to take the mug from him. Erica would say Todd needed to serve her for both of their sakes, and allowing it was a way of showing appreciation for his thoughtfulness. But she still felt ashamed.

When the water was hot, River dropped the tea bag into the mug and watched it leak yellow.

"Are you feeling better?"

She nodded. Having someone with her was always better than being alone. Besides, this Christmas they had a new baby on the way, so there was lots to be excited about. Maybe she should make a stocking for the baby, with matching ones for her and Todd. Todd might think it was dumb since the baby wasn't coming until early spring, but she wanted to practice. If she was going to be a good mom, she'd have to figure out how to give her baby the kind of Christmas she'd never had.

LIBBY

THE MERMAID TAVERN

LIBBY HIT the curb with the back tire as she pulled into the parking lot of The Mermaid Tavern. The windows of the bar were covered with black paper, but someone had hung strands of Christmas lights around the edges that peeked through the gaps, offering a strange mix of the comforting and the forbidden.

Libby swung the old Taurus into a spot and grimaced. She needed more practice getting the turns right. Oh well. The night air was cold against her legs when she opened the door. She was wearing a skirt—not as short as she would have liked, but short enough. She hugged her denim jacket tight against the wind and hurried to the entrance.

The wooden door was scratched and scarred from a lifetime of use, opening to people coming to drown their sorrows or meet a special someone. Libby was hoping for both.

She felt a little thrill as she stepped inside and reached for River's wallet. People never gave her any trouble when she tried to pass as the older woman. Especially when the light was low.

People weren't very observant.

Libby went to the bar and ordered a beer with a full head, then settled at a table in the corner where she could watch the room. She still didn't know the right people in this town yet. The last time she'd tried to get a hit, the guy had roughed her up a bit.

Todd had been so mad. As if it were her fault. As if she'd asked for it.

Todd hated her. He only put up with her for River's sake, but she was pretty sure his patience was wearing thin. That was fine with Libby. The feeling was mutual. She didn't trust his devoted husband act. She'd known too many so-called devoted husbands. Might even meet one tonight in this bar.

If only she could get away from River and Todd both. Stop them from controlling her life.

Libby dipped her finger in the foam and licked it off.

A man sitting at the bar glanced in her direction meaningfully. She sized him up, taking in his thinning hair. Could he be the connection she needed? Maybe. He looked to be in his late 20's, maybe early 30's. Not bad looking, but she wasn't sure she wanted to get entangled with an older man. Sometimes they could be really demanding. Someone young, like her, would be best. Someone who could get her what she was looking for but didn't care if she'd be around next week.

Problem was, the guy at the bar was the youngest one in. Maybe it was a bad night of the week.

Maybe it was a bad town.

He looked at her again, and she looked away, but it

was too late. He slid off his stool and made his way over to her table. A little unsteady as if he'd already had too many. Definitely not what she was looking for, but maybe she could pick his pocket.

"Hey, sugar," he said by way of greeting. "This seat taken?"

He stood with his weight on one leg, like he thought he looked cooler that way. Libby hid a smile.

"Just waiting for my friend." She tapped the laminate table for emphasis.

"I could be your friend." He had nice teeth when he smiled. Libby cocked her head, wondering if she should give him a shot.

"You think? What sort of friend do you think I'm looking for?"

"I think you're looking for someone who respects you and will treat you right. But also knows how to show you a good time."

Libby smirked. "And that's you?"

He smiled again and took a drink. "Maybe."

"What's your name?"

"Stewart, but you can call me Stew. What's yours?"

"Maria." Libby took another drink. Across the room the door opened, drawing her attention.

Todd.

He peered into the darkened room but didn't see her sitting behind Stew. After a quick glance around the room, he headed toward the bar.

Libby slipped out of her chair. "I've gotta run to the bathroom really quick. Back in a jiff."

She hurried down the small hallway and was relieved when the door was unlocked. The bathroom doubled as a closet with a yellow mop bucket taking up half the space. The concrete floor had a large drain in the middle and graffiti and unidentifiable stains mottled the walls, making Libby glad she wasn't seeing it in the light of day.

She looked at her reflection, considering what to do. Todd was getting better at finding her. She'd have to switch things up. This might be the last time she visited the Mermaid.

A knock sounded on the door.

"Just a minute!" She turned on the tap. Maybe she could sneak out the employee entrance in the back. She took her time washing her hands and opened the door.

Todd stood in the hallway, his eyes dark with fury.

Libby laughed.

"Hey Todd, you come for a drink?"

"What are you doing here?" Low, through clenched teeth.

"What does it look like?"

He looked back at the table where she'd been sitting. Stewart was gone.

"It's not what you think. We were just chatting. Perfectly harmless."

Even in the dim light, she could see the red under his skin. Or maybe that was from the neon Budweiser sign overhead.

"Give me the keys and get in the car."

Libby frowned. "Don't talk to me like that. You're not my father."

"No, I'm not. But you're acting like a child. Hand them over. I'm taking you home now."

Libby considered testing his patience further. But what was the point? So he could call the cops on her? If she caused a scene, everyone in the bar would remember her. She didn't want that. And she especially didn't want to make an impression on the cops.

She dug through River's purse and found the keys, then passed them over and stalked past Todd to the door.

Out in the parking lot she bypassed the front seat and reached instead for the back door—the one that had been replaced, but hadn't been painted to match, so it stood out, dark blue against gray. She sat in the back, wanting to put as much distance between herself and Todd as possible.

He didn't speak as he started the engine and backed out of the lot, but Libby could feel his eyes on her in the rearview mirror. She stared out the side window, avoiding eye contact.

Once they were on the main road, he finally spoke.

"This has got to stop. I don't know what else to do, but you can't keep going on like this."

Libby didn't answer.

"I had to ask Josh for a ride. Got him out of bed because you stole the car."

"I never asked you to come get me," Libby snapped.

Todd laughed sourly. "What am I supposed to do, just let you destroy your life? It's not just your life you're screwing with here."

"You don't have a right to tell me how to live my life. All you care about is River and the baby. Admit it."

Todd humphed a sound like a would-be laugh. "Yeah, it's true. I admit it."

"See? Why would I trust you when you don't care about me at all?"

"Of course I care about you. I wouldn't be here if I didn't."

Libby settled back against the seat, feeling a slight buzz from the alcohol. It wasn't quite what she'd gone looking for—she'd hoped to hook up with something harder—but she would take whatever she could get.

When they got home, Todd parked in the carport and went inside without even waiting to see if she followed. He didn't open her door like he would have if River had been there. What a tool.

Libby stayed in the car until she had to pee. When she finally went inside, the door to the bedroom was closed and the light was off. Todd must have given up and gone to bed. Good. At least he wouldn't yell at her until tomorrow. She grabbed a blanket to sleep on the couch. He still had River's keys, so she wasn't going anywhere.

But there was always tomorrow.

DECEMBER 14

FRIDAY

1 DAY AFTER DISAPPEARANCE

GRACE

GRACE ZIPS her ankle boots with the tortoiseshell buckles and straightens, eyeing herself in the full-length mirror. She's curled her hair to hang in soft waves around her face, a lengthy process that gave her plenty of time to wonder about the evening and if there are any rules she needs to know about dating a pastor.

She tries to remember her first kiss with Max, but it happened at a party when she was a little tipsy and the details have faded with time. Besides, Evan is nothing like Max.

She trusts him, but still she pulls up River's number on her phone.

> Hey, just checking in for safety. E will be picking me up soon.

River doesn't usually reply quickly to texts, but she must already be on her phone because the response comes almost immediately.

That's right! Where are you going?

Captain's Quarters

Nice. Didn't think pastors made that kind of money.

Grace squirms a little at that. River and Todd get by, but they probably can't afford to eat out very often, let alone at the nicest restaurant this side of Coos Bay.

Shore Acres after that, so it'll be late, but I'll check in when I get home.

River's response comes in the form of a gif showing a child in a party hat wriggling with excitement. It helps Grace relax a little. She's feeling off tonight and worries the date is doomed before it's even started.

A knock sounds at the door a few minutes before 6:00 pm and Grace opens it to find Evan on the stoop holding a bouquet of flowers. Red roses and white daisies dominate the color scheme, with gold-tipped ferns and a shiny ribbon giving it a festive air.

"They only had Christmas arrangements, so I hope you don't mind." He's dressed in a gray sweater and slacks, and his hair is pulled back, exposing the short undercut. As much as Grace likes his loose curls, this look emphasizes his high forehead and strong, sloping nose.

For the first time all day, she feels a little thrill.

Grace smiles and reaches for the bouquet. "I've been eating and breathing Christmas since Thanksgiving. They're perfect. Come in."

Grateful she took time to tidy up, Grace goes to the

kitchen and grabs a vase while Milton inspects the newcomer. The water rinses off the lotion she put on just before Evan arrived, so she quickly reapplies hand cream before joining him in the living room.

Just in case.

Evan is looking at the tree that stands in the corner, bedecked in silver and white decorations.

"It's lovely."

Grace feels a twinge of shame.

"Thank you. I'm always partial to themed trees. But when my mom passed away, I inherited all her decorations. Crafts we kids made when we were little, stuff she and my dad collected over the years, that sort of thing. A part of me feels obligated to use them instead of keeping them stored away in a box, but I just can't bring myself to embrace popsicle stick chic. Does that make me a bad daughter?"

Evan's mouth pulls up at the corner. "Maybe you need two trees."

Grace laughs.

"I'm serious," he insists. "Then you don't have to choose between what's an expression of you and what's a meaningful way of honoring your mom."

"How about your parents?" she asks, turning the conversation to Evan as they head out to the car. He opens her door, and he does it in a way that seems effortless, as if he doesn't even have to think about it.

"Mine are both still living," he answers. "I'm the youngest of four, so there will be plenty of others to share the sentimental load when the time comes."

As they drive out of town, Evan talks about his older siblings, his growing number of nieces and nephews, and how noisy his family gets when they're all together over the holidays. Grace's plan to spend the break sleeping in and catching up on Hallmark movies feels a little anemic by comparison.

The weathered wood of The Captain's Quarters restaurant stands out in proud lines against the fading light of the expansive sky, where clouds tinged pink near the western horizon mark the last light of the setting sun. Perched on a cliff overlooking the ocean, the restaurant features a one-hundred-eighty-degree view with insets and angles so virtually every table has a window seat.

Grace and Evan are seated in a quiet corner with a view of the Ellis Cove lighthouse to the south. It's become Grace's favorite, its distinctive red glass making the Fresnel lens flash alternating beams of white and red lights. Perfect for the holidays.

In spite of the high ceilings and full length windows, the room is warm and Grace stifles a yawn.

"I'm sorry!" She laughs at Evan's expression.

"I'm boring you already? That doesn't bode well."

"No, not at all! I just didn't get a lot of sleep last night."

"Concert stress?"

Grace shifts in her chair, the wood hard against her back. What would happen if she told him what had really kept her up last night? If she told him her suspicions about River? As a member of the clergy, would he keep it to himself?

But she dismisses the thought. It wouldn't be fair to River, even though it's burning her up inside.

"The concert...Diana...there's a lot going on right now."

Evan nods gravely. "I know how much you tried to help her."

Grace looks up, thinking for a split second he's talking about River. But the sorrow in his eyes makes her realize he's talking about Diana. Shame twists in her middle, as familiar as the weight of the pendant around her neck. She fingers it as she considers her response.

"It wasn't enough. It wasn't even close to enough." The words sound more bitter than she intended. She reaches for her water glass to stop from saying anything else.

"We're holding a candlelight vigil tomorrow. Have you heard?"

"That's a great idea. At the church?"

"School, actually. I talked to Marilyn about it today. More people might come if it's not a church thing."

"Do you..." Grace begins, pauses, then makes herself finish, "...need any help?"

His eyes soften, and the dimple in his chin makes a brief appearance. "Actually...I'd love your help, but for something kind of specific. Do you think your choir might sing? Just one of the numbers you did for the senior citizens, nothing special."

A wave of impossibility washes over Grace. The last thing she wants to do is attract attention during a candlelight vigil meant to show support for Diana's family.

"I don't know, Evan. That would be...tough. Really tough. I don't know how I'd get the word out on such short notice, and we'd be at the mercy of whoever showed up that night. With no time to practice beforehand."

"So it wouldn't be your best performance. That's not what it's about. You said yourself how much Diana loves being in the choir. You don't have to decide now. Just think about it."

A waiter brings their meal, and the conversation turns to safer topics. Grace doesn't have much of an appetite, but she makes herself take a few bites of her hazelnut crusted lamb chops. The huckleberry balsamic sauce is perfection, but she can't savor it. Not tonight.

"There's that yawn again," Evan points out as they look over the dessert menu. His eyes glint in the light of the votive candle burning on the table between them.

"I'm sorry. It really isn't you."

"We don't have to do the lights tonight. If you'd rather, we can go after school gets out for the break."

"No. I'd like to go tonight. I missed it last year, and I'm afraid I won't have the courage to go alone."

He raises a questioning eyebrow.

"I used to take my mom every year," Grace explains. "It was kind of our thing. Last year I didn't go because it was the first Christmas without her. But I want to go back."

Besides, the alternative is sitting at home alone with her thoughts.

By the time dessert comes, full night has descended and only the white fringes of cresting waves are visible. Lights wink on the horizon from boats returning to the harbor. They appear out of nowhere. First, only darkness, with no separation between sea and sky. Then, small pinpricks of light ever so slowly drawing closer to shore.

When Grace stares out at the horizon, she can understand why it was once commonly believed that the world was flat. Her eyes tell her the same thing. There's an edge out there as far as her eyes can see. Beyond that, it's easy to believe a person would fall into oblivion.

All day she's felt that nameless oblivion lurking just out of sight, and now that it's dark it feels closer than ever. She takes Evan's arm as they leave the restaurant, seeking an anchor to keep her grounded as they face the night.

EVAN

EVAN SHIFTS into a lower gear as the road tightens into a winding two-lane highway closed in by evergreen trees and lush rainforest. He notices Grace's grip on the door handle and backs off the gas.

"Maybe I should have taken the 101. You doing okay?"

She nods and manages a weak smile. "I don't get car sick, but these roads make me nervous in the dark. You never know what's coming around the corner."

"That's fair," he observes as they pass a Deer X-ing sign, the reflective paint illuminated by the headlights.

Fog creeps across the road from the shoulder, and Evan slows further. Occasionally the forest parts, revealing open sky above a pulsing sea, the gray of the water fringed white, and a shy moon hiding behind a bank of low clouds.

Grace's mood seems natural enough, but it's almost too natural. Like she's making a concerted effort to keep things light. Diana's disappearance hangs between them, and they're both working too hard to pretend it doesn't.

As if reading his mind, Grace says, "Police were at the school today asking questions about Diana and her family. It's funny, you spend every day with these kids, and you feel like you really get to know them. Then someone asks you whose house they might have gone to after school or whether they like to hang out at the beach or the park, and suddenly you realize you don't know them at all. Not really."

"I know what you mean. I went to see Nora today and felt like I was wading through an alligator swamp, never knowing what might turn up if I stepped wrong. Did she need comfort? A listening ear? Counsel? And who am I to think I'm qualified to give any of those things?"

He feels Grace's eyes on him and keeps his gaze fixed on the road, tension winding up his shoulders with his confession.

"Of course you're qualified to do those things," Grace says gently. "You're her spiritual leader. That's your job."

"I don't know. I never felt so out of my depth. People look to me like the words I say are going to bring healing and peace. It's my job to fix things, but how can I fix this? What do I say to a parent who's lost a child? Literally lost her." It feels good to say out loud the things that have been bothering him all day. "I knew that choosing this calling would mean taking on the burdens of others. I welcomed it. Funerals, divorces, miscarriages, affairs, all the pain and the heartache this life of sorrows brings. But I don't feel prepared to deal with something like this."

"I'm not sure anyone is ever prepared for this kind of tragedy until it happens."

Grace gazes out the window at the trees, flashes of ghostly white pillars appearing in the bright headlights before disappearing just as quickly into darkness. Her profile accentuates her upturned nose and round cheeks.

Evan thought her pretty enough the first time they met, but spending time singing with her these past weeks has ignited something in him. She's more than just a pretty face. It's the beauty of her soul that he's falling for, and seeing her concern for Diana makes his heart swell. He looks back at the road, hoping she won't notice his admiration.

When she speaks, it's with the weight of someone needing to unburden herself.

"I can't help but wonder if things might have been different for Diana if I'd reported my suspicions two weeks ago. I was there at her house. I saw the way they lived. But I was trying not to let my biases push me to unfair conclusions."

Evan reaches out and squeezes her hand. It's small and soft, and he searches for the right words to say.

"You can't blame yourself. You did what you thought was right."

Nice one. Comforting, but not very romantic. He sounds like a pastor. He wants to hold her hand as a friend, or maybe something more.

Definitely something more.

"Besides," he continues, "even if you'd made that call, it might not have made a difference. I don't think Nora and Leo are responsible."

"I guess it depends on how you look at it. Whether she ran away or something else happened to her, they share some of the blame for not providing a safe home in the first place. Don't you think?"

Evan moves his hand back to the wheel to navigate a tight turn. "I don't know. Children disappear all the time and parents think it's their fault. That sort of guilt could eat a person alive and doesn't bring the child home."

"They still failed her." Grace's voice hardens. "I failed her too. She trusted me and I tried to help, but I only made things worse. If I'd never gotten involved, maybe she wouldn't be missing."

Evan reaches for her hand again. "That doesn't matter now. All that matters is finding her. You've talked to the police about your concerns?"

"Yes."

"Then that's all you can do."

She holds his fingers loosely, and Evan hopes he isn't being too forward. He wants to give her space but also make his interest clear. He worries that he rushed things last night at the church. Maybe it was good they were interrupted so he didn't do something he would later regret.

For a long while, the only sound is the hum of tires on the road. They finally pull to a stop and Evan flicks his turn signal. "Sorry, this isn't great date conversation."

"It's all right. I don't think either of us can really think about anything else right now."

"Sure we can. Tell me what your plans are for Christmas. Will you be staying in the area? Going to see family?"

The pull to a mundane topic shifts the mood in the car like a whiplash.

Smooth, Sheppard.

"I...I haven't decided. Last year I went to my aunt's in Seattle, but I'm not sure I'm feeling it this year."

"You have an older brother, right? Where's he at?"

"He's in Texas, so I would've had to get tickets months ago. There's no way I could afford them now. But his wife doesn't really like me, so it's probably good."

"How could she not like you?"

"I don't know. We've just never gotten along. She's nice enough, but our interactions always feel forced. Their house looks like something off Pinterest, and she's very trendy. Really active on social media. Whenever I visit, I feel like I'm tracking the proverbial dog poop into her sacred influencer space."

Evan chuckles. "Sounds like Christmas would be a delight."

"Right. Get ready for your photo shoot before you get out of bed. Ugh." Grace shudders. "My nieces are pretty great. But the oldest one has already started her own makeup channel."

"How old is she?"

Grace hesitates. "Twelve? Thirteen? I'm not sure"

Evan whistles. "Get their image issues started young, I guess."

"In fairness, I think she knows more about makeup than I do. Maybe I should watch it."

"This is the part where I'm supposed to say you look more beautiful without makeup, right?"

"No! I wasn't thinking that at all."

Evan grins. They're descending a sharp hill toward Sunset Bay on the final approach to Shore Acres. "It's fine. I got it. I do think you're beautiful without makeup, so it's not even a stretch."

Grace snorts. "You've never seen me without makeup."

"What are you talking about? You never wear makeup."

"Yes I do! Not a lot, but I do."

Evan squints and leans toward her. "It must be very subtle then."

"Stop staring at me!" Grace buries her face in her arms.

"I can't help it. Your natural beauty overwhelms me."

"Stop it!" She laughs freely, and the sound cracks through the gloom of their earlier conversation. "I'm really not fishing for compliments."

Brake lights shine in the darkness ahead, and they slow to a stop behind a long line of cars waiting to get into Shore Acres.

"I appreciate all kinds of beauty," Evan says, his voice tinged with humor. "God made you the way you are and He did a good job. A very good job. If you choose to embellish His work, that's up to you. It's not anyone else's business."

"Thank you," Grace says with a sly smile, her eyes bright in the red glow of tail lights. "He did a good job with you, too. Just saying."

At last, it's starting to feel like the evening he hoped for.

GRACE

SHORE ACRES SITS on a large promontory owned by a rich lumber baron in the early twentieth century who built a lavish mansion on the edge of the exposed bluff in the early part of the twentieth century. Stepping out of the car, a dull roar greets Grace from unseen waves pounding against the cliffs. The wind gusting from the sea tosses her hair and makes her regret taking the time to curl it.

Evan notices her struggling to keep it out of her face and smiles, his white teeth flashing in the dark. "Let's hurry. It'll be less windy inside."

He grabs her hand and jogs to the entrance and she laughs in spite of the pinch in her boots.

Once they pass through the entrance to the gardens, Grace is hit with a sudden wave of sadness so sharp she catches her breath. Lights festoon bushes, trees, and low hedges lining the walkways. Two children stand in the path, pointing toward an animated whale which rises out of the grass in the distance, arcing through the air before splashing into the darkness. The gardener's cottage—the only original structure remaining—is outlined in white lights and a line has gathered to tour the interior.

Evan waits as a young family passes, pushing a stroller with an infant wrapped in a fuzzy fleece blanket. He sees Grace's expression and his smile fades.

"Is this a bad idea? We don't have to do this if you…"

Grace blinks and forces a smile. "No, I'm fine. Just thinking of the last time I was here with my mom. I didn't know it was our last Christmas together." She cringes at how it sounds. "I'm sorry. I don't mean to be a killjoy. You're going to regret bringing me."

The path clears and Grace walks forward determinedly. Evan falls into step beside her.

"Do you regret coming?"

"Of course not!" But she wonders if it sounds a little too earnest. She takes him by the arm. "There always has to be a first time. I'm glad it's with you."

They pass the fountain that stands at the crossroads to the cottage. Evan looks at the line of visitors bundled against the cold.

"Do you want to go in?"

"Sure."

Grace's mom hadn't asked. She'd expected it. But she'd been so weak, she could barely walk a few minutes without having to rest on one of the long wooden benches lining the hedgerows. Grace had eyed the steps leading up to the cottage. She knew that just inside a steeper, narrower staircase led to the second floor.

"We should have brought a wheelchair," Grace said, annoyed at herself for not thinking of it. "You're worn out as it is. I'm not going to risk you falling on those stairs."

Her mom gave her a disapproving look, her lips pressed together in annoyance. "Don't I have a choice? I know my own limits." She'd regained her speech after the stroke, but when she was tired like this she sometimes slurred her words.

"You mean like how you almost pitched headlong down the stairs to the Japanese pond?" When her mom's feet had tangled up, Grace had nearly had a heart attack trying to catch her. She didn't want to ruin the night with a fight, but she wouldn't budge.

They didn't tour the cottage.

It was the final sour note to an evening riddled with worry and disagreement.

Now, as the line moves forward, Grace looks for something more pleasant to think of. "Was this a tradition for you growing up?"

"Of course," Evan answers. "Five dollars for a whole car load? Cheapest entertainment of the season. Not that my teenage self appreciated it. I lived in fear that I would run into kids from school, never considering that if I did, it would only be because they were here with their families too."

"Worried about your image?" Grace smiles at the thought of a young Evan who was too cool to hang out with his family in public.

The light from the cottage bathes his face in a soft glow. He smirks. "I was one of only two Black kids in my graduating class. Of course I was worried about my image."

The revelation feels like a gap between them and Grace squeezes his arm, unsure what to say.

"So, when did you know you wanted to be a pastor?"

Evan is silent so long she thinks maybe her words were lost against a backdrop of laughing children as a large group passes, their hands cupped around steaming hot cider that sends plumes of steam trailing behind them.

"I had a roommate in college who was set on proving God was only a cultural myth perpetuated by ancient civilizations for our species' survival. He claimed that since we've evolved enough to understand the world through science, it was time to let the myth go. I'm not sure I had a single conversation with him that first semester where he didn't inject some jab against my faith."

"Sounds like a lovely guy."

"He was an obnoxious little punk. Not because of what he believed, but because of how he treated those who believed differently. But that second semester, as I got further into my Poli Sci major—"

"Politics!" Grace blurts incredulously. "You were going to be a politician?" She tries to picture him in a business suit standing behind a different kind of lectern and preaching a different kind of message.

Evan's chuckle sounds more than a little self-effacing. "I don't know. I didn't have a firm plan. But I wanted to make a difference in the world. That seemed like a good place to start."

"Until you realized you'd have to sell your soul to the devil, you mean."

An older man in line turns around and shoots her a dark glance.

"Don't worry," Grace says loudly. "He's a pastor. He gave his soul to God."

Evan stifles a laugh.

"So, what happened to turn you from politics to preaching?"

"Hard to believe, isn't it? I wonder sometimes how much I would have hated it."

"Nah. I think you would have been good at it. We need more politicians with integrity and principles."

"That's what my roommate said."

Grace raises an eyebrow. "Your jerk roommate?"

"Our second semester his brother got diagnosed with ALS, and it turned his world upside down. Had a hard lesson in mortality and started wondering if there was more to life. Instead of dreading our nightly discussions, I looked forward to them. A lot. That feeling of being able to bring hope to someone who was lost in despair was something else."

Evan's voice rolls through Grace like the swelling tide, and she wants him to keep talking and carry her away. But they've reached the cottage front door so they ease their way inside. The tiny house is packed with people and the balustrade of the narrow staircase is festooned with heavy pine boughs trimmed with seafaring icons; shells and starfish interspersed with poinsettias. A Christmas tree decorated in pale pink and white lighthouses brightens one corner. It's a lavish treatment for such a small space, and the abundance is enough to lift even Grace's spirits.

They join a queue for cider and a cookie, then escape the cramped, overheated cottage to the cool outdoors.

As they wander toward the Japanese pond Evan takes

her hand, and this time it feels different. This time it feels like a man who likes a woman and doesn't care who knows.

Grace's heart flutters. She's grateful for the anonymity of the darkness and hopes they won't run into anyone from Ellis Cove.

They talk more of Evan's teenage years spent in Coos Bay and what it was like to adjust to the coastal weather after spending his childhood in the desert of southern California.

"I'm a California girl myself," Grace confides. "Sacramento, though, so not the same as Bakersfield."

"Shh," Evan says, looking around him in mock alarm. "Don't let anyone hear you."

"I know, I've learned. I tell people I'm from Portland because my last teaching job was there."

"That's almost as bad, girl!"

"Nothing's as bad as California. You can commit no greater sin."

"Ain't that the truth!" Evan's laugh warms her.

They wander around the pond and Evan takes her hand again, lingering on the wooden bridge. Dark silhouettes move around the water's edge, but for a moment they have the little corner to themselves. Tall evergreens rise behind them, shielding them from the buffeting wind.

"It's a lovely necklace," Evan says, looking at the chain twisted around her finger.

"Oh, thank you." Grace hadn't realized she was fidgeting with it again.

"What is that, a heart?"

"Yes, good eye. Most of my students think it's a fancy

y." Grace holds it up so he can see the stylized heart engraved into one side of the round disc, then flips it over to see the scripture reference.

"Matthew 25:40," Evan murmurs appreciatively. "It's a favorite of mine too."

"My mom gave this to me the Christmas before she had her stroke. It was one of her favorite verses." Jess was given a matching one, but Grace had never seen her wear it.

Evan steps closer, a smile teasing his full lips, and Grace wishes for a breath mint after the bite of the cider.

Her breathing is shallow and her pulse quickens.

"Evan!"

Grace starts, and Evan releases her hand. She feels adrift without his touch.

An older woman, with graying hair pulled up in a knot at the back of her head, approaches along the path that circles the pond. She holds the arm of a man who is slightly stooped and wears a knitted beanie against the chill. Lights shifting along the water illuminate her eyes, and Grace recognizes Evan in them.

His parents?

So much for worrying about running into someone from school. This is so much worse.

Evan greets his mother with a hug. She's taller than Grace, but he's taller still and she has to reach up to kiss him on the cheek.

"Hello, Mom. Dad."

His mom turns her gaze to Grace, and she wants to look away from the question in the older woman's eyes. Instead, she steps forward and offers her hand.

"Hi, I'm Grace. I'm a friend of Evan's."

Evan's mom wears soft gloves and something flickers in her eyes at the word 'friend.'

"Maureen. This is my husband, Donald."

Donald has kindly eyes behind rimless glasses. "Nice to meet you. We won't crash your party here. Just wanted to take advantage of a night without rain. Have you been to the cottage yet?"

"That was our first stop," Grace says.

"We're saving the best for last," Donald says knowingly.

"We heard about that missing girl in Ellis Cove. Do you know her?" Maureen's question punctures Grace's tenuous joy.

"They're in my congregation, yeah." Evan glances at Grace, his eyes full of apology.

Maureen doesn't seem to notice. "Police are looking for a man they think might have been involved. They showed a sketch. Makes me glad I'm not raising kids right now, but I worry about Petra and Acacia."

"Grace teaches music at the elementary school," Evan says with the clear effort of trying to change the subject. "You should come to the concert next week. You'd love it. The things she can get those kids to do is amazing."

Grace wonders if he'll mention the duet they sang together last Sunday, but he doesn't, so she says nothing.

"That sounds wonderful," Donald says enthusiastically.

But Maureen's smile is barely polite. "That's nice. Acacia is performing a solo for her choir next week. That girl has a set of pipes like you wouldn't believe. She was a runner-up in the state competition last year…as a sophomore!"

"That's impressive," Grace says, trying to hold back a yawn. Whatever energy she's absorbed from Evan is passing, leaving her drained.

As if reading her mind, Evan catches her eye. "We'd better be heading back. We're helping with a candlelight vigil tomorrow so it'll be a busy day."

"Oh, that's good of you," Donald says.

Maureen's eyes soften. "We won't keep you, then. Nice to meet you, Grace."

"You too." Her smile feels more genuine when she looks at Donald.

They follow an exit near the pond that leads them into the forest serving as a buffer between the gardens and the headland where the mansion once stood. The lights of the garden disappear behind a tall cedar fence and they use the light on their phones to find the path. Pine needles soften the ground underfoot, making it springy with each step.

"Sorry about that," Evan says. "I didn't know they were going to be here."

"Don't apologize. They seemed nice."

"My mom takes a little while to warm up. It's not your fault. She's like that with everyone."

Great. Grace searches for something positive to say. "She seemed like someone I'd want to have on my side in a fight."

Evan snorts. "That's for sure."

"You're lucky. She obviously loves you."

Ahead, an orange security light illuminates the back of the public restroom near the parking lot. Grace pauses. "Do you wanna go to the cliff before we leave?"

"In the dark? There's nothing to see."

"Sure there is. Come on, it's cool."

She takes his hand and pulls him toward the trail on the left. The forest path gives way to open lawn lit only faintly from a distant lamp post. Out of the protection of the trees, the wind hits them full force, making it hard to breathe. A mournful clanging sound rises from a cable hanging on the empty flagpole nearby, rising over the roar of wind and sea. They head toward the low wall that serves to keep visitors from walking off the sheer cliff into the violent waves below.

And they are violent indeed.

In the dark, it's disorienting trying to discern where the waves are. They boom relentlessly against the rocks and saltwater mists the air. Occasionally, white spray catches the faintest hint of light in the night sky as the waves pound against huge monoliths a short distance off the cliff edge. Close enough to touch, it almost seems. But Grace knows better. The treacherous chasm between them and the rocks is wider than it looks.

Grace exhales, trying to release the tension she's been carrying all day, envisioning the wind cleansing it from her pores, taking it from her lungs. But thoughts of Diana still cling to her. Thoughts of River. Nora and Leo. Her mother. Maureen.

She senses Evan's presence and edges closer, imagining his arms around her. Desire aches in her at the thought, but he keeps his hands firmly in his pockets. Does he regret last night? Is he waiting for a sign from her that his advances are welcome?

Are they welcome? She doesn't know anymore.

Suddenly she feels so alone. So burdened. The wind stings her eyes, drawing tears. She wonders at the power of the ocean. Relentless, even cruel. It's intoxicating, but also terrifying. She wants to lean into Evan, to feel his strength behind her as she faces the pounding surf. If he touches her, she just might tell him everything.

That's a scary thought.

"It's mesmerizing, isn't it?" He asks, his voice low and alluring in a way that makes her want to melt against him.

"I feel like I'm standing on the edge of the world," Grace answers. "Like the darkness is almost tangible. Can you believe they only have a short wall to keep people safe? One step and you'd be lost. Into the void." She sways on her feet. Saltwater stings her tongue.

A steadying hand brushes her back.

"Let's get you home. I've kept you out long enough. You need to get some sleep before tomorrow."

"I'll sleep when it's all over," she says. But as she turns her back to the cliff, she wonders if it's true.

BESS

BLANKIE

I STUFF the corner of my blankie into my mouth. It's wet and smells of spit, but it doesn't calm me. I close my eyes and suck and suck and suck and suck, but I can still hear them.

They've been screaming for a long time. It started as soon as he came home. I knew it was going to be one of those nights from the way he smelled and the way he looked at Mama.

Mama barely even noticed when I took my blankie and slid off the couch and went to my room. I got myself ready for bed and brushed my teeth and crawled under my blankie without going back out to the living room to say goodnight.

I didn't want them to see me.

His voice is loud and comes through the walls like he's right here in my room. Hers is loud too, but not in the same way. It's harder to hear, and I don't know what she's saying.

I don't want to know.

I just want them to stop.

My blankie is soft in my hand, except the part where it's torn. I've had it as long as I can remember, and some pieces are so thin that when I hold it up to the light I can almost see through it. He says I'm getting too big to drag an old blanket around with me everywhere I go. I don't tell him I need it most when he's around.

I'm rubbing it against my chin while I suck, but it's not making me feel better. The mattress is stiff under me. Light creeps under the door from the living room, and a nightlight across the room paints the wall a pale yellow. Usually the light makes me feel safe at night, helping me see that the strange shapes in my room are just the dresser with the shiny cover that's peeling off, the plastic hamper, and a basket of toys.

But tonight I don't feel safe.

If I stay in my room with the light off, he won't come in. It's like he forgets I'm here, and as long as I don't remind him then he'll leave me alone. I like it that way.

A clattering sound like something breaking makes me lift my head. The door stays closed.

I don't like it when he breaks things. Once he gets started he doesn't know how to stop. And when he's finally finished, he won't clean up the mess. She'll have to clean it up, even though it wasn't her fault. Even though sometimes her eye is so swollen she can't see right and her fingers can barely hold a rag.

The last time they fought this long Mama couldn't use her arm for over a week. I thought she should go to the doctor, but she didn't. I had to brush her hair and put on her shoes and make my own sandwiches. I wonder what he'll hurt this time. Her arm? Her eye? Her mouth?

Something in her stomach that makes her gasp when she tries to stand up straight?

There's a sound like someone's fallen, and I know it's Mama because he's never the one who falls on the floor like a broken doll.

The screaming stops and at first I'm relieved. Maybe it's over now and he'll leave.

But then I hear other sounds that are worse than screaming. Sounds that remind me of animals. Moaning. Grunting. Growling.

It's a long time before the house finally gets quiet.

Maybe Mama will check on me now.

But no one comes.

NOVEMBER 30

FRIDAY

2 WEEKS BEFORE DISAPPEARANCE

GRACE

"MISS MILLER! DARREN STOLE MY SHOE!"

Josie hobbled toward the bus, one foot bare and the other strapped in a silver shoe with a heel so high that even Grace wouldn't have attempted it. She was trying to look indignant, but her face flushed with laughter.

Darren looked at Grace and froze, then tucked the evidence behind his back and gave a sheepish grin.

"Hand it over, Mr. Price."

Grace turned back to her attendance sheet, checking off the members of the chamber choir as they gathered outside the bus. Its engine was already running and the smell of diesel filled the air. Clouds hung low in the sky over the surrounding hills, promising rain later.

Girls in Sunday dresses and boys in button shirts and ties filed onto the bus until there was only one name not yet checked off.

Diana Beck.

Grace climbed the bus steps and was greeted with the

cacophony of children charged with nervous excitement and the promise of missing school.

"Darren, I want you sitting over there. Nope. Right there. Thank you. Has anyone seen Diana today?"

"She's absent!" a voice called from the back.

Grace couldn't see who had spoken. The bus seats were too tall, and a few students stood in the aisle negotiating seats.

"Yeah, she's absent today," someone else verified.

A pang of sorrow thrummed in Grace's chest. The outing would have been so good for Diana, giving her a chance to be part of something special. Had she stayed away because she dreaded Grace's disappointment when she didn't have her permission slip?

It felt like betrayal to drive away without her, but Grace had arranged with Barb to practice in the sanctuary beforehand and she didn't want to miss the window. She still needed to make it a meaningful day for the rest of the choir.

The bus driver was a surly man who spent the short drive to First Hope Church lecturing Grace about the students not leaving any trash behind. He parked the bus near the gravel pile at the back of the parking lot.

Grace eyed the puddles between the bus and the door and thought of Josie and the other girls tottering in their ridiculous heels.

"Can you drop us off any closer?" she asked the driver.

"Nope. With those cars there I'd have to back up, and that's not allowed."

Grace didn't point out that even still, he didn't have

to pick the farthest place to park. She didn't need the conflict this close to a performance.

The senior home vans hadn't arrived yet, so they still had time to warm up. She reminded the children that they were preparing to enter a house of worship and needed to show appropriate respect as they filed off the bus. Some of the students probably attended church here, so she wanted to make sure no one misbehaved and made them feel uncomfortable.

River waited for them in the foyer, dressed in a simple black dress that stretched tight over her pregnant belly and a knit sweater for warmth. Her music bag sat on the floor by her feet. She was talking to an older woman with auburn curls whose eyes lit up behind thick plastic glasses when Grace entered.

"You must be Grace," she said excitedly, stepping forward as quickly as her long pencil skirt would allow. "I'm Barb. We've been chatting back and forth. It's so good to meet you in person!"

Grace smiled warmly in return. The secretary had been making the arrangements for the special concert for seniors in the area. Her warmth had leaked through in her emails, and Grace was delighted to hear a trace of a southern accent.

"We're so excited about today's concert. You know, these folks miss out on so much during the holidays, and it's so nice to do something special just for them. They're going to love hearing your choir sing. Look at them! They're so precious." She beamed at the boys and girls filing past.

"We're honored to be asked. Thank you. And thank you so much for being willing to save the Christmas concert. I'm sure your month was already crammed full, so this is truly an act of generosity."

Barb waved away her gratitude. "It wasn't me. Our pastor, Mr. Sheppard, really believes in being there for the kids. What did God give us this beautiful building for if not to open it to those young voices singing praise for his birth?"

"Will we have time to warm up before the audience arrives? I want the choir to get used to the space. For most of them it'll be the first time singing in a hall so large."

"Absolutely! Let me show you where to put your things. If you'll follow me, there's a classroom just down the hall."

River joined them as they walked. "Apparently the Taylor family canceled their musical number. But the bagpiper is still coming and there's also someone who'll be playing the marimba."

"No kidding." That wasn't a common instrument even for larger communities, and Grace wished she could hear the performance.

"The Taylors were scheduled to take twenty minutes, though, so if we have anything that will fill extra time..."

Grace sighed. Of course things couldn't go as planned. She mentally ran through their repertoire. "We could add in one of our numbers from the fall concert. What do you have the music for?"

While River looked through her bag, Grace directed the choir students to drop off their jackets in the classroom and line up by the doors to the sanctuary. They'd practiced this several times, but when she brought them out to the risers, some of the kids still found themselves needing to switch places with their neighbors. Josie and Savannah had to shuffle to hide the space where Diana should have been.

"Let's try that again. Remember, you're not elephants. Step lightly. And if you're starting a new row, make sure you step up all the way before walking across. It's a small thing but you'll look much more professional and it will really help set the tone. All right, Xander, take the lead."

As they filed off to make another attempt, a Black man stepped through the doorway, greeting them as they passed. He was dressed in dark jeans and a trim, wine-colored button-up shirt. He turned to Grace, and at the sight of his brilliant smile and cleft chin just visible under a close beard, her mind went blank.

"You must be Ms. Millar." He shook her hand with both of his in a grasp of familiar affection.

"Please, call me Grace." She felt her cheeks warming and hoped he wouldn't notice.

"Evan Sheppard."

"You're the pastor?"

"That's me. Thank you so much for accepting our invitation to sing today."

"It's our pleasure. This is a lovely space. It'll be a wonderful opportunity for the new members of our choir." She glanced toward the arched ceiling soaring overhead. Lovely, but horrible for acoustics. The challenge would be encouraging the students to sing out when they couldn't hear the sound bouncing back to them.

"Well, we're honored for you to join us. But don't let me get in the way. I just wanted to welcome you personally."

Grace thanked him, her eyes sliding to his bare left hand as he moved away. She couldn't remember the last time she'd even bothered to check.

River was setting up her music at the piano, a smile pulling on her lips. Grace shook herself, focusing on directing the students back to the risers. But she was keenly aware of Mr. Sheppard's deep voice as he visited with Barb in the back of the sanctuary.

Focus.

She led them through the warm-up exercises, then started their opening number, *Ding Dong Merrily on High*. It was supposed to be delivered with a punch, but the students were timid and unsure. Grace cracked a few jokes to put them at ease, and didn't make a big deal when the altos missed their entrance. The best thing to soothe their nerves was increasing their confidence. Pointing out flaws this close to performance time wouldn't do any good.

They only did a partial run-through of the other songs before exiting back to the classroom to wait for their turn to perform. The fifth and sixth graders settled in chairs, pulled out phones, and clustered together in excited groups. Some showed their nervousness by fidgeting with hair or shirt collars. Grace couldn't sit, even though her feet would regret it by the end of the day.

"Where's Diana?" River asked, looking out over the classroom.

Something shrank in Grace. "She didn't come today. I went to her house last night hoping to get her permission slip signed, but her mom wasn't there. I hope she didn't stay home because she thought I was going to be mad."

"You, mad? I wouldn't think so."

"I don't know. Kids are weird that way. I'm disappointed, but only for her sake. Not for mine."

A funny expression crossed River's face. "I doubt it had anything to do with you."

Grace cocked her head. "You think? Why's that?"

River turned back to watch the students. The tip of her nose was pointed and sharp, reminding Grace of an elf or woodland creature from a fairy tale. "I'm sure you meant well, but they probably didn't appreciate you interfering."

"Why do you say it like that? Like I did something wrong."

River blew out a small breath. "It's not your fault. But that doesn't mean they won't blame Diana for involving you."

Grace swallowed, her enthusiasm souring. She'd been trying to make things easier for Diana to get the permission slip signed. Had she made things worse instead?

A soft knock sounded on the door, and Barb poked her head in. "They're arriving now. About ten more minutes."

Grace's smile felt forced. Try as she might, with fresh concern over Diana, her heart simply wasn't in it now.

RIVER

RIVER REGRETTED her sweater by the end of the first song. It wasn't a large group, no more than fifty senior citizens from the assisted living homes in the area, but playing for an audience was always stressful. She felt too warm and her armpits were sticky. She'd have to dress cooler for the big concert in three weeks.

The first half dozen rows of the sanctuary were filled with men and women who had come dressed for the occasion wearing Christmas themed sweaters, vests, or even a hat trimmed with holly. They watched the kids with obvious pleasure. As the choir sang, members of the audience occasionally sang too, their warbly voices creating a small hum behind River. It made her smile and helped her think of something besides Diana and what had kept her home that day.

River was amazed at how calm Grace could be during a performance. She pushed the kids hard enough in practice but knew when it was time to back off and let them enjoy it. The throw-back to the fall concert—*I'll Give My*

Love An Apple—was a little rough, since they hadn't sung it since October. But all in all, they did very well.

After the final number, the audience clapped and several of the more spry members rose to their feet. Grace offered a gracious nod and gestured to the choir, who beamed. Then she turned to River and the choir kids all joined in the applause.

River blushed, unsure what to do. She settled for an awkward half bow, her neck sticky with heat.

Evan took Grace by the hand as he publicly thanked her and the choir. Grace's eyes were bright and River fought a smile. She'd noticed Grace's reaction when she'd met Evan. The man could leave an impression, for sure. River loved to hear him preach on Sunday. His voice held a music and rhythm that she could listen to all day.

As they ushered the students off the risers and back to the classroom to pick up their things, River pulled Grace aside.

"Can I get a ride home? Todd needed the car today so he dropped me off."

"Of course," Grace answered. "Nice job today. Sorry that we rushed the last song, but you did a great job of keeping it from running away."

They were halfway across the parking lot when they heard Grace's name. Evan was jogging toward them.

"Beautifully done, ladies. What a gift for our elderly community. River, sublime job, as always. And you have a gift, Ms. Millar."

"Please, call me Grace. They've worked very hard this year. I'm proud of them, especially the ones who started out not even knowing how to read music."

"I loved my time in choir as a kid," Evan said,

placing his hand over his heart for emphasis. "There's something so powerful about uniting your voice with others. It's like a prayer, don't you think? I feel it deep in my soul in a way that spoken worship doesn't match."

"I know what you mean," Grace replied, her cheeks turning pink in the cold. "I don't know if it's the sound waves or what, but there's something about a choir that takes my breath away."

"Yes! In fact, I have a pretty big favor to ask of you. And it's okay if you say no. I don't want to put you on the spot."

"Mr. Sheppard, you've saved our Christmas concert. I'm pretty sure I owe you big."

Evan's dark eyes sparkled in the beguiling way he had. River didn't think he meant to be so irresistible. He couldn't help it. She'd seen time and again how people melted for him.

Now his eyes widened in a pleading way. "I'm looking for someone to sing a duet with me for our service in two weeks. I was listening to you practice with the kids and wondered...would you be willing?"

"Sing with you?" Grace stammered. "Well, I guess. I mean, I love to sing. What did you have in mind?"

The color in Grace's cheeks heightened, and River suddenly felt like an intruder. She edged toward the bus to give them privacy. The air inside where the kids were waiting was muggy and the interior of the windows had fogged over.

River settled into a seat, watching Grace chatting with Evan. Her head tilted to the side, almost flirtatiously, and River smiled as Evan's deep laugh rang out.

When Grace joined her a few minutes later, she wouldn't meet her eyes.

"It's nothing," she insisted.

"Hmm. I like the look of that 'nothing.' Just saying."

Grace smiled but didn't say anything more.

The bus seat was made of stiff foam and River was grateful it was only a short ride to the school. She kept her feet braced against the floor to counteract the bouncing. At least she was short so her knees didn't push against the seat in front of her. How did teenagers manage to fit on these things?

Grace stood and called the kids to attention as they pulled up to the school. "Well done, ladies and gentlemen. Your hard work has paid off. I was proud of how you represented yourselves and our school today. Enjoy your weekend, and on Monday, we'll start auditions for the *In Dulci Jubilo* solo."

A few of the girls gasped with excitement, and the energy increased further as the students jostled each other to get off the bus.

River came last, helping the driver pick up forgotten pieces of trash. By the time she joined Grace in the parking lot, only a few students remained. Most of the parking lot was empty, the staff having already left for the day.

A man in a blue dress shirt and khaki pants exited the school, then made a beeline to where they were standing.

"Miss Millar! How did the performance go?"

Grace's eyes brightened politely, but River sensed the exhaustion underneath. She knew the feeling well. She would be useless the rest of the day.

"They did a wonderful job. Have you met River

Vincent? She's my accompanist. Mr. Knight is one of our fifth grade teachers."

"Call me Matthew. Nice to meet you, Ms. Vincent."

River shook his hand and it felt limp and sticky in hers. She fought the urge to wipe her palm on her skirt.

Matthew leaned over and ruffled the hair of one of the students sitting on the curb, waiting for his parents. The boy looked up in surprise and scowled. Matthew didn't seem to notice.

"Such good kids. I've been talking to Marilyn about starting up a robotics group after school, but I don't want to interfere with what you've got going on with the choir. How often do you do little events like this?"

River felt Grace bristle at the term "little," but her tone didn't change.

"Eventually I'd like to have performances once a month, but we're not there yet. As long as we coordinate our schedules, I'm sure we can work it out."

"That would be great. I'd hate to make them choose. It's a great time of life to explore lots of interests."

"Absolutely."

The conversation died as a blue pickup truck pulled up to the curb, the passenger window rolled down and country music blaring.

A teenager with hair curling around his ears and wearing aviator sunglasses yelled from behind the wheel. "Come on, Xander! Move your butt!"

Xander stood up from the curb and picked the seat of his pants out of his crack.

Grace jumped forward. "Hold on, Xander."

She walked to the passenger side and leaned in to get a better view of the driver.

"Are you Xander's brother?"

"Yeah."

"The permission slip specified that we could only release the students into the hands of a parent or responsible adult."

The teen sighed. "Well my mom's still at work so good luck with that."

"Can I see your ID?"

Xander fidgeted on the curb while his brother fished his license out of his wallet.

Grace took the license and made a show of reviewing it. "Wonderful. Nice to meet you, Micah. Will you please let your mom know that in the future if she can't pick up Xander herself, I'd appreciate a note giving permission for you to do it instead?"

"Fine, whatever. Can we go now?"

Grace moved aside and smiled at Xander as he climbed in. "Well done today, Xander. Have a lovely weekend."

Matthew grimaced as he watched them drive away. "It's hard to see what they'll turn into in a few years. You couldn't pay me enough to teach high school."

River thought about Libby's destructive anger and silently agreed.

Grace joined them, looking thoughtful. "It's a shame Diana missed today. She was looking forward to it all week, but she couldn't get her mom to sign the permission slip."

Matthew let out a soft breath. "Ah, Diana. Such a sweetheart, but she's got an uphill battle if she wants to make something of herself. So much working against her."

"It's true. But that's part of what makes our jobs so great. We get to make that battle a little easier, right?"

Matthew glanced again at the students sitting on the curb and pitched his voice lower. "Yeah, just be careful. I had a run-in with Leo in September. You're better off keeping your distance."

Grace frowned. "What sort of run-in? Anything I should be aware of?"

Matthew's cheeks grew splotchy with color. "Maybe it's not as bad since you're a woman. But I'd try and deal with Nora and avoid Leo if at all possible. Nora's got her own issues, but you'll get further with her."

River wandered away to sit on the low concrete wall bordering the sidewalk. She couldn't handle standing for that long in one position and her head hurt. Lichen grew on the rough concrete, tinging it with a faint green hue. By the time the last student left and Matthew said goodnight, early dusk was descending with the low clouds.

"Sorry about that," Grace said, hurrying to her black sedan. "I don't know why parents can't seem to get here on time."

River settled into the passenger seat, relaxing against the leather.

Grace exhaled and started the engine. "I hope Diana will be back on Monday. She specifically asked me about auditions last night."

River didn't respond. Grace cared so much, but she had no idea what Diana was dealing with if missing an audition was Grace's worst fear.

"I don't know what to do for her," she continued. "She loves being in the choir, and I want to support her, but if it's creating conflict at home I don't want to make things worse."

They pulled out of the school parking lot and onto the street. The town's holiday decorations, vintage shapes made of tinsel—a toy soldier, a candy cane, a stocking—hung on electrical poles. A tinsel banner reading SEASON'S GREETINGS spanned the intersection at Main Street, but the base of the second "e" had detached so it read SEASON'S GREFTINGS.

Thoughts of Bess pressed against River's mind. Pushing. She reached for her music bag, trying to find her tin of Altoids in the pocket. Hurrying, before Grace noticed.

"Are you okay?"

Sharp peppermint flooded her nose as she popped the mint in her mouth. It burned on her tongue. That was good. She took a deep breath.

"Sorry. Just thinking. Diana reminds me of me sometimes. I worry about her."

"What do you mean?"

River felt Grace's gaze on her, measuring. Looking for the malnourished waif, the street urchin that River tried so carefully to hide.

"My home life was really dysfunctional."

That was putting it mildly. *Dysfunctional* didn't adequately describe the time she brought home a sandwich she'd found in the dumpster behind the grocery store and it made her so sick she threw up. Grandma Billie had made her clean it up, then eat the vomit, swearing at her for thinking she was too good for the food she gave her.

Or what about the fact that River wouldn't eat chocolate because the only time she had chocolate was when Gene gave it to her after she'd been in the pink room?

Dysfunctional. Such a polite word. Appropriate for civilized company.

She sensed Grace waiting for more, so she added, "My mom ran off when I was little. My dad couldn't take care of me so I was raised by my grandma. But she was...she wasn't very nice."

Just mentioning Grandma Billie made her voice loud in her head, and River pushed away the memory. She felt that familiar sense of detachment as she looked out at the houses with their decorative lights on roofs and porches.

The car was quiet except for the thrum of tires on the road.

River's fingers tightened around her left wrist.

"I'm so sorry," Grace said weakly, as if she sensed how inadequate it was.

But River appreciated her effort. "Thank you. It's over now. In the end, I won, not her." *I hope.*

They pulled into the trailer park, the headlights swinging over the Harbor Lights sign. River's house was two streets over. Before she got out there was one more thing she had to say.

"Don't...don't say anything to anyone, okay? No one knows except Todd and my therapist. That's it."

Grace's eyes shone in the reflected headlights shining on the house's siding. "Of course I'd never tell. It's nothing to be ashamed of. It's not your fault how you were raised. But if you want to keep it private, that's your right. Just let me know if I can do anything for you." She seemed earnest, and River almost allowed herself to hope that it was true.

Would it help to have a friend to confide in?

But she knew she'd never do that to Grace. No matter how strong Grace seemed, River wouldn't put her in that position. She'd already had two therapists fire her because they couldn't handle her. If she was too complicated for the professionals, Grace didn't stand a chance.

DECEMBER 15

SATURDAY

2 DAYS AFTER DISAPPEARANCE

GRACE

GRACE HAD HOPED to sleep well after her date with Evan, that their time together would counter the heaviness pressing against her temples so insistently that sometimes she can't see straight. That feeling like something is stalking her just out of sight and if she lets down her guard it'll catch her. But in spite of exhaustion, she can't completely surrender to the darkness and instead watches TV late with the Christmas tree lights casting a comforting glow around the living room. Finally, in the early hours of the morning, she dozes on the couch with the volume low and the screen flashing blue light against her eyelids.

She dreams fitfully of Jess. Jess and her teenage boyfriend whom Grace suspects first introduced her to drugs at fifteen. But in the dream, the boyfriend wears the face of the man at the park and Jess is dressed in the wolf sweatshirt Grace last saw Diana wearing. She wakes feeling like she had too much to drink.

A shower and cup of coffee help, but Grace still wishes she could curl up in bed and throw the covers over her head. But she told Evan she would help with the candlelight vigil, so she slips on her jacket and grabs her purse.

Everywhere she goes—from the dollar store to pick up tea lights, to a local coffee shop who donated the cups to hold them—Diana's face looks at her from "Have You Seen Me?" posters. Stapled to utility poles, taped to storefront windows, and lining the chain link fence near the school playground. Diana's haunted eyes watch her from the colored photos. The eyes that betray the smile, turn it into an expression of uncertainty.

Grace's despair increases with every photo. Did the poor child ever know a day of true joy? Did she ever feel safe, like she could enjoy life without it coming back to hurt her?

After a while, Grace stops looking at the posters.

Eyeing the party section at the grocery store, she texts Evan.

What was Diana's favorite color?

Grace catches herself before she sends it and changes "was" to "is". Everyone knows that the more time passes, the less likely Diana will be found alive. But still, dogged optimism is necessary. She doesn't want to be the first person to publicly give up hope.

After a few minutes, Evan responds.

Nora says it's orange. Why?

Picking up tablecloths. Trying to personalize it for Diana.

Good idea. Thanks. BTW I'll be at the school at 4 to set up. Have you decided if the choir's gonna sing?

Evan's request has been niggling the back of Grace's mind, but she isn't ready to commit either way. She doesn't respond.

Marilyn sends her four addresses of parents willing to loan hot beverage servers, and Grace picks them up on her way home. Hot chocolate and coffee will help keep the gathered crowd warm.

As she pulls into her driveway, Sonya is backing out of her garage. She waves cheerily as Grace gets out. Maybe that's what she should do over the Christmas break. Clean her mom's stuff out of the garage so she can park her car inside.

The prospect is more depressing than spending the time alone bingeing Hallmark movies.

By the time Grace figures out how to work the beverage servers and calls as many of her choir members as she can, the sun is peeking out from under a bank of black clouds to paint her kitchen walls a watery yellow.

Milton whines as she heads toward the door.

"Sorry. I know I've left you alone all day. I promise I'll make it up to you later."

When she arrives at the school, Evan and Matthew Knight are already there, carrying out a long table from the building. Grace feels unexpectedly nervous seeing Evan again, with thoughts of the previous night on her mind. She almost wishes she could do the whole evening over again. He was so thoughtful and solicitous, but she'd been distracted and wrapped up in thoughts of Diana.

Evan's back is turned to her as he leans over to open the table legs and lock the braces. What should she say? She imagines herself in a rom-com wearing a cute knitted hat and scarf, sneaking up behind him and doing a flirty feint to one side, maybe running a hand along his waist as she flashes a megawatt smile. But she isn't wearing a knitted hat and her hands are full holding plastic bags from the dollar store.

As she stands there debating what to do, Matthew calls her name.

"Hey there, Grace!"

Evan hefts the table into place and turns around. Grace feels caught like a deer in the headlights.

"Hi." Her eyes flit to Evan's and she looks away again, pretending interest in the bags as she lays them on the table. Anything to avoid eye contact. "Here are candles and tablecloths; there are hot drink servers in the car."

She drops her keys next to the bags and Evan grabs them.

"Looks like you've been busy. Matthew, wanna help?"

It takes the men only a few minutes, but that's enough time for Grace to collect herself. When they return, she's composed and ready for conversation.

"I hope there's a good turnout," she says. "With it only being two weeks until Christmas, people are going to have plans. It'll be hard to drop everything last minute."

She reaches for a tablecloth as Evan and Matthew position another table near the first one.

"It's true," Evan says, "but what better time of year to get outside of yourself and show love to a neighbor? Nora and Leo could really use the support."

To Grace's annoyance, Matthew—not Evan—joins in to help her tape the tablecloth edges down so the orange plastic won't fly away in the breeze. It seems inappropriate, somehow, to have such a cheerful color at such a somber occasion. But Grace doesn't say so.

She smells the faint sheen of sweat that Matthew's worked up from carrying tables and chairs. She turns her head away from his body odor.

You're too tired to be out among people, she thinks to herself. *You're going to say something you'll regret if you're not careful.*

"What did you decide to do about the choir?" Evan asks from the other table. He watches her steadily, his dark eyes probing in that way he has that tells her he's giving her his complete attention.

Grace screws up her face in a grimace. "If this is a disaster, don't say I didn't warn you."

"You mean you'll do it?" It's the first real smile she's seen from him, and she wants to see it again.

"We'll try. But I hope you've got some extra miracle points stored up because you're gonna need 'em."

Matthew laughs too loudly, and Grace edges away on the pretense of gathering up the trash and stuffing it back into the plastic bags. He doesn't usually rub her the wrong way but something is off tonight.

She's off.

As if Evan can read her mind, he asks Matthew, "Do you know where to find a large garbage can?"

"There should be one or two in the cafeteria."

Grace seizes the opportunity to follow Evan inside, her hands full of discarded packaging.

As soon as the door closes behind them, Evan says, "You're a good soul, Grace. I know how you feel about Nora and Leo. It shows true Christian love that you're willing to do this."

"I'm doing it for Diana, not for them. But I know a little about how it feels to lose someone you love. I wouldn't wish that on anyone."

He waits expectantly, and she senses the pastor in him coming out in his patience.

"My sister ran away for the first time when she was sixteen," Grace explains. "I was away at school, so I couldn't do anything to help except take my mom's frantic phone calls. She was a mess for weeks until my sister came home." How strange that she can talk about this in such a detached way. It's like she's reporting on someone else's life.

"How are things with your sister now? You said that was the first time."

"Jess is Jess. There's no helping her until she decides she wants it." Grace cringes at how much she sounds like Greg.

Evan nods. "God himself won't make us change if we don't want to. He offers His help, but He won't force it on us."

Grace *had* tried to force it. After a couple years of Jess stealing from her mom, disappearing for months at a time, and always returning with a promise to do better,

Grace had offered to let Jess live with her. She'd even taken out a hefty student loan to pay for rehab.

She's still paying off that loan.

They find the large trash can, and when they wheel it out the doors, Marilyn has arrived and is placing a wooden easel to support a large picture of Diana glued to black poster board. It isn't a candid shot like the one from the "Have You Seen Me?" posters. It's a school portrait, staged against a standard blue background. Her smile is forced, but her eyes don't have the same haunted look. She doesn't seem as afraid of whoever stood behind the camera.

She's wearing a light pink sweater with purple stars. Her hair looks limp and unwashed, but she has two little hoop earrings in her ears, as if she wanted to make a special effort for picture day. The sight of the earrings pains Grace.

While Evan and Matthew go in search of a microphone and speaker, Grace places candles in cups and lines them up on the tables. Clouds are gathering overhead and the wind gusts as people start arriving.

Grace works to light the candles with butane lighters, listening to snatches of conversation centered around a news story from earlier that day. Law enforcement haven't released much information, but they shared a sketch of a bearded man who might have been on Main Street that evening. Witnesses placed them together sometime after Diana left the church.

Grace's ears perk up. She's been so busy she hasn't taken time to catch up on the latest news. To be honest, she doesn't really want to.

A police-issue Tahoe drives into the parking lot, and

Marilyn greets the officer who emerges. It isn't Williams this time, but a woman with a thick ponytail and a slight limp.

Marilyn brings her over to the table.

"Grace, this is Sergeant Polaski."

"Good evening, Sergeant. Would you like a candle?"

"No thanks. I'll leave them for others. Can I have a word with you, Miss Miller?"

"Millar," Grace says automatically, her stomach sinking.

She hands the lighter to Marilyn and moves away from the table and the gathering crowd. They stop at the breezeway, the covered area where students can move from one building to another without getting soaked by rain.

Sergeant Polaski offers her hand for Grace to shake. Her fingers are long and thin. "Mr. Sheppard says you recently had some concerns about Diana Beck and her family. Can you tell me more about that?"

Her words stoke the shame that is a constant burn in Grace's gut these days.

"I'm not sure what you want to know. I already talked to Officer Williams. I stopped by Diana's house a couple of weeks ago to get a permission slip signed and was concerned about what I saw. The house itself didn't look fit for children, and Leo showed a lot of contempt for the children."

"Do you frequently make house calls?"

"Not frequently, no. But we had a performance that Diana was really excited about attending and I wanted to support her. It seemed like Nora kept forgetting, so I thought it might be easier if I brought her the form and she signed it right then and there."

"So you went to the house?"

"Yes."

"And after you saw the state of their living conditions, you didn't call DHS?"

Grace's face feels hot in spite of the chill. "I wasn't sure if I should or not."

Sergeant Polaski's expression doesn't change. "Did Diana ever tell you about abuse in the home?"

"No. The first indication I got that there might be more than poverty or even neglect going on was when she shared a letter from her mom. She was proud of it, but it made me sick. If I'd gotten a letter like that from my mom, I would have been horrified."

"Do you still have the letter?"

"No, she kept it. I told all this to Officer Williams."

"Did anyone else see this letter?"

Grace falters. River saw it. But the last thing Grace wants is to give the police an excuse to question River.

"Not that I know of. You might ask her teacher, Matthew Knight."

As Polaski scratches away on her pad, Grace's guilt gives way to anger. Anger at herself for not acting sooner. Anger at Sergeant Polaski and her judgmental questions. And anger at Nora for not taking better care of her own children.

Grace's mother wasn't perfect, not by a long shot. She was stubborn and, especially in the years after Grace's dad died, demanded more and more of Grace and Greg. But she would have done anything for her kids and always put their needs before her own.

"Listen, Sergeant. I was concerned about Diana, but I didn't want to overreact. I worried that without something more concrete my concerns would be dismissed, which wouldn't do those children any good. I thought it would be better if I wrote down some clear examples of neglect before I reported anything."

"Do you have a copy of your notes?"

"It's...I just made a memo on my phone."

"I'd like to see it if you don't mind."

Grace pulls up the note on her phone and hands it over. Polaski must be a master poker player, giving nothing away as she copies Grace's notes down on her pad. It doesn't take long, since Grace only started the list two weeks ago.

"Thank you, Ms. Millar. One last thing. What time did you leave the church Thursday night?"

Grace stills, trying to think. Why is she asking this? "It was pretty late. The students left at around six o'clock. Mr. Sheppard came to help, and we worked a couple more hours before he got a phone call and had to leave."

"Do you know what time that was?"

"Eight? Maybe nine? I wasn't keeping track of the time."

"Do you know who called him?"

Grace frowns. "You'd have to ask him. I'm sure he'll tell you."

"I'm wondering what he told you that night."

"He didn't tell me. It wasn't my business. But he had to leave and I left not long after that." She hopes the sergeant won't push her on that. Did she already talk to Evan? What had he told her?

"And what time would you say Diana left?"

Grace has never been good at lying, but again she feels like she shouldn't be completely honest. Was it wrong of her to let Diana stay later than the other students?

"We wrapped up at around six, but it took parents a little while to pick up all their kids. Diana wasn't getting picked up, so she was the last one to leave. Maybe six-thirty?" That doesn't sound so bad, right? Even though Grace knows it was later.

If Polaski suspects she isn't being completely truthful, she doesn't say so. Again, Grace wonders what Evan said. She looks past Polaski to where cars are filling the parking lot.

"If that's all, Sergeant, I really need to get the rest of the candles ready."

"Thank you, Ms. Millar. If you think of anything else that might help us figure out where Diana went after she left the church the night she disappeared, please let me know."

Grace takes the sergeant's card and quickly stuffs it in her pocket to hide her trembling hands as she walks away.

Evan looks up from unrolling an orange extension cord as she approaches.

"What was that all about?"

Grace shakes her head and continues out to the parking lot as quickly as she can. She needs a chance to breathe.

Dusk is falling and bringing a fine mist with it, making everything feel damp. Grace appreciates the darkness. It'll be easier to stay in the background that way. She can't handle any more unwanted attention.

She goes to her car and sits for a few minutes, watching families arriving for the vigil. So many parents with children. Some bringing stuffed animals or balloons. Should Grace have brought a gift? She feels foolish for not thinking of it. Is that something only people with kids understand?

She stays in her car as long as she thinks is reasonable. She isn't in a hurry to get back, even to see Evan. Maybe especially to see Evan. She doesn't want him to read the emotions on her face. They're too ugly for her to contemplate, let alone share.

When the whine of a microphone echoes out over the parking lot, Grace sighs and finally returns. Evan is fiddling with the mic while Matthew adjusts a portable speaker. Grace spots a few of the kids from choir and waves, mentally taking note of how many have shown up. If there are one or two strong singers for each part, they can carry the rest.

Hopefully.

Dozens of people have gathered already, and Marilyn is struggling to keep up with the demand for new candles. Grace settles in beside her and quickly goes to work, grateful for something to do with her hands.

She senses someone standing nearby and looks up to see River and Todd, bundled up against the cold with hands shoved into pockets.

"Hey, Grace," River says with a weak smile.

"You made it. Here." Grace hands them both a candle.

"Thanks."

River looks over Grace's head and her smile fades.

Grace follows her gaze.

An old Grand Am has pulled up to the curb and Nora Beck is stepping out. Her ruddy face is pinched and haggard in the waning light. Leo emerges from the driver's side while Daniel slips out from the backseat, his ripped pants too short to cover his ankles and his jacket unzipped.

The crowd goes quiet at their arrival. An older woman steps forward, grabbing Nora. A sharp sob breaks the air.

Grace looks away. "I don't understand how they can be so grieved when they mistreat her the way they do."

The crowd parts, making way for the little family.

River watches them, a mystified look on her face. "Love is complicated. Some people just aren't very good at it."

This makes Grace go quiet.

"Thank you, everyone, for coming." Evan's deep voice coming through the microphone grabs everyone's attention. He stands near Diana's framed picture. "I know it's hard to change your plans on a Saturday night, especially this close to Christmas, but we're all touched by your show of support for Diana and her family. We're grateful to the school for letting us gather here, and for businesses who provided the candles and supplies. Please, if you see anyone from these organizations, be sure to give them a warm thank you.

"As you know, we're here to join in showing love and support for Diana Beck, who went missing Thursday night. Many of you know Diana from school or church. Maybe you work with Nora or Leo. Or maybe you don't know the family at all but feel this loss as a wound in our community, and you've come here seeking healing. In that way, tonight, we're all family."

Evan looks out over the crowd to make eye contact with Grace. "Diana is part of another special family, a chamber choir led by Grace Millar, the music teacher at the elementary school. Members of the choir have generously agreed to sing for us tonight."

Grace takes a deep breath. She walks to the front and motions to the students to come forward. There are fourteen students, a pretty good showing under the circumstances. She hopes it will be enough.

Evan tries to hand the mic to Grace, but she shakes her head. She doesn't want to say anything to the crowd. The sooner her part is over, the better.

She arranges the students in a loose semicircle, keeping the shorter kids in the front. They're all holding candles and the light makes their faces glow. Grace tries to keep her face neutral so the kids don't read her emotions and falter. This is their most challenging piece because it's sung a cappella, but without a piano it's the only one that seemed appropriate.

Grace hums a quiet note, raises her arms, and brings her hands down for the start.

Nothing happens.

Grace pauses. The students shuffle awkwardly.

Josie looks stricken.

"Do it for Diana," Grace whispers.

They shift again. Some of them straighten.

She hums the starting note again a little louder, offers a brave smile, and tries again.

This time, they sing. Softly. Timidly. But gaining strength and power as they continue.

Grace smiles encouragingly, gesturing to bring out more sound. It's easier to shut out the people behind her and focus on the song. The harmonies. The moving dynamics. She doesn't have to think about anything except these sweet children who haven't yet experienced the dark horrors of life. The lucky ones who will go home tonight to loving parents who will keep them safe against the evils of the world.

RIVER

THE BABY KICKS.

River reaches for Todd's hand and places it over her shuddering belly. He looks at her, and his bloodshot eyes soften a little around the corners. He wraps one arm around her shoulders and rests his chin on her head.

The crowd is somber in the way that only music commands, even children and babies quiet and attentive. What a great idea to have the chamber choir sing. River watches Grace lead them through *Lux Arumque* by Eric Whitacre, an atmospheric piece that always takes her breath away. They start to go flat and Grace brings more energy to recover. It's an ambitious piece, and River knows that Grace spent much of September simplifying the arrangement for her fledgling choir, trying to get it just right. She wanted the boys and girls to get a taste of what was possible, to raise their sights beyond folk songs and children's tunes. Hoping to give them a gift of music that would shape them forever.

Grace has taken Diana's disappearance hard, and River suspects it's because she second-guessed herself about whether or not to report Nora and Leo. It isn't fair, of course. What about Matthew, Diana's teacher? Or Evan, their pastor? Diana has many adults in her life who could have intervened. It isn't fair of Grace to take so much on herself, thinking she can hold up the world. Like Atlas. Forgetting that she can only do so much, that some people can't be saved.

The harmonies merge into unison and the volume crescendoes. The children's voices reverberate against the metal overhead structure. It's a mournful sound, a mixture of youthful sweetness and the eerie passage of music through an open space. River notices a woman nearby wiping at her eyes.

Grace would be pleased. She always loves it when music evokes emotion from the audience. But as the song ends, Grace simply nods and excuses the choir to shuffle back to their parents. She doesn't even turn around to make eye contact with the crowd.

"Wow." Evan breaks the silence. "What a beautiful tribute. Thank you to Grace Millar and the chamber choir for sharing your talents with us tonight."

His voice, even in this somber setting, carries the edge of the public speaker. He's clearly comfortable before a microphone. River always enjoys his sermons, especially since he likes to draw out other perspectives from the Bible—people who were looked down on and lived their lives on the fringes. By the time Evan is finished bringing their stories forward, they seem admirable. Even noble.

He's doing the same thing now. Taking Diana and bringing her out of the shadows. Giving the people someone to care about. Someone to want to protect. Someone to fight for.

Grace moves around the edge of the crowd and comes to stand by River.

"They sounded great," River murmurs.

Grace smiles wanly. The flickering light of River's candle accentuates the dark circles under Grace's eyes, making her look tired and worn. River feels a pang of guilt for being so flaky the past few weeks. The Christmas concert is only a few days away, and River can't even get her own crap together well enough to show up consistently.

Evan finishes his remarks and hands the mic to Nora.

Nora wipes at her cheeks and takes a deep, shuddering breath. Her voice comes out loud and with a strong rasp against the mic that makes River cringe.

"Thank you for coming here tonight. And thank you to the police who are working so hard to find our Diana. She's the sweetest…" Nora's voice rises and chokes off.

Evan steps to her side and puts a steadying hand at her back.

River realizes she hasn't asked Grace more details about her date with Evan. Or has she? Last night is blank. She itches to check her texts but leaves her phone in her jacket pocket. Nora is talking again, sharing a memory from the day Diana disappeared. How she'd been so cheerful leaving the house that morning for school.

River listens as Nora spins a tale of a loving home life. River knows better. She knows that Diana probably left without eating breakfast, far earlier than she should have, then took her time wandering through town until it was time to be at the school.

That's what she would have done.

Grace catches River's eye with a sidelong glance. From what River knows of Grace's childhood, she's never seen the darker side of family life before. Her parents were loving and provided a stable home. Yes, she had the tragedy of losing her dad when she was a young teen, but even then she had the support of extended family and friends.

River can't imagine it. But that's what she wants for her baby, so knowing it was possible for Grace gives her hope.

Evan frequently glances in Grace's direction. Does she notice? Will they become a couple? He seems like the kind of guy Grace would end up with. Solid and kind and with so much belief in the goodness of people that he makes the world brighter just by being in it. And people are coming along. When Evan first started the men's group at church, Todd had scoffed at the idea. But now he's made some real friends there. It's the first River has seen him connect to other men outside of work.

She leans against Todd and he squeezes her shoulder. Things have been hard for him lately with her dissociation getting so bad. But he never complains that she isn't a good wife. He never complains that he would have been better off marrying someone else. Someone normal. But surely he has to think it sometimes, right?

She'll never ask.

Still, she wonders sometimes if he keeps as much

from her as she keeps from him. How would she even know?

Nora finishes and an officer takes the mic. Tension creeps into River's neck the way it always does whenever she's around a police officer. The officer talks about reporting any sightings of Diana from that day. Apparently she was last seen going past the Shell station at 4th and Main.

River shifts uncomfortably. When she drives to the school, her route takes her to that intersection. Did anyone see her there that day?

She hopes not.

"Are they about done?" Todd asks in her ear, his breath warm on her neck. He didn't want to come to the vigil in the first place.

River keeps her eyes fixed on Evan, who is back at the mic thanking everyone who came and preparing to lead them in a moment of silence.

They all bow their heads and the crowd quiets. A baby fusses and two kids nearby snicker. River tries to empty her mind and pray, but she feels awkward with all those strangers nearby. Her mind keeps going back to that day. Erica will be back in a few days. Hopefully they can talk about it then.

"Thank you," Evan says, releasing the tension that built as the silence stretched on. "That's all we have planned this evening. You're welcome to visit with the Becks and share your love and support. Sergeant Polaski is available to answer questions or if you have anything to share that may help with finding Diana. Please dispose of your trash in the garbage cans. And God bless."

River relaxes a little as the crowd starts murmuring and breaking up.

"Now can we go?" Todd asks.

River wants to talk to Grace, but Grace is busying herself at the table cleaning up the unclaimed candles.

Disappointed, River lets Todd pull her away.

GRACE

FOG HAS ROLLED in with the oncoming night, the water droplets hanging heavy in the air of the dimly lit parking lot. Grace carries the last bag of trash to the dumpster on the far edge of the parking lot, lifting the lid only as much as necessary to swing the heavy bag inside. She wipes her hands against her jeans, wishing for the sanitizer she keeps in her car. Only a few cars are left in the lot—Evan's gray Subaru and Marilyn's white Honda among them.

Grace doesn't feel bad leaving Marilyn to lock up the school, knowing Evan will make sure the older woman makes it safely to her car before he leaves himself. But she hesitates, torn between returning to the school or going to her car, a black Camry which sits alone in the dark space between the pools of orange light cast by two lamp posts. She hadn't consciously intended to separate herself from the others when she parked, but it seems fitting somehow.

She's relieved the evening is finally over, and she's anxious to return home.

Except...

The thought of going back to her empty house and enduring another wretched night alone fills her with dread. She feels a pull back to the school, toward Evan and Marilyn—and even irritating Matthew Knight—and the warmth of human companionship that's suggested by the murmur of their voices drifting out over the parking lot.

On a night like this even the simulation of friendship can soothe a troubled soul.

River's the closest friend Grace has here in Ellis Cove, but she and Todd left as soon as the vigil ended. Grace had noticed the broken turn signal as their car had passed, and for a moment she'd forgotten how to breathe. Thinking of it now makes her decision easy.

She turns her back to the school and heads to her car.

She doesn't notice the small piece of paper pinned under her car's wiper blade until after she's already settled into the driver's seat.

It's torn from a flier announcing the vigil, just a small scrap and moist at that. So when she turns on her wiper, hoping to knock it loose, it clings stubbornly to the glass. Annoyed, Grace climbs out of the car and reaches for it.

Two words are scrawled across the paper.

I KNOW

A jolt courses through her. She glances up, scanning the parking lot.

Who left it?

What does it mean?

And what do they think they know?

Grace squeezes the scrap into a tiny ball and shoves it into her jeans pocket. It's just a slip of paper, but her heart pounds as she slips back into her car and locks the door. Shrubbery clusters around the school building—burning bushes and Oregon grape forming pockets of shadow the dim light can't reach. Big enough to hide a person.

Is someone watching her now?

She feels almost naked with the interior lights of her car's cabin shining overhead, exposing her like prey to a predator, so she quickly starts the engine to make them go dark. She breathes deeply to ease the jittery feeling in her stomach. It could be nothing more than a practical joke.

It could mean anything.

But still, the hairs rise on the back of her neck and she drives the long way home, passing her house twice before she's confident the street is empty and it's safe to park.

With the wadded note in her pocket, she locks her car and hurries into the house to face another sleepless night.

LIBBY

STRANGER

LIBBY PARKED on the east side of the Shell station near the car wash. The air was tinged gray with morning mist, and the mournful sound of the foghorn on the jetty seemed amplified in the gloom. Pulling her hood up against the damp chill, she fingered the twenty in her pocket and hurried toward the convenience store entrance.

If Todd suspected she'd taken it last week, he hadn't said anything. He usually complained about everything she did, so he must not have noticed.

She could have used River's bank card, but that was easier to track than cash. The less River and Todd knew, the better.

The clerk was a balding man with a bushy goatee that hung past his neck. He looked disapprovingly at the pack of cigarettes she laid on the counter, but he said nothing. His fingers brushed hers as he reached for the pack, and she flinched at their coarseness. Coarse skin didn't always mean rough hands. Sometimes the men who showed up with Gene wearing ties and with hands soft from sitting at a desk all day liked to hurt her the most.

Gene's hands hadn't been soft. They'd been coarse and stained black, with grease under the nails. He'd smelled like a mixture of fir and gasoline from the lumber mill where he worked as a millwright. Libby's palms still sweated whenever a diesel truck passed her.

The clerk accepted River's ID and the twenty, and Libby held his gaze, careful to keep her expression neutral and not look like a teenager with something to hide. That's one thing she learned from Gene. Don't give people a reason to ask questions. Not your teachers. Not the woman who lived next door. Not her cute seventeen-year-old son who offered to take Libby for a ride when he bought his first car.

The clerk dumped her change on the counter and Libby slid the coins off into her hand, feeling a sudden urge to wash. When she got outside, she realized she'd forgotten a lighter. She swore and was about to turn around when a shape crossing the parking lot caught her eye.

A small figure in black corduroy pants. The girl bent to pick something off the ground. Slipped it in her pocket before continuing to the nearest trash can. Bent to check its contents. Moved on to the next one.

"Hey, kid!"

A man standing next to a green pickup truck reached in the passenger window. "You hungry?" he asked.

Libby stiffened. The girl seemed familiar. River worked at the school; she would know who she was. But Libby couldn't think of her name. She was glad the girl paused. Wary.

"It's all right; I'm not gonna hurt you." There was a playful tone to his voice.

Diana. That was her name.

Libby stepped forward before she knew what she was doing.

"Diana! Hey there."

Diana's eyes widened to see Libby.

The man looked up and saw her, then tossed the paper sack to the ground. "Take it or don't take it. Makes no difference to me."

Diana grabbed for the sack and scampered over to Libby. She withdrew a half eaten breakfast burrito wrapped in the paper from the local diner.

Libby could almost taste the processed cheese melted over the eggs.

"Don't they teach you stranger danger in school?" The irony of those words coming from Libby wasn't lost on her.

Diana shrugged and took a bite. "I wouldn't have gotten in his truck or anything."

"I guess you didn't have breakfast."

"Danny's hungry too. I'll save him some."

Libby watched as she took two more bites, wrapped the rest of it, and returned it to the sack. She reached in her pocket for the change from Todd's twenty dollar bill.

"Here." She thrust the bills out to Diana. "I don't need it. Maybe you can get some bread or cereal."

Diana pulled back as if she wanted to bolt. "I don't think I should."

Libby sighed. "Look, it's your life. But I'd suggest you figure out how to get what you can when you can. If you're worried about getting in trouble, you need to learn to hide things better."

Diana squinted at her, considering. "Okay. Thanks." She took the change and stuffed it into her corduroy pocket. "What are you doing here?"

Libby fingered the package of cigarettes in her hoodie pocket. She itched for a smoke, but something told her not to do it in front of Diana. "Nothing. Just needed to use the bathroom."

"I like the one at the park. It doesn't have doors, but it's always open and you don't have to ask for a key."

Libby suppressed a smile. "Thanks for the tip."

"There was a man this morning sleeping on a picnic table. At first I thought he was dead 'cause he didn't look like he was breathing at all. But I poked his leg and he yelled at me."

"Why'd you poke his leg? I'd yell at you too."

Diana looked abashed.

"Look, you'd better take that burrito home to your brother. And stay away from strangers. They aren't all as nice as I am."

Diana laughed. "You're no stranger."

"That's not the point. Go find a good place for that money and don't tell anyone where you got it."

"Okay, I promise."

Libby watched her go, then headed toward the car. Now that she didn't have any money left, she couldn't pick up a lighter. But maybe the man sleeping at the park would have one and she could trade him some smokes. Of all the things Libby was afraid of, strangers weren't high on the list anymore.

DECEMBER 5

WEDNESDAY

1 WEEK BEFORE DISAPPEARANCE

GRACE

PIANO MUSIC DRIFTED out of the sanctuary, and Grace paused in the doorway to listen. Evan was sitting at the black baby grand, shoulders hunched as he moved with the music. He was playing Bach's *Ave Maria,* a fitting piece for a religious man. The melody welled up inside Grace and she was tempted to join in singing but resisted. No one liked a prima donna.

He played well, and for a moment she gave herself over to the music, letting the melody wash over her as if it were a tangible thing, working out the tension of the day. After two days of rehearsals, she'd given the soprano solo to Layla. She had the right range for it and had clearly been practicing. But it was always hard to break the news to the others.

Diana had packed away her hurt feelings so fast, if Grace hadn't been looking closely, she wouldn't have noticed. She'd pulled Diana aside after practice and given her a copy of a piece she planned for January, excitedly telling her that it would be perfect for Diana's range and she wanted to give her a sneak peak so she could be ready for the solo auditions after the break. But the light in Diana's eyes didn't rekindle, and the rest of the day Grace had felt like Scrooge ruining Christmas for Tiny Tim.

The sensitive piano solo was like a balm to her soul. She leaned against the doorframe to the sanctuary, wondering how Evan had learned. Wondering how many nights he sat at this piano and enjoyed the open stillness of being alone in the cavernous space.

He played from memory, his eyes tracking his hands on the keys, oblivious to his unseen audience of one. The low light made his strong profile look regal, his springy locks dancing as he moved. His fingers traveled deftly over the keyboard, with just enough power and sensitivity to awaken something in her that she hadn't felt in a long time. Something that made her want to know how it felt to hold those fingers and feel their warmth.

She shifted the music book in her arms and smiled at her own silliness. Music had always held too much power over her.

The song came to its final conclusion, as familiar to Grace as a pair of well-worn shoes. She was almost sad to hear the last chord, knowing the spell would end. The final notes lingered in the air as they found their way to the high ceiling above, with a faint creak from the piano bench as Evan shifted.

Grace breathed in, gathering courage to break the spell. But before she could speak, Evan attacked the keyboard with gusto, pounding out the unmistakable, iconic chords from *Bohemian Rhapsody*.

Grace burst out a laugh before she could stop herself.

Evan looked toward the door, pulling his hands away as if he'd been stung.

"Don't stop on my account," Grace said, walking up the nearest aisle toward the piano. "I love Bach as much as the next person, but there's always a time and a place for Queen."

Evan grinned, the dimple in his chin deepening. "Maybe not in a place of worship, though. Sorry. That was inappropriate."

"You don't have a piano?" Grace guessed.

"Someday. This one, though, it's a beauty."

"It is. You play it well."

"Thanks." Evan ducked his head as if embarrassed. "Not as well as I'd like. My mom always warned me that someday I would wish I had practiced more, and she was right."

"Wise woman," Grace said with a sly smile. "Sorry I'm late. I stopped by to pick up River but she had an appointment in Coos Bay and isn't home yet. I don't think she'll make it, so we'll have to make do with my playing."

"That's fine. I appreciate you coming so late on a school night. With youth group, I couldn't get away any sooner."

She waited for him to vacate the bench, but he only slid over a few inches, making just enough room next to him. She slid onto the bench, her heart skipping a beat at his nearness. In the dim room, lit only by a few direct lights overhead, it felt like they were in a much smaller space. She was suddenly glad that River hadn't been able to come after all.

Anxious to start playing and disguise her nervousness, Grace started out with the intro to their duet. It was a contemporary song by Lauren Daigle, meant to be performed as a solo with a choir. But Grace had spent the weekend arranging it for two voices, and the result wasn't half bad. Evan's voice was so much richer than hers, but she hoped the different timbres would complement each other.

With Evan sitting so close, she couldn't help but bump against him as she played, and he leaned forward, poised to turn the pages for her. He smelled masculine and clean, and when he started singing, his voice resonated through her, sitting as close as he was.

As she joined in, every part of her hummed with the music. It was intoxicating. She became aware of his eyes on her and resisted looking at him. Instead, she kept her gaze fixed on the music and hoped he couldn't see the heat rising in her face in the low light.

When Evan transitioned into falsetto for the strong climax, she couldn't keep the smile from her lips. The music thrummed through her, resonating her whole being like a tuning fork.

The final note died out and she finished the last bars, feeling a release at the end like she'd been holding her breath.

"Girl, I'm smitten!" Evan blurted, his eyes bright. "My chills got chills! Let's do it again."

And so they sang again. And again. By the third time, Grace's heart was beating normally again. Everything felt right. Natural and normal. Comfortable as if they'd known each other forever.

After thirty minutes, Evan sighed and got up, looking for his water bottle. The air felt cooler in his absence.

Grace took the opportunity to stretch and get a drink herself. Evan found his water near the pulpit and sat on the floor to drink, leaning against the polished wood. Grace followed suit, pulling her legs up cross-legged.

"You have a gorgeous voice," she said. "What's your music background?"

"Nothing like yours. My family was musical growing up, but I wasn't as into it as they were. I've got a couple of nieces who put me to shame. Still, it's something I enjoy. No matter where you go, music can connect you to others."

"That's so true. It's a universal language."

"Absolutely. Especially this time of year. Everywhere you go, you hear praises to God. In the grocery store. On the radio—"

"Ugh." Grace wrinkled her nose. "I have such a love-hate relationship with popular Christmas music. I don't care how many records you've sold, that doesn't mean you have any business singing a pop version of *O Little Town of Bethlehem*."

Evan pointed an accusing finger. "You're a Christmas carol snob!"

"Guilty as charged!" Grace laughed. "Some of them are just awful."

"All right, now you have to tell me. Which is the worst?"

"Easy. *Santa Baby*."

Evan choked on his water. "You hate *Santa Baby*?"

"Despise it."

"It's a classic! Granted, a misogynistic classic with questionable motives. Which, come to think of it, applies to a lot of classics."

"How about you? Name a Christmas song you hate."

Evan settled back with a grin. "Hmm. Hate's a strong word, but I don't care for *Mary Did You Know*."

"Really? What sort of self-respecting pastor are you?"

"I know, it seems like it should be part of the pastor creed, right? But I can't stand it."

"Well, you are an enigma."

In the companionable silence that followed, Grace's joy was dampened by the knowledge that after they sang together on Sunday there would be no more long evenings rehearsing together. The more she got to know him, the more she wanted to know.

"Question time," she said, twisting the silver chain of her necklace around her finger. "What do you love most about being a pastor?"

Evan looked up at the large cross looming over them on the wall. "I think what gives me the most joy is helping people connect with Jesus. He wants to give us so much if we're just willing to take it. But we let our own fear stop us from reaching out to him. When I can help someone see themselves the way God sees them, that's when I know I'm really doing his work."

Grace smirked. "A little *Bohemian Rhapsody* in church doesn't hurt either."

"All right, all right," Evan laughed, looking sideways at her through his dark eyelashes. "Are you going to use that against me?"

"It depends. What leverage can I get over a pastor? Extra brownie points at the pearly gates? A deduction in the collection plate?"

"How about a date?"

He said it so bluntly and unexpectedly that Grace froze and it took her a split second to recover.

"Oh. I—"

Evan looked away. "I'm sorry if that was too forward. You don't have to—"

"No! I'd like to." Grace's face burned. "I was just surprised."

"I'm sorry, that was really clumsy of me."

They tripped over each other apologizing until they both ran out of things to say, and Grace wasn't sure if the offer still stood or not.

"So, did you have anything specific in mind?"

"There's a performance of Carmina Burana in Eugene in January."

"Oh. January." That was ages away.

"I figured I was already tying up too much of your time here, I couldn't ask you to give up another evening this close to the holidays."

His solicitousness made her smile.

"Well…I haven't gone to see the lights at Shore Acres yet."

Evan's eyes brightened. "Then let's go. How about next Friday? We could do dinner before if you're sure you have time."

"That sounds perfect."

They went through the piece one more time, and although Evan didn't join her on the bench, he did stand behind her and leaned over her to turn the pages. She didn't want the night to end. Every nerve seemed attuned to him. She was afraid to touch him because she thought there might be visible electricity if she did.

Or worse. That there wouldn't be.

But as they said goodnight and the cold sea air washed over her face, waking her up for the drive home, Grace couldn't help but feel like something magical had happened. It was the beginning of something new. Something exciting. She didn't know where it would lead, but for now, she just enjoyed the hope that there might be someplace for it to go.

BESS

SHOE

IT'S BEEN quiet for a while, and I almost think I'll be able to go to sleep. I want to forget what I've heard.

But just when I can't tell what's real and what's a dream anymore, something thumps against the wall, making me jump. It's a bad sound. I don't know what it is, but it makes goose bumps on my arm and my throat feels tight like a scream got stuck in there.

I wish they would stop. I wish *he* would stop, because I know Mama isn't fighting anymore. She stopped fighting a long time ago.

Sometimes he'll go away after a big fight, and I wonder if this will be one of those times. Maybe I'll wake up in the morning and he'll be gone and I'll ask Mama where he went and she'll tell me to eat my oatmeal and not worry about it. He always comes back.

I want to see Mama and know that everything's going to be okay. I want Mama to tell me I'm safe, and no matter what happens, she and Daddy still love me and will always take care of me. That's what usually happens when they've been fighting.

But not this time.

Someone is moving outside my room. I don't think it's Mama because the steps are quick and heavy and she moves more slowly after one of their fights. But I imagine it's her. I want it to be Mama and I want her to come in and tell me goodnight.

When the door opens, I lift my head and can see from the shadow that stretches across my bedroom floor that the person standing there isn't Mama. It's Daddy. He's bigger than Mama, and right now I'm afraid of him. I'm afraid of the sounds I heard. I'm afraid of what he's done.

"Get your blanket. We're going to sleep at Grandma's tonight," he says.

He sounds calm now, but I know his niceness is only as thin as a lightning bug's wing. So I do what he says, even though I don't like visiting Grandma Billie. She's cranky and smells funny and smokes in the house. Mama doesn't like to visit her either.

I get my blanket and Daddy holds out his hand and I take it. We walk down the hallway and I look for Mama as I pass their open bedroom door. It's dark in there and Mama isn't in their bed.

"Where's Mama?" I ask.

"She's gone. She's not coming with us," Daddy says, and anger pulses through the calm. He sounds like he'll yell at me if I say anything else, so I don't ask anymore questions.

Even when I see that a table in the living room has fallen over and one leg is broken. Even when I see a hole in the wall like something big hit it. Even when I see one of Mama's shoes on the front step.

If Mama went somewhere, why wouldn't she wear both of her shoes?

The air in the car is cold as I climb inside. The hum of the tires against the road makes me feel sleepy. By the time we get to Grandma Billie's, I'm so tired that I don't care that her house is stinky. She's waiting for us and shows me a sleeping bag on the floor where I can sleep. I climb inside and wonder where Daddy will sleep. But he doesn't come in the house. He drives away again.

As I drift off to sleep, I wonder where Mama is and wish I could have told her goodnight.

DECEMBER 16

SUNDAY

3 DAYS AFTER DISAPPEARANCE

GRACE

Service is at 10 today, in case you want to come. I meant to invite you last night but didn't get a chance to talk after the vigil.

GRACE SITS CURLED up on her couch under a blanket. It's 9:15 a.m. Evan sent the text at 8:00 that morning, but she hasn't responded yet.

Last Sunday, she was there for his service, performing with him the duet they'd practiced. It was powerful and she enjoyed his sermon, enjoyed listening to the rise and fall of his voice as he preached about the signs of the birth of Jesus.

A week ago she wouldn't have hesitated. But now...

A lot has happened in a week.

She likes Evan. She likes him a lot. But it's hard to think straight these days. Everything has changed since Thursday night. Grace wishes she hadn't gone to the vigil last night. Too many people. Too public in their anxiety for Diana. And she can't help but think it's her fault.

For a moment, she imagines going to Evan's service today and joining with Diana's family and River and all those other faces from the vigil. She lets herself imagine what it would be like to see Evan standing at the front of the sanctuary in his vestments. She imagines listening to him give a message of hope and love, perfect for the Christmas season, but also tailored to the recent tragedy.

Could she be brave enough to ask him for some private time to talk? Could she tell him everything that keeps her up at night? Would he be able to make any of it better?

Grace rubs her eyes with her knuckles. No. He wouldn't. No matter all his nice words and steady faith, he can't fix anything. She's on her own.

Grace thumbs her phone to reply.

> Feeling a bit low today. Thanks anyway.
> Good luck!

She spent the night on her couch again in the glow of the Christmas tree lights with the TV on low. Her back aches from the foam cushions, but she can't bear to leave the light of the tree for the darkness of her room.

Shifting to relieve pressure on her hip, she opens the news feed on her phone. She finds a story about the candlelight vigil and an article saying that police have taken Diana's parents in for questioning again.

A video on the local morning news shows footage from the vigil, together with interviews of members of the community. Here's something new. A security camera near the bank has footage of Diana walking toward Park Street the night of her disappearance, the opposite direction from her home. The news story ends with a plea for anyone who thinks they might know anything to come forward.

Grace connects her phone to her bluetooth speaker and turns on a Christmas playlist, looking for something else to distract her. A pile of silk flowers sits in a basket near the TV. Grace picked them up the day before while running her errands, thinking to make a couple of holiday bouquets for the Christmas concert.

She sits on the floor and reaches for them, then begins stripping off the leaves, leaving only one or two behind. Inspired by the bouquet from Evan that graces her table, she's chosen an assortment of red roses, white Gerbera daisies, gold berries and sprigs of fir. She wishes she had some floral spray paint, but this will have to do. She settles her back against the couch with the flowers sorted in piles in front of her.

Two gold, bowl-shaped vases serve as the bases. Grace intends to place one in the foyer where the audience will enter and one in the sanctuary, near the pulpit. She'll leave them there for Evan's congregation to enjoy throughout the season, a thank you gift of sorts.

She places green floral foam into the bottom of each bowl to hold the stems, then reaches for the longest rose. Placing it standing tall in the center, she then adds four more to form the arms of a cross. It's a subtle design that probably no one else will notice, but seems appropriate for the setting.

Her phone buzzes. She tries to ignore it, but suspects it's Evan and curiosity wins out.

Thanks. Sorry you don't feel up to it. Maybe we could have lunch sometime this week?

Grace chews on her lip. She can't keep putting him off. Milton crawls into her lap and kneads his paws against her thigh while she types her response.

Sure, let me get through the concert and then I should be able to breathe.

She should have just told him no.

The flower arrangements might have been too much. During college she worked at a floral arranging shop, but that was a long time ago and she's out of practice. She restarts twice before she's happy with the foundation. Fortunately, silk flowers are more forgiving than fresh, so they aren't any worse for wear.

My Favorite Things comes on the speaker and Grace is immediately flooded with a memory of Jess as a girl singing in the school talent show, dressed in a light blue sundress. She'd practiced the song for a month and couldn't talk about anything else as the day drew near. The talent show was one of the last celebratory traditions before school let out for the summer.

Grace—five years older and in the high school choir—had coached her vocals. She looks back at it now and grimaces. She didn't know anything about proper singing then and is sure all her advice was bad.

What's worse, Jess's voice had cracked on her last long note. The look on her face had been pure devastation. Grace's heart still squeezes at the thought. She'd wanted to run to her, to be there for her sister when she came off the stage, but only performers were allowed in the wings. So she'd waited in agonizing impatience for Jess to make the long walk back to the auditorium.

When she exchanged a look with their mother, she knew she was thinking the same thing. It was such a big deal for Jess to do this in the first place. They hadn't expected her to win, but at least hoped she would be proud of herself.

When Jess finally made her way down the row toward her family, she had to squeeze past the knees of a dozen other people first. Several of them whispered, "Good job," or, "You did great!" But every time they acknowledged her, the crust hardened. By the time she got to Grace, her pain was buried behind a wall of hostility.

Grace didn't know what to say.

"I'm so proud of you," Mom said, offering her a hug.

Jess shrugged her off and sat down.

Grace knew how much her little sister looked up to her and realized in that moment she hadn't done her any favors by pretending to know everything about singing. Jess had a fine singing voice, but Grace knew she would never sing a solo in front of a crowd again unless Grace could think of the right words. Right now.

Grace leaned over to Jess and placed an arm around her shoulder. "Wow, I just love listening to you sing," she said. Jess looked at her then, anguish shining through the cracks of her veneer. And a hint of something else. Hope.

Grace smiled. Jess smiled back. They held hands through the rest of the show.

The playlist moves on to another song and Grace unfolds her legs and stretches. She goes to the bathroom and pulls her hair back into a ponytail, looking at her face critically in the mirror. What does Evan see when he looks at her?

What would he see if she told him what she was most afraid of?

She just has to get through this week. That's all.

And then what? a small voice asks.

Then Christmas. Alone.

Then back to work.

The thought makes her stomach tighten. All she wanted to do last night was be home and get away from people. But now, the thought of being stuck here alone is driving her crazy.

Maybe she should book a flight somewhere. Florida? San Diego?

Her phone rings, and she ignores it. She can't talk to Evan right now. She worries she'll agree to something she'll regret. She needs to be alone. But at the same time, she doesn't really want to be.

She flips on the TV and pulls up her list of favorite Christmas movies. Nothing grabs her attention. Everything is romance with cheeky puns, and she can't handle either right now.

Her phone rings again and she reaches for it to silence it. But the number is one she doesn't recognize.

Feeling a little spike of fear, she answers.

"Hello?"

"Grace?" A man's voice.

"Yes?"

"This is Todd."

Grace's insides turn to mush. "Yes?" she asks warily.

"I can't find River," Todd says. "She said she was going for a walk, but she took the car. She must have turned off her phone because I can't locate her. Is there a chance she went to your house?"

Grace peers through the closed blinds and looks out onto the street. It's empty, except for the backpacker she saw at the park. He's sitting on the curb, eating a sandwich.

"No, she's not here. I haven't heard from her."

Todd swears. "I can't even look for her without the car."

"I'll see what I can do. I'll let you know if I find her."

"Thanks. What am I going to do with her?"

Grace can't answer. Todd sounds pushed to the brink. But she can't worry about him right now. If River is in danger, she's all that matters.

LIBBY

THE WIND BLOWS Libby's hair, whipping it across her face. The sun is shining and it's a glorious day.

She stands on a small outcropping accessed by climbing over the guardrail at the top of the cliff and working her way through the wild huckleberry and sea grass. Below her, waves crash and swirl into a small bowl with jagged rocks known as Devil's Teeth. Across from Devil's Teeth, perched on a rocky promontory, the Ellis Cove lighthouse stands white against a blue sky, its lens flashing red and white in a slow, measured rhythm. Tiny shapes in bright colors are people milling around the base. Libby wonders if they can see her in her baggy black sweatshirt. Probably not. They're probably all looking out at the wide expanse of gray-blue ocean and seagulls circling over the water.

It's a beautiful December day.

A glorious day to kill them all and finally be free.

Bess is crying, as usual. She's so weak. But what would you expect from a child?

River is the worst, though. Always telling Libby what to do. Telling her to stop stealing money from Todd. Stop driving the car when she's had a little bit to drink. River acts like she's in charge, but she isn't. She's as weak as Bess. How could someone like that be in charge?

Libby will get rid of them once and for all. The question is, how to do it so that she doesn't kill herself? Sea spray blows across her face. The sound of the pounding waves echoing against the cliff almost drowns out their voices.

Almost.

She parked the car up the road at a different turn-out. If Todd is looking for her, he won't find her in time. He'll be furious, but that's nothing new. He's always mad at Libby.

A car crunches onto the shoulder and Libby looks up. She recognizes the black Camry. How did Grace find her?

"River!" Grace shouts from up above on the road.

Libby doesn't respond. Maybe Grace won't look down. But of course she does. Grace isn't stupid.

"River!" she cries when she spots Libby. "Thank God I found you! Are you okay?"

Libby looks back out at the ocean. Seagulls circle lazily overhead. She thinks she can make out sea lions bobbing in the water, but it might be nothing more than seaweed.

She hears Grace making her way down the narrow trail. It isn't an official trail, just a small path that people with more adventure than good sense have worn through the foliage to get a closer look at the tempestuous whirlpool of Devil's Teeth.

She waits until Grace reaches her to speak.

"You didn't have to come for me."

"Of course I did! What are you doing?"

"Just enjoying the view."

"And why did you turn off your phone?"

Libby smirks. "I wanted some alone time."

Grace narrows her eyes. She suspects. Good. Libby would be disappointed if she didn't.

"Why don't you come back with me? It's not safe here."

"Of course it isn't safe. That's the point." Libby spreads her arms out and tips her head back, closing her eyes. "I could end it all right now and be free!"

"Or you could come back with me and go home to your husband."

"He's not my husband. I'd rather get rid of the others and then...go to Vegas or something. I've never been to Vegas."

Grace hesitates. "So...you're Libby?"

Libby doesn't answer. It's always so inconvenient when people can't tell them apart. Embarrassing.

"If you jump from this cliff, there won't be any Vegas."

"Sure there will. I'll be fine. It's the rest of them who will be dead. I'm not trying to kill myself." What a ridiculous idea. She has no intention of killing herself. She has so much to live for, if she can only get free of them.

"River's my friend."

"I don't know why. She's so boring."

"River's cool. You just don't know her the way I do."

Talking about her now makes River's voice louder in her head. Libby grabs her hair and growls. "She's annoying and bossy and thinks she knows everything. I just want to get away from her!"

Grace lifts her hands as if to stop Libby. But she doesn't touch her. "Okay, that's fair. How old are you, Libby?"

"Fifteen."

"Right. So, when I was sixteen, I figured I was old enough to make my own decisions. I went with some older friends on a day hike. My mom told me to bring extra water and a jacket just in case, but it was a hot summer day and we knew where we were going. Until we didn't."

Libby snorts.

"There wasn't any cell service in the backcountry, and it turns out we were all crap at reading the map. We planned to jump on another trail that was supposed to loop around back to the car, but when we couldn't find it, my friends decided to turn back. I didn't want to because we'd already been hiking for hours, and I just knew when we hit that other trail it would take us straight to the car. So I kept going."

Libby looks at Grace properly for the first time. "You went alone? Even I know that's stupid."

Grace grins and tucks her hair behind her ear. "Yeah it was. But I thought I would make it back to the car hours before they did. I ran out of water and food, but I didn't really get scared until the sun set and I started freezing."

"So, what did you do?"

"Fortunately for me, I ran into two bikepackers who were camped up there for the night. They shared their food and water, and the woman let me share her sleeping bag. It was a little awkward, but they probably saved my life."

"So it worked out after all," Libby points out with a smirk.

"Yeah, it did. The problem is, I was only thinking of myself. How was I going to get back home? Had my friends left me without a car? That sort of thing. I didn't even consider how worried my friends would be. Or how my mom would call Search and Rescue and stay up all night praying that they'd find me. Or the men and women who spent all night risking their own lives looking for me."

Libby frowns. "Then they should have just stayed home. You were fine. They should have trusted you and let you figure it out."

Grace's smile fades. "That's not how it works when someone loves you. We don't get to choose how hard they fight for us."

Libby is quiet for a minute. Grace is so naive, living in her little dreamland where people do noble things for those they love. She doesn't understand what it's like to only be able to count on yourself.

"I don't need anyone telling me what to do."

"I know. The thing is, Libby, you're very smart. You deserve to live the life that matters to you. But River deserves to live her life too."

Libby shrugs. "Not my problem."

"And what about the baby?"

Libby squints at the sun. "Why should I care about the baby?"

But she doesn't mean it. Grace senses it too.

"You couldn't do that to River's baby. No matter what River's done to you, you know her baby is innocent."

Libby grits her teeth and takes a step forward. "I just want to be free!"

"I know. I want you to be free too. I promise. But if you do this now, you'll hurt an innocent baby. And I don't think you would ever do that."

Libby steps back and growls. Grace is right. Of course she's right.

"Fine. But only until the baby's born."

"Okay. I can work with that. You wanna come with me back to the top?"

"I guess."

Grace waits for Libby to go first. A part of Libby is glad she came. Grace doesn't even seem mad, not like Todd would have been.

"Are you going to tell Todd where I was?"

"Probably. He'll need to know."

"He's just as nosy as River."

Grace snickers. "Someday you'll understand."

"I seriously doubt it. You don't know him the way I do."

Libby reaches the top and stops, turning around. What would Grace do if she pushed past her and flung herself over the edge?

But Libby likes Grace. She doesn't want to cause her trouble.

And Grace won't always be there to stop her.

DECEMBER 9

SUNDAY

4 DAYS BEFORE DISAPPEARANCE

RIVER

DIANA WAS WAITING for River when she got home from church. Todd was helping Josh work on some car repairs, so River had gone alone. She was annoyed that Todd missed Grace and Evan's duet, but now, as she recognized the dirty blond head bent over the knobby knees, she was glad he wasn't there.

When Diana looked up, she was smiling.

"Hi Mrs. Vincent!" she called out before River had even turned off the engine.

"Hey, Diana," River greeted as she braced her feet to pull herself out of the car. "What's up?" Diana didn't seem to notice the wariness in her tone. Boundaries were hard enough for River to set in the first place, she didn't want to get entangled with someone who didn't know how to respect them.

"I brought you something," Diana said. "I thought you could use it for the baby."

It was a rattle toy shaped like a crab, with grips on either side for little fingers.

It was clearly used. The cheerful face paint was scratched and grime caked the grooves for the finger holds.

"Oh, thank you. This is really thoughtful." River wondered where Diana had gotten it. Was it an old toy from when she or her brother were babies? Or had she nicked it from the thrift store?

She started moving up the steps, hoping Diana would go home, but Diana followed her. River turned back at the door. Diana waited expectantly, clearly hoping for an invitation to come in.

"Well, I'm going to make dinner, and it's probably good for you to go home too."

Diana's face fell. "Can I see the baby's room again?"

She looked so hopeful that, against her better judgment, River nodded.

"For a few minutes."

River let her inside but didn't set her purse on the table. She knew that if Diana stole from her, it would be out of desperate need, not maliciousness. But she still didn't want to give her the opportunity. River didn't have much to spare. Besides, it would complicate Diana's life if she started stealing so young. If she waited until she were older, she might be smarter about it.

Instead, River led the way down the hallway, and while Diana veered off to the nursery, River put her purse in her bedroom and closed the door.

When River returned to the nursery, Diana was sitting on the floor, staring at the nightlight. It projected stars onto the wall and ceiling, cycling through an array of colors.

"It's so cool," she breathed.

"I think the baby will like it too."

"Before my window broke, I liked to look out at the stars at night."

"What happened to your window?"

Diana didn't answer right away and River thought she could guess. Not an errant toy or excited play. Someone got angry.

"It has a board there now. But it gets really cold in the winter."

"Do you have enough blankets? I have an extra one you could have if you need it."

"Really?" Diana's face lit up.

"But only if it won't make your mom mad." She thought of how Grandma Billie would get if she ever brought home gifts. Sometimes the office at school would call her down and give her groceries or clothes. At the time she didn't know why, and only later understood that there were probably other kids getting the services too.

Diana's expression clouded over. "My mom probably won't get mad. But Leo will. Unless..I think I can sneak it in so he doesn't notice."

River was torn. Show the girl some kindness and help her be warm during the winter? Or risk making things worse by attracting attention?

Grace would probably have told Diana to ask her mom first, but River knew better. Asking was never the better choice. You either got away with it or you didn't. Drawing attention to yourself was always the worst possible option.

River got an old comforter out of the closet. "Tell you

what. Maybe hide it somewhere outside first and then wait until Leo is gone before you bring it in the house."

Diana squeezed the blanket. "Thanks. I know just the spot. I have lots of secret places I like to go. There's a place in the rocks down by Fool's Beach that's my favorite spot. You just have to be careful not to go out too far because if the tide comes back in you can get trapped."

River didn't know where Fool's Beach was, but there were so many private beach access points along the coast that it could have been anywhere.

"Are there tide pools there?" she asked, moving to the kitchen to get started on dinner. Diana followed her.

"Yeah, but they aren't very big. Not like the ones at the cove. Tara in my class says she saw an octopus in one once!"

River reached for a knife and hunted for the last half of an onion in the fridge. She wished Diana would go. Her muscles were tensing up the longer Diana stayed. If she didn't leave soon, River was going to end up having a flashback, she just knew it. She could feel it creeping on the edge of her mind.

Finally, she laid down the knife.

"Thanks for coming, Diana, but you'd better hurry home before it gets dark."

"Oh, I don't mind the dark."

"Still, I would feel better if I thought you could be safe."

She hated the hypocrisy of the words. Of course Diana wasn't safe. And here was River, making the lie worse because she knew Diana wasn't safe but she was pretending that she didn't. Just like every other adult who saw what they wanted to see instead of seeing the truth.

But River wasn't like other adults, because she knew.

And she hated herself for pretending.

EVAN

EVAN LOCKED UP THE CHURCH, threw his bag over his shoulder, and walked home with music in his head. Man, it had been a good service. While singing with Grace the rafters at First Hope had rung like choirs above were joining in. Afterward, sweet old Gertie Hammer had clutched him in an exuberant hug.

"I swear I could feel God today like I never have before. Thank you. What did we ever do without you?"

He knew he shouldn't enjoy those affirmations as much as he did. He'd learned as a running back in high school that when he got too full of himself, God had a way of reminding him just how fallible he was. But for a second he'd indulged in the sweet satisfaction of acceptance after the years he'd spent trying to earn his place in this mostly White town. Football success only went so far off the field when your skin was Black.

But this…this was a good day. He hummed as he crossed the parking lot, eyeing the pile of gravel and making a mental note to ask Deacon Thomas about it at the next board meeting. They would need those spots for the Christmas service, when Evan expected the lot to be full and overflowing onto the street. He wanted to give Deacon Thomas a chance to fill his leadership role, but he was half tempted to take matters into his own hands if that's what it took to get the pile spread once and for all.

A wooded lot bordered the church property, and the western sun cut through the tops of the evergreen trees. Wood smoke filled the air, making the setting sun's rays shine like lighthouse beams, and Evan couldn't resist taking a detour into the forest. A walking path wound nearly half a mile before connecting with the trail that ran along the river, and Evan followed it now, even though it would take him a little longer to get home.

He had initially invited Grace to sing with him almost on a whim. From the first time he'd met her, he'd felt a connection. That inexplicable something that happened sometimes when meeting someone new, when everything about the moment seemed super clear, as if his brain or his soul or the Holy Spirit was saying, "Pay attention! This person matters."

He'd felt almost desperate to see her again and had seized the idea to invite her to sing with him. She could have said she was too busy. She could have looked at him like he was crazy.

Instead, she'd said, "What do you have in mind?"

Grace had a good soul, worthy of her name. The way she cared so deeply for her students, her generosity toward others, and her seasoned faith drew him to her. Evan was looking forward to their date on Friday, a chance to spend time with her away from the church. To set aside the pastor and see how they got along.

The shadows under the cover of trees were deep and somber. Leaves and pine needles covered the path and English ivy climbed the tree trunks. Everywhere thick moss clung to bark and hung from drooping bushes. The air was thick with moisture and the scent of rich earth and decaying things. It was so different from the dry desert where Evan had spent his young childhood. The coastal climate had worked into his blood, and he knew now he would never leave.

A figure was sitting on a bench, and Evan watched as he approached to see if it was someone he knew. It was a man dressed in a bulky jacket with a large camping backpack strapped to his back. The backpack was so overloaded, Evan wondered how he stayed upright when standing. The man's face was heavily bearded and his hair was covered by a coarse beanie. Evan didn't know him, but as he drew near, he recognized the girl sitting on the other side.

"Hello, Diana," Evan greeted. "Missed you at church today."

"Mom was sleeping. She worked late last night."

"Ah. And who's your friend here?"

The man's eyes flitted to his, then up to his hair and back down on the ground. He didn't speak.

"Hey there, brother," Evan addressed him. "How are you on this fine Sabbath evening?"

The man grunted.

"This is Jim," Diana said. She poked at a hole above the knee of her sweat pants. "He says he's on his way to San Francisco."

"Is that right? I love San Francisco."

The man threaded his fingers together, resting his elbows on his knees.

"Where are you staying, Jim?"

Finally Jim spoke. "I think I'd better get going."

He stood and Evan offered his hand.

"Can I get you a warm meal before you go? Maybe a cup of coffee? Share a message of hope for the season?"

Jim looked at Evan's hand suspiciously, as if he couldn't remember what the gesture was for. Up close, Evan realized he was younger than he'd appeared at first glance. Looking past the dirt caked in the creases of his skin, Evan suspected Jim wasn't much older than he was. He smelled like he hadn't bathed in months.

"No thanks." Jim started to walk away.

"Wait. Here." Evan reached in his bag for his wallet. He only had a few bills, but he handed them over.

Jim looked at the bills, then at Evan. His eyes were rimmed with red. "I'm not a beggar."

Evan held his gaze. "I didn't say you were. I believe the word I used was 'brother.' Take it."

Jim lowered his eyes to the bills and snatched them. He stuffed them in his pocket and shuffled away.

Evan sat on the bench where Jim had been sitting before. "He seems nice."

Diana picked at a chip in the bench's paint.

"What did he want?" Evan asked.

"Nothing."

"How do you know him?"

"I see him at the park sometimes. He chased away a dog that was barking at me once."

"That was nice."

The sun slipped away, leaving a golden hue in the air.

"Diana, I don't want to scare you, but just because you know somebody's name doesn't mean you can trust them."

"I know." She sounded defensive.

"Just be careful, okay? Try not to spend any time alone with Jim or anyone else you don't know very well."

"Like you?" She pushed her hair out of her eyes and squinted at him.

Evan smiled. "Sure. Even me." He stood and slung his bag over his shoulder. "Be safe, Diana."

RIVER

RIVER DIDN'T SAY two words to Todd over dinner, but he didn't seem to notice. He was on his phone the whole time. He barely noticed when she cleared his plate and washed the dishes. The water burned her hands, and by the time she finished they were angry red. She left the dishes to dry in the small drying rack.

"I'm going to bed," she said quietly.

Todd looked up. "You feeling okay? Do you need anything?"

What did she need? To be able to sleep without nightmares. To not be afraid of the dark.

"No thanks. I'm just tired."

But after she brushed her teeth and crawled between the cold sheets, she couldn't get her mind to rest. Bess's memories were strong, and River kept slipping back to the house on Vine Street.

A woman with curly red hair sat in a chair in the corner of the bedroom. She threw back her head and laughed like she didn't have a care in the world. River wanted to go to her, but she was afraid. Why was she afraid? The woman was kind. She liked River. She would hold her on her lap and she smelled like vanilla.

But seeing her there, in the corner, fills River with terror.

Why?

"Come here, Bess," the woman says.

River knows that voice. Knows it like she knows her own skin.

She is Bess, of course. Her name before she changed it. The name that her mother gave her.

Mother. That is the woman in the chair. She's River's mother.

Her mouth is wide with straight teeth. She doesn't look like someone who would have married Gene.

"Why did you run away?" River asks.

"What are you talking about? I'm right here. Come give me a hug."

Bess obeys. She climbs out of bed and crawls into her mother's lap. The fabric of her blouse is rough against her cheek. Mama wraps a soft blanket around her shoulders. The edge is silky smooth and Bess fingers it.

"You ran away."

"Don't be silly. You've had a nightmare. I'll never leave you, little bug."

"I don't want you to go away."

"Don't worry. I'm not going anywhere yet. And when I do, you're coming with me. We're going to get a little house in the mountains far, far away. Maybe by a lake. We'll swim in the lake in the summer and watch the snow fall in the winter while we drink hot chocolate by the fire. Doesn't that sound nice?"

Bess nods and closes her eyes.

"But you can't tell Daddy. It's our little secret. You can't tell him about the lake or our plan to go away. You promise?"

"I promise."

The weight of her mother's chin settles on Bess's head. She rocks back and forth. "Someday, little bug. Someday soon."

River woke with her heart pounding. She held perfectly still, trying to remember where she was. This was her room. She was River Vincent, married to Todd Vincent and expecting their first child. She lived in Ellis Cove on the Oregon coast, and no one—not even Todd—called her Bess.

Had she been asleep? The dream was fresh. So real. She knew that place. Her blanket with the silky binding. The green carpet in the hall. Mom hated that carpet.

She remembered her mom. How she smelled. The sound of her voice.

Her mom loved her.

She had to tell someone.

Todd lay next to her in bed, breathing deeply. She looked at the clock. It was almost 1:00 am. If she woke him now, he would be too tired to work the next day. But she had to talk to someone.

She grabbed a blanket and her phone and gently let herself out of the bedroom. She crept down the narrow hallway to the living room and dialed Grace's number as she curled up on the edge of the couch. She probably wouldn't answer. She was probably sleeping.

"Hello?"

River relaxed.

"Hi, Grace."

"Hi, are you okay?" Grace's voice was sharp with anxiety.

"I don't know. I just need to talk to someone. I've been having dreams. Dreams or memories, I don't know which. About my mother."

"Oh. Tell me about it."

Bless her for not telling her it could wait until morning.

"I didn't realize that's who it was at first. But tonight somehow I knew. I didn't think I had any memories of her, but now I do. She had curly hair."

Grace murmured appreciatively. "I'm so glad. That's got to mean a lot to be able to remember your mother."

"I know why she left now. At least, I think I do."

Grace was silent on the other end of the line.

River was whispering but her throat felt hoarse trying to hold back the urgency.

"I remembered the night we left. We left, Gene and me. Not Mom. They'd been fighting. It was horrible. Screaming and shouting so I couldn't sleep. I went to check on them once and ask them to be quiet, and she was sitting in a chair. She was tied up and gagged and the strap made her mouth all wide like she was smiling, but she wasn't smiling."

"Oh, River," Grace whispered.

"Gene sent me back to bed. Later I heard crying. Then he came to my room, and we went to Grandma Billie's that night. I never saw my mother again."

There was a long, expectant pause. Finally, Grace asked hesitantly, "What do you think happened?"

"I don't know. I know she planned to leave, and she

was going to take me with her," River insisted. "We were going to live in a house in the mountains. I was supposed to keep it a secret. I think Gene must have found out and stopped her. That's why he was so angry."

"I don't know, River—"

"*I* know. I know how it feels for this child to grow inside of me. I would protect it with my life, and it doesn't even have a name yet. She wouldn't have left me behind."

"Maybe she didn't have a choice."

"Maybe my dad made that choice for her."

Grace was silent for a long time before finally asking, "What do you want to do?"

"I don't know. But I had to tell someone. I can't go to sleep. Every time I close my eyes I see her there."

"Do you want to go to the police?"

"No. I can't."

"River, if he did something to your mom—"

"I don't want him to know where I am. I can't risk it. My name…my name isn't River. I changed it when I left. His sentence is up in a few years. I can't let them know where I am."

"Of course. I understand. You need to be safe."

River's pulse pounded and every creak in the house sent her heart racing. She felt anything but safe.

"What I can't decide is how much Grandma Billie knew. She always said my mom ran away. But surely she suspected. She knew him for what he was. Did she know he was capable of that?"

Grace was quiet for a long moment.

"I'm so sorry, River. I'm glad you called. You shouldn't keep something like this to yourself."

"Well, thanks for answering. I didn't know who else to call."

"Will you tell Todd?"

River ran a hand through her short hair. "I don't know. Maybe eventually. But not right now. I don't want to make things worse for him."

"I'm sure he won't mind. He loves you. He wants to take care of you."

"Yeah, but…not yet."

River couldn't explain it. But if she told Todd what she'd dreamed and he dismissed it like it was nothing more than a meaningless nightmare, she might lose that thread to her mother.

Her mother who hadn't left her. Her mother who didn't run away.

Her mother who loved her.

DECEMBER 17

MONDAY

4 DAYS AFTER DISAPPEARANCE

GRACE

GRACE SLOWS near the harbor to wait for a school bus. Her windshield wipers make a rhythmic counterpoint to the music playing over her car speakers. She usually times her drive to the school to avoid getting caught behind a bus, but she was a bit frazzled this morning and left late.

The night before, after Grace found River on the cliff overlooking Devil's Teeth, she told Todd where to pick up the car and then brought River back to her own house.

Milton settled on River's lap like an old friend, and after a few minutes of cat therapy, River came back to herself, to Grace's relief. She stayed until after dark, sharing more details about her life. When River was fifteen, Grace learned, a well-meaning piano teacher had reported his suspicions of abuse. His report had aligned with an ongoing investigation into a local child sex ring, leading to the arrests of her father, grandmother, and five others.

It surprised Grace to hear River talk about the police

investigation with such hostility. In Grace's mind, the police were the heroes. They'd rescued her from being trafficked by her own father. But being ripped from the only family she'd known hadn't felt like rescue to River.

She'd been placed in foster care for a while, until running away at sixteen and living on the streets. It was rough, but not as bad as where she'd come from. There wasn't much she hadn't already suffered.

Eventually, she'd hitchhiked her way across the country and joined a youth support group in Phoenix. From there, she'd been able to change her name, get a job, and earn her GED.

That was the surface story. Underneath, Grace saw a young woman running from a past that would never leave her, no matter the college degree, husband, or baby.

At one point, River had grimaced. "You met Libby? Isn't she such a brat?"

Grace pulled back. "No, I don't think so at all. She's smart and funny. Has an attitude, sure, but I think she's got a right, don't you?"

"It sounds like you like her."

"Yeah, I do. And, more importantly, she listened to me when I needed her to."

River looked at her like she was crazy. But Grace couldn't explain how she'd recognized River in Libby. How she'd sensed the same intelligence and humor. Felt the same desire to protect her.

The school bus slows again for two kids waiting with an adult under a massive umbrella. Red lights flash, and the stop sign signals the children to duck out from under the umbrella and make a run for it. On rainy days like this, as much water is stirred up by passing cars as falls from the skies, making it even harder to see.

Grace checks the time. She doesn't have a first period class, but she still has lots to do. She needs to get itineraries out to the teachers and parent volunteers who are going to be escorting the children during the concert. They'll wait in shifts in the church's classrooms, and it will be up to the adults to make sure the groups get to the waiting area on time and lined up in height order so everyone in the audience can see their child.

Grace almost feels a flicker of excitement at the prospect. Almost. What a strange month it's been. Ordinarily she would be eating, breathing, and sleeping the concert. But this year the concert is just something to get through. If the rest of the community gain seasonal joy from it, great. But she can't feel anything.

Her phone buzzes and the car audio system announces the caller.

Max.

Her stomach does that same unpleasant squeeze it does every time he calls. She initiated it this time, though, having left a message on his phone before she left the house. But this is a phone call she doesn't want to have while driving. She silences the call.

At last, the bus turns off into the trailer park and Grace speeds up. A police cruiser is parked at the entrance to Harbor Lights. She tenses momentarily until realizing it doesn't have its lights on. It could be anyone, for anything. It isn't necessarily about Diana.

Grace parks at the school and reaches for her phone. A call like this requires complete privacy, so she doesn't want to risk calling from her classroom. Max answers on the second ring.

"And a Merry Christmas to you too," he says by way of greeting.

"Hi Max. Is this a good time?"

"Let me guess. You're getting collection calls for your sister and need help tracking her down?"

"No. Not this time. But I do need help finding someone, if you've got the time."

Max sighs and Grace can picture him running a hand through his mop of white-blond hair. "Sure, I've got the time. It just so happens that I'm home recovering from surgery this week anyway." His voice holds a bitter note and Grace wavers. Should she ask about his surgery? Is that too personal coming from an ex-girlfriend?

"I'm sorry to hear that. I hope you get feeling better soon." It sounds as lame and disinterested as she feels and she bites her lip with shame.

Max notices and shifts into business mode. "So, who am I looking for? Name, birthdate, last known residence, that sort of thing."

"Her name is Janice Ketchum. Or it was, twenty years ago. I'm guessing she's going by a different name now if she's still alive. Lived in Florida in the early 90's and was married to a Eugene Ketchum. Had a daughter named Elizabeth, born in 1993. That's all I know."

"No maiden name or birth year?"

"Sorry."

"So, what's her story? Who is she and why are you trying to find her?"

Grace fingers the tassel on her purse's zipper. "She's my friend's mom. Left when she was little, probably fleeing an abusive marriage. My friend's expecting her first baby and it would really mean a lot to reconnect with her mom."

"You know they have private detectives for this sort of thing."

"I know. If you can't do it, that's okay. I don't want to impose—"

"It's okay, I'm on it. But if you're going to make a habit of playing Nancy Drew, it might be good to use a professional. Especially one who's not popping oxy."

Grace smiles. "Thank you, Max. I owe you big."

"Yeah you do. Next time you come to Portland, you can take me to lunch."

"Sure. That would be nice." She hopes her enthusiasm doesn't sound false. "And Max, one more thing."

"Yeah?"

"If you…Try not to use the name Elizabeth Ketchum if you can. I wanted you to have it for context, but don't, like, use it in any way that could get back to you."

"The daughter? Why?"

Grace falters. "Just…look at the arrest records for Gene and Billie Ketchum and you'll figure it out."

"Hmm…curiouser and curiouser. All right, I'll let you know what I can dig up."

"Thank you, Max. I really do appreciate it."

Grace sighs in relief as she hangs up and grabs her bag. That went better than she expected. Last time she asked Max to help her find Jess, he'd been coming off a breakup and bordered on hostile.

Grace uses her key to get in through the back entrance closest to the music room. Buses will start arriving soon, and she doesn't have time to visit at the office.

Charlie McGee waits outside her room, his hair still damp from the rain.

"Hi Miss Miller."

"Good morning, Charlie."

"I was wondering if I could play your xylophone this morning."

"Sorry, not today. I've got some other things I need to do this morning. Maybe tomorrow, though, hey?"

His shoulders droop. She watches him go, slumping dejectedly, and feels a tug to invite him in anyway. But the library is always open before school, so there are other places he can go.

Grace unlocks her classroom door and shoulders her heavy bag. She boots up her computer and plugs in the scented diffuser that sits near her desk. One of the swags of tinsel garland she hung up after Thanksgiving has come loose and droops in the corner. Is it worth calling custodial to borrow a ladder to fix it? She'll just tear it down in a few days anyway.

"Oh good, she's here."

Marilyn's voice sounds out in the hall, followed by the murmur of another voice.

Grace stands just as Marilyn and Sergeant Polaski enter the room. Grace's insides flip at the sight of the officer.

"Good morning, Grace," Marilyn says. "We missed you at our staff meeting this morning."

Grace winces. "Was that today? Sorry."

Marilyn raises a hand to silence her apology. "Don't worry about it. I know how it is this time of year. Grace is in charge of the Christmas concert at First Hope tomorrow night," she explains to the sergeant.

"Your choir performed at the vigil on Saturday night," Polaski observes.

"Yes."

"And that's the choir that Diana Beck is a member of?"

Grace moves away from the desk and pushes in her chair, gripping the back of the seat.

Present tense.

"She is. That's why she was helping decorate at the church the afternoon she disappeared. But you already know that."

Marilyn glances at the clock. "I'll leave you to it, then. Let me know if you need anything else."

Polaski thanks her and turns back to Grace. "How well do you know River Vincent?"

Alarm shoots from the back of Grace's neck to tingle in her fingers. "Pretty well. We've been friends for a couple years. We took a Jiu-Jitsu class together in Coos Bay and now she's my pianist."

"Is she here today?"

"No. We don't have students until second hour, so she won't come in until closer to ten." And then, before she can stop it from slipping out, "Why?"

Polaski doesn't answer her question directly. Instead, she asks another one. "Are she and Diana close?"

The question gives Grace pause. "Close? No, I wouldn't say that. But she's kind and compassionate, especially toward kids who are disadvantaged in any way."

Polaski notes this in her notebook. "Does Diana frequently visit Mrs. Vincent at home?"

Grace blinks. "Not that I'm aware of. A lot of kids in this town wander the streets, though. It's a small town. Safe. I have students knocking on my door a lot, and I don't live as close to Main Street as River does."

"Has Diana ever come to your house?"

"Sure." Grace saw Diana pass by her street once or twice, hadn't she? "I don't invite them in, of course. I just say hi on my doorstep, sign up for whatever cookie dough fundraiser they're selling and leave it at that."

"You're talking about Diana?"

"And the other students. It's really pretty common."

"When was the last time Diana visited your house?"

Grace hopes her discomfort isn't evident on her face. She feels warm and worries her cheeks are flushing. "Let's see...I don't know. Maybe sometime around Halloween? I have a black cat and she wanted to hold him. Yeah, it was probably around then."

Sergeant Polaski betrays nothing in her expression. Grace feels like she's facing an exam and suspects she's failing.

The first attendance bell rings.

Polaski looks at the clock. "What time did you say Mrs. Vincent would be in?"

"Maybe nine forty-five? But everything is crazy right now. We've got the concert tomorrow and the holidays are coming up. And she's got the pregnancy of course."

Polaski nods. "Danny Beck says Diana was excited about the baby. Said she'd been to the Vincents house to see the nursery."

What? River didn't mention that. Grace tries to keep her expression neutral.

"Like I said, Diana responded well to kindness."

Polaski fixes her probing gaze on her. "What do you mean by that?"

Does she have to look so stern? Grace can barely meet her eyes. "Just that...if she'd gotten kindness at home, she never would have had to look for it elsewhere."

The tardy bell rings and River walks in, bundled in a coat and carrying a bag that makes her lean with the weight.

She stops in the doorway. "Oh. Sorry."

"You're early." Grace watches her carefully and reads the tension in her face.

Sergeant Polaski notices too, her focus shifting. "Are you River Vincent?"

"I am," River says, and the wariness in her tone makes Grace want to shield her from the police officer.

Polaski steps forward to shake her hand and River shoots a panicked look at Grace.

"Is there somewhere we can talk in private?" Polaski asks

"I..."

"You can stay here," Grace offers. "I won't have students for another forty-five minutes."

"I'd prefer to speak to Mrs. Vincent alone," Polaski says firmly. Did the woman never smile?

But Grace can be stubborn too. She takes River's bag and looks her directly in the eye. "River, do you want me to step out, or would you like me to stay?"

"Stay please," she says gratefully. "Those are treats for the kids. For after the concert."

Grace peeks in the fabric bag and spies dozens of candy cane reindeer complete with pipe cleaner antlers, googly eyes, and red pom-pom noses.

"Thank you. They'll love them."

Grace pulls out three chairs so they can sit. The plastic is hard and unyielding and shaped for smaller bodies. She hopes it will encourage Polaski to keep her questions brief. She sits next to River, facing the policewoman together.

"Mrs. Vincent," Polaski begins, "when was the last time you saw Diana Beck?"

"It must have been the day before she disappeared."

"The day before. Wasn't she decorating at the church that day?"

"Yes, but I didn't go. I wasn't feeling well."

"Hmm. And you didn't see her later at your house?"

River frowns.

"No. I didn't."

"Did you go anywhere that day?"

River pauses. "I was going to go to the store. But I changed my mind."

"Why?"

River shrugs. "I wasn't feeling well."

Sergeant Polaski eyes her and River shifts.

"Where do you live, Mrs. Vincent?"

"The trailer park near Main."

"Diana was seen near the Harbor Lights trailer park that evening. Are you sure she didn't come visit you?"

River blinks a little, and shakes her head. "No. No, she didn't."

Grace fidgets with the fringe on her scarf. She understands why River isn't telling the sergeant everything.

She wouldn't either, and River is a far more private person.

"When is your baby due, Mrs. Vincent?" Sergeant Polaski licks her thumb and turns a page in her notepad.

"Um...mid-February."

"Boy or girl?"

"We don't know yet. It's a surprise." River tugs at the shirt straining over her belly.

"Will there be anything else?" Grace interrupts. "I need to get ready for class."

Polaski looks her over. "Ms. Miller, isn't it school policy that when you have an activity after hours that the students have to get permission from their parents to attend?"

"Yes."

"And did Diana Beck have permission to be at the church that day?"

Grace hesitates. "Of course. I wouldn't have let her be there otherwise."

"Can you show me the permission slip?"

"Uh...I don't think I have them any more. Let me check." Grace moves to the desk, her hands trembling slightly. "I don't hang onto them past the activity, otherwise they get mixed up." She makes a show of flipping through the stack of folders that house the permission slips for the concert. "I must have shredded them."

Polaski is unmoved. "Shredded them? Or recycled them?"

Grace catches River's eye. "We're supposed to shred anything with personal information on it."

"Ms. Miller, my wife is a school teacher. I understand

that just because you're supposed to shred documents doesn't mean it always happens."

Grace folds her arms. "I might have put them in the recycle bin. I don't remember. But it would have been emptied on Friday."

"Thank you, Ms. Miller."

"It's Millar."

"I'm sorry?"

"Millar. Not Miller."

"Excuse me. Ms. Millar. Mrs. Vincent. Thank you for your time. Please call me if you remember anything else about that day."

Grace follows Polaski to the door and closes it behind her. She breathes out audibly in relief.

"I'm so sorry, River. I didn't know she was going to be here. But you did so well."

River is rubbing her arm distractedly. "Did I?"

"Yes. You did great."

"Do you know why she wanted to talk to me?"

"I think she's just checking with everyone who might have seen Diana that day. Do you...do you remember anything about that night?"

"Just what I told the sergeant. Why? Do you know something I don't?"

River's voice has an edge of challenge to it and Grace doesn't trust herself to answer. Does River suspect? Grace shouldn't have said anything.

"No, I was at the church all night. Can you help me sort out these itineraries? I have the lists of parent volunteers here somewhere..."

She glances out at the parking lot, but River's Taurus

with the mismatched back door isn't there. Todd must have dropped her off. That's probably for the best.

In the last few minutes before the students arrive, Grace organizes itineraries by grade. River helps whenever Grace gives her something to do, but she moves slowly. When she doesn't have a specific task, she stands still. Listless.

"River? You okay?"

River nods uncertainly, but her eyes are vacant. Empty.

Grace's heart sinks.

Dozens of footsteps sound down the hall.

"The students are coming. Can you play the piano?" Grace asks helplessly. "Tell me how to help you and I'll do it."

River moves to the piano bench and sits down. Grace helps her get out the piano music for the fourth grade just as the students enter the room. River stares at the sheet music.

"Good morning!" Grace calls cheerfully as the students settle into their chairs. "Mrs. Vincent is going to be doing some work for me to get ready for the concert, so hold on a minute while we get situated."

She wraps an arm around River's shoulder and murmurs in her ear. "River, Bess, or whoever you are, come on over to my desk. It's okay, just come with me."

River stands and obeys. Grace leads her to the desk and sits her down.

"Good. Just like that. Just hang tight here while we sing for a while, okay?"

She turns the piano a bit to block the view of River

from the students, even though it makes it harder for her to make eye contact with the class.

"Wonderful! Let's get started with a nice warm-up. Who wants to pick today?"

By the time the period ends, Grace is sweating like she's run a 5K.

As the students file out of the room, she turns her attention back to River. Her head is moving in brief passes as if tracking something in the air ahead of her.

"I think we should call Todd. Do you have his number?"

River doesn't answer.

"Where's your phone? Is it in your purse?"

Grace finds the phone in River's purse and hands it to her, but River looks at it without recognition.

"Here, just..." Grace helps her activate the security thumbprint to unlock the phone. She swipes through River's favorite contacts and finds Todd at the top.

Grace texts him from River's phone.

This is Grace. River's having a hard time.
I think she needs to go home.

Todd's reply is quick.

Can she stay for a bit? I can pick her up
on my lunch break. 30 min.

Yeah, that's fine.

The next class goes a little smoother now that Grace knows what to expect. As the second graders leave to go to the cafeteria for lunch, Todd ducks into the room. He's wearing work boots and a Carhartt jacket. Grace can't look him in the eye.

"Come on, River. Let's get you home." He sounds weary and more than a little annoyed.

River goes with him without question.

Grace turns away and busies herself sorting through the mail from her box. A flyer from the PTO announces a family Christmas craft night the previous week. She tosses it in the recycle bin.

She senses Todd hesitating at the corner of her vision, like he wants to say something. But she doesn't want to hear whatever he has to say. Especially if he's going to thank her.

She doesn't breathe easily again until he's gone.

DECEMBER 12

WEDNESDAY

1 DAY BEFORE DISAPPEARANCE

GRACE

GRACE'S PHONE lit up where it lay on the counter next to the kitchen sink. She leaned over to read the incoming text as she poured a boiling pot of pasta into a colander. It was from River.

Do you have time to chat?

"Siri, send a text to River."

What's the message for River? Siri's soothing voice replied.

"Sure."

She ran cold water over the pasta and waited for River's reply.

K. I'll pick you up in a few minutes.

Oh. Grace had expected a simple phone call. This was more than just a chat.

Grace shook the colander to finish draining the pasta,

then tossed it with a bowl of sliced veggies. Pouring Italian dressing mix over it all made her mouth water, but she could eat after she got back. It would taste better chilled anyway.

When River's gray Taurus pulled up to the curb out front, Grace was already waiting with her coat and purse. She opened the passenger door and slipped into the seat. The lights from the instrument panel illuminated River's tired smile.

"Thanks. I hope I'm not interrupting anything."

"Nothing that can't wait. I just made a killer pasta salad in case you're hungry."

River gripped the steering wheel and didn't respond. Grace didn't say anything more. Whatever River wanted to talk about, Grace would let her take as long as she needed.

The headlights illuminated trees and bushes whipping in the wind as they drove through town. A trash can rolled against the curb, its lid skittering across the road. It was a terrible night to be out. Grace wondered if she should have invited River to come inside instead.

"Is Todd home?"

"No, he's out with his men's group."

Grace looked at her. "A men's group?"

"It's through the church. They get together once a month."

"Like a Bible study?"

"Sometimes. Other times it's just to relax and watch football. It gives them a chance to hang out with other men in supportive ways."

"Huh. That's cool."

"Yeah. There's a women's group too, but I've never been."

Grace's church had a women's group too. She'd gone a couple of times when her mom was alive. But it seemed that all the conversations ended up commiserating about husbands or children, and Grace couldn't relate to either.

River took Main out of town to Oceanview Drive. They passed The Captain's Quarters and a small hotel before reaching the parking lot for Devil's Teeth. Huge seastack rocks hulked out in the darkness, like leviathans coming out of the deep.

To the north, the Ellis Cove lighthouse perched on a knoll, keeping watch with its steady beam swinging out over the waves. Red. White. White. Red. The foghorn moaned gloomily in the night.

Grace loved this spot during the day. The north end of the lot was dedicated to a fenced viewpoint that overlooked the lighthouse and the violent churning bowl of Devil's Teeth. But the south side held a staircase that led to a calm beach with a wide stretch of soft sand. It was a favorite spot for tourists, but this night, with a storm brewing, the parking lot was empty.

River shut off the engine and switched off the headlights. The air immediately began to chill and Grace was glad she'd worn her warmest coat. The wind buffeted the car, shaking it with every gust.

"I've been remembering some more things about my mom," River said. "About the night she either left or...he killed her."

Grace waited, offering River the space to say what she needed to say.

"I remember...I remember trying to stop him. She

was crying and I hid in my room, wanting it to be over. Not able to go to sleep."

She twitched a little.

"That must be..." Grace couldn't think of the words to describe it.

"I was so scared." River held the long sleeve of her sweater and rubbed it against her face.

She twitched again.

"Can you make them stop?"

Grace looked at River sharply. Her voice sounded smaller, somehow. Weak. She looked at Grace, and ice trickled down Grace's spine. River's eyes looked...wrong, somehow.

Afraid, but also...blank.

"They're so loud." River covered her ears with the long ends of her sleeves.

Grace sat, frozen in place. Her lips parted to speak but no words came.

River started. "I have to get out of here. He's coming. We have to go!" She pawed at her seatbelt.

Grace finally found her voice. "River, we're okay. No one's here but us."

Seatbelt unlatched, River reached for the door.

Grace didn't know what to do except follow. She opened her own door and hurried around to the driver's side of the car. River was already halfway across the parking lot, her door left hanging open. Grace reached in and grabbed the keys, then shut the door and locked it.

When she turned, the darkness made her blind.

"River?" she called, but the wind snatched her words away.

She turned on the flashlight of her phone and caught

River's form walking toward the wooden staircase that led to the beach.

Grace ran to catch up. "Let's go home. It's too wild out here tonight. The beach isn't going to be safe."

High tide or not, when a big storm like this came in, the waves could be fierce. High surf warnings urged residents to stay away from beaches. At night, it would be throwing yourself at nature's mercy.

River started down the stairs, methodically. Not in a hurry, but deliberate.

The wind whipped Grace's hair and stung her eyes, making them water. She shone her light toward the beach. Was that water she saw down below? Or sand? She couldn't tell.

"Come on, River. Come back."

At a turn in the stairs, a sign warned about sneaker waves. *Great.* The lightness on the beach was moving. Waves foaming and cresting. Not sand.

Still River followed the stairs down. The wind made it hard to breathe. Grace hurried after her and reached her before she hit the last turn. She grabbed River's arm and pulled her to a stop.

River looked at her, but still her face didn't register emotion. Just that blank, empty stare.

"We have to go back," Grace shouted over the wind. "It's dangerous down here."

River mumbled something Grace couldn't hear. But she obeyed and started climbing back up the stairs.

Grace sighed in relief. Cold rain started pelting her back. She stayed behind River, making sure she didn't turn around again.

When they got back to the top, Grace put her arm

around River, guiding her back to the car. Her hair clung to her forehead, and she struggled to see through the driving rain. She brought River around to the passenger side and crawled into the driver's seat herself. Her jeans were damp against her skin as she adjusted the seat for her height.

River didn't comment as Grace started the car and fumbled to turn on the windshield wipers. Rain spattered in noisy bursts across the windshield, passing in waves with the gusts of wind. Grace kept an eye on River as she circled the overlook and pulled back onto the main road.

River's short hair was plastered against her brow. She didn't seem to notice the water leaking down her temples.

"Are you okay?" Grace asked. "River?"

River turned to look at her, but her eyes seemed distant. "Who's River?"

The question was so unexpected, Grace laughed at first. But River didn't smile. What was going on? Whatever it was, Grace was out of her depth.

"Uh, River is my friend," she said seriously. "Who are you?"

"Bess," River answered. "And you're Grace. Grace is my friend." She turned back to the window and settled back against the seat.

What was that *supposed to mean?*

"Do you know where my mama is?" River asked in a small voice.

"I'm sorry, I don't."

"Mama says we're going to go away. We're going to go to the mountains where it snows."

"That'll be fun."

Grace's voice sounded forced in her own ears. She clenched the steering wheel, her heart pounding. She couldn't cover the miles fast enough, but the wind blew debris across the road forcing her to be cautious. Streetlights appeared in the distance as they neared the city limits.

As the silence stretched long, River covered her ears again.

"He's so loud," she complained. "Yelling and yelling. I think he's hitting her."

Grace looked at her in alarm.

"Stop!" she shrieked. "Stop hurting Mama! No, I don't want to go away. Tell him, Grace! Tell Daddy I don't want to leave Mama!"

"I'll…I'll tell him."

But River wasn't even listening. Suddenly she grabbed Grace's arm and the car swerved toward the gravel shoulder. Grace yelped and corrected, getting the car back on the road.

"Mama's in the chair. She can't talk. Something's wrong with her mouth. I'm scared."

Grace's breath came in shallow gasps. "It's okay, Bess. We'll call an ambulance and they'll take care of Mama."

River shook her head. "No, they can't. Daddy won't let them."

They were finally in town, and Grace slowed as the speed limit dropped. River pulled her feet up onto the seat and wrapped her arms around her knees. She twitched again.

"It's okay, Bess. We'll get some help." Grace hoped it was true.

The trailer park was close. Grace had never been so

happy to see the Harbor Lights sign. A couple blocks further and she pulled the car into the carport.

Stuffing River's keys into her coat pocket, she ran around to the passenger side to help River get out, hovering over her but uncertain what to do. River didn't seem to notice. She seemed completely ambivalent toward Grace.

"I don't want to go with him," she said again.

"You don't have to. Just stay with me; I'll take care of you."

"You promise?"

Todd opened the back door before they'd reached the steps. He sighed in relief. "I've been calling and calling. Where did you go?"

River didn't respond, so Grace volunteered.

"We went for a drive. I don't think she's feeling very well."

"You okay, babe?" Todd asked, holding River by both arms. A look of resolve settled over his face. He'd seen this before.

Grace stepped into the small kitchen and placed River's keys on the counter. It smelled like lemon-scented cleaner and something faintly musty, like damp wood that had never fully dried.

"Thanks for bringing her home. I never should have left her alone."

"It's fine."

"Come on babe, let's get you to bed," Todd said, shepherding River toward the bedroom.

Grace felt a surge of gratitude for Todd. Not many men would be that comfortable with their wives going off the deep end.

No, that wasn't fair. River wasn't crazy. Whatever had happened tonight was strange, for sure, but River was still River. And whatever happened wasn't her fault.

Grace pulled out her phone as Todd was busy in the back, suddenly wishing someone was worrying about her. Waiting for her to come home. Wishing she had someone to talk to about what she'd just been through.

There was a text waiting from Evan.

> How about Baby it's Cold Outside? If that song isn't problematic, I don't know what is.

Evan's playful reference to their ongoing conversation felt like a lurch to another life. She wished she could tell him what had happened. But it wasn't fair to River. She tried to think of a pithy response, but her mind was blank.

The floorboards creaked to announce Todd's return. He stopped when he saw Grace in the kitchen, as if he'd forgotten she was there.

"Do you mind giving me a ride home?" Grace asked apologetically. "I don't have my car."

Todd looked back over his shoulder. "Yeah, just a minute."

He returned to the bedroom and Grace heard the murmur of voices. A few minutes later he emerged with a set of car keys.

Grace followed him out to the car and climbed into the passenger seat.

"So, you met Bess tonight?"

He said it so matter-of-factly that Grace was taken aback.

"I guess. Does this happen…frequently?"

Todd shrugged and ran a hand over his five o'clock shadow. "More and more often lately. Her therapist is trying to help her get it under control, but nothing seems to be helping."

"So, who *is* Bess?"

"It's her as a kid. She changed her name after her dad was arrested for pimping her out. Her real name was Elizabeth Ketchum."

"So Bess is actually River? Not like a made-up person or anything?"

"She's a version of herself. But she's trapped in that time when she was a kid."

Grace paused, letting it settle. She had so many questions.

"How do you get her to…go back to being River?"

"She comes out of it on her own usually. It's worse at night. Where did you say you went?"

"She texted and said she wanted to talk and then she came to pick me up. I'm sorry, I didn't know she shouldn't be driving…"

"It's fine, you couldn't have known. She probably didn't want to tell you what was going on. Sometimes it really freaks people out."

Grace *had* been freaked out. But now she was glad she knew. It made her heart ache for River, keeping it to herself the way she had.

"She said some things…some really serious things. Are they memories from her past?"

Todd looked grave. "I don't know. She thinks they are."

"She was telling me some stuff about her parents tonight."

"Yeah, it gets pretty messed up sometimes."

"Will she remember? When she…wakes up?"

"Maybe. I don't know. She doesn't like to talk about it."

Grace thought about what River had said about her mom. What had Bess witnessed? And what Todd had said about River's dad…Grace didn't know anything about River's past, but she never would have guessed she'd been trafficked by her own father.

The thought made Grace shiver. Suddenly Grace's own history that once seemed so tragic—father died young, sister a drug addict—felt really pedestrian. What easy problems she had.

"I'm sorry, Todd. This must be so hard for you."

"Uh, yeah. It's hard. It wasn't always like this. Her therapist thinks that maybe the pregnancy has something to do with it. She hopes that after she bonds with the baby, it'll be a way of working out her own grief over her mom."

"Do you know what happened to her mom?"

"Just what River told me. That she left her when she was six and River never heard from her again. She was raised by her dad's mom, who made things pretty rough for her. Then her dad started selling her to the highest bidder when she was maybe eleven or twelve."

Grace tried to reconcile the ugly words with her kind and generous friend. "How…how does one person survive all that?"

Todd didn't reply. They drove in silence until they turned onto Grace's street.

"That's me, with the black Camry."

Todd stopped in front of her house.

"Thanks for taking care of her tonight," he said. "The car was gone when I got home and she hadn't texted to let me know she was leaving. She's usually good about checking in with me. I was so worried..."

He didn't finish but Grace thought she knew what he was going to say. She thought of River's insistence on walking down the stairs to the tumultuous beach below. Had there been other nights that Todd worried she might not come home?

"Next time I'll make sure we stay put," Grace said as she stepped out into the rain. She closed the door behind her and Todd pulled away. Grace suspected he was in a hurry to get back to River, but she wished he'd stayed long enough to make sure she got in all right. The world felt like a more sinister place tonight and she felt very much alone.

She flipped on the light as soon as she got in, but it didn't chase away the darkness creeping at her mind. She hung up her coat and shook her wet hair, grabbing a soft throw and settling onto the couch. She felt weary, but her mind buzzed. There were a few things she needed to know.

She Googled multiple personalities and scanned through a few pages about Dissociative Identity Disorder, or DID. But everything she read was broad and clinical. Nothing described what she'd experienced with River.

Then she did a search for Gene Ketchum. Eugene Ketchum. Judith Ketchum.

It was a long shot, since she didn't know where or

when they were arrested. Google served up some obituaries and a few Facebook profiles, but nothing useful.

Milton whined and appeared from around the corner of the couch.

Grace turned off her phone. "Come here, baby. Give me some love."

His big green eyes stared at her without blinking but he didn't move.

Grace sighed. Useless cat. There would be no comfort for her tonight. She was on her own.

LIBBY

DANGEROUS

LIBBY TWISTS the doorknob all the way to the left so the latch won't scrape against the metal plate. She pushes the door open silently and distant light from the living room cuts across the carpet to the foot of the bed where Todd sleeps. The room smells of sleeping breath and dirty laundry. His snore is a deep rattle, slow and steady.

Libby steps across the worn carpet, avoiding the boots and damp socks Todd left near the bed last night. A stack of plastic drawers doubles as a nightstand, and Todd's phone sits charging on top. Libby unplugs it and gently lays the cord down so it doesn't scrape against the plastic surface. Then she slips just as quietly out of the room, pausing to make sure Todd's breathing continues uninterrupted before closing the door.

It's strange the way Todd has access to River's phone but she doesn't have access to his. River always seems more worried about making Todd's life better than she is about whether he makes life better for her. Never mind it's River who did all the packing for their last move.

River who pays their bills and buys the groceries. River who files their taxes and argued with insurance when they wouldn't pay the anesthesiologist for Todd's shoulder surgery. But she isn't allowed access to Todd's phone when he has access to hers?

It sickens Libby. Fortunately, she's more observant than River and figured out his passcode, then added her own thumbprint to his security. He hasn't realized it yet. Neither has River.

Libby sinks into the couch and unlocks Todd's phone. The screen opens to YouTube and Libby scowls at the suggested videos. She really doesn't want to know about his porn habit, but she scrolls through his history anyway, wondering if she should tell River. She could send her a text right now from Todd's phone. Show her that video right there of the girl who doesn't look any older than Libby.

Libby smirks a little thinking about how River would react. She thinks she's so smart, always telling Libby what to do. So mature. So experienced. But she doesn't even know about her own husband's kinky fantasies.

Libby doesn't send the text. She'll save the knowledge for another time. Maybe she can use it against Todd somehow. Gene always kept videos of his clients. Insurance, he called it.

Libby's skin crawls thinking of the men who came to the pink basement room. Their faces were lost in the haze of heroin Gene gave her afterward. But heroin didn't take away the scars between her legs or the gagging reflex that hits her any time she smells artificial strawberry scent.

Todd has problems, but he's nothing like Gene.

Libby leaves YouTube and pulls up the app Todd uses to track River's phone. He set up a notification to alert him whenever she leaves the house at night, but it takes only a few seconds to shut it off. As long as his phone is right where he left it when he wakes up, he'll never guess what she did.

She creeps back into the bedroom and returns the phone without a hitch, indulging in a small self-satisfied smile as she closes the door quietly behind her. The pickle jar she's saved for a week is hidden in the back of the cupboard under the bathroom sink. It's still there. No one has discovered it yet.

A knife would be easier, but Todd hid the only sharp one in the house. Broken glass will have to do the job.

She'll wait to break it until she's down the street away from the house. Maybe all the way to the park. The park isn't lit well at night. A few lamp posts rim the playground and parking lot, but at night the area near the baseball diamond is hidden in deep shadow.

Already she imagines the relief she'll feel when the blood starts to flow. The cool of the damp grass seeping into her clothes. Surrendering to oblivion.

Libby grabs a jacket and tucks the jar under her arm. She opens the back door slowly, just a crack.

A shape stands on the sidewalk across the street, watching the house.

Bulky and large like a man, he's silhouetted against the lamplight, his head covered by the hood of his coat.

She pulls the door shut, her chest squeezing with alarm. She fumbles with the lock and deadbolt. Libby isn't easily spooked, but something about the faceless shape feels like a threat.

She leans against the back door, breathing fast. There's a window in the door covered by a tattered mini blind that doesn't rise anymore. Libby lifts the blind slightly to peek out.

He's still there, not even trying to hide. He stands out in the open as if challenging her. Daring her to leave.

Who is it? What does he want with her? A faint glow under the shapeless hood suggests the embers of a cigarette. She gets a glimpse of a heavy beard before the glow fades. Does he know her plan? Is he there to stop her leaving the house?

For a wild moment she thinks maybe Todd asked a friend to come watch the house in case she tried to leave. But he isn't that creative.

Libby checks the time and swears under her breath. It's almost 2:00 a.m. Todd will be waking up in a few hours. If she's going to make it to the park, she needs to do it soon. Or else put the pickle jar back and wait for another night. She doesn't dare try to break it here in the house. There's no way Todd would sleep through that.

Why don't they have proper knives? This is ridiculous.

She peeks out the blinds again. The man is right outside the carport now, on this side of the street. Libby gasps and drops the blinds. She sinks to the floor under the window. Bess is crying now. Of course she is. Bess is afraid of everyone.

River is yelling at Libby to go wake Todd, but Libby refuses. She tries to push them both away. But she can almost sense the man climbing the back stairs, reaching for the doorknob. Would he try to break in? Would he hurt her? Of course he would. Why else is he there?

Maybe Gene found her after all this time. He'll kill her this time. Or worse, drag her back to the house on Vine Street.

She sits on the floor of the kitchen, trembling.

Bess is so close. When a floorboard creaks, Libby nearly slips away.

River looks up in fear. Todd stands in the faint light at the end of the hallway.

"Hey. You okay?"

River looks down. She's dressed in boots and a jacket, like she's planning to go out. She senses it's late. She tries not to let her confusion show. Todd hates it when she loses control.

"Yeah, I'm okay. Sorry to wake you."

Todd turns on the lamp near the couch. It casts heavy shadows over his face.

"What are you doing? Geez, River, it's three in the morning."

Is it? There isn't anything River can say. Her tailbone hurts from sitting on the hard floor, and her feet tingle painfully when she struggles to stand.

"What's that?" Todd asks, and River follows his gaze.

An empty pickle jar sits on the floor near the door.

And then she understands Libby's plan. But what she doesn't understand is what stopped her.

"I don't know. It looks like it needs to go out to the recycling."

River leaves it on the floor. She doesn't want to pick it up right now with Libby so close. Let Todd take it out in the morning.

Why didn't Libby go through with it? It wouldn't be the first time River had woken up covered in her own blood. But Libby had stopped. River feels a sudden urge to check out the back door.

But when she pauses and turns back, Todd stops her.

"Come on. You've got a big day tomorrow."

That's right. It's the day of the concert. She follows Todd, but can't quite shake the feeling that something dangerous is just outside the door.

DECEMBER 18

TUESDAY

5 DAYS AFTER DISAPPEARANCE

GRACE

IT'S the morning of the Christmas concert and Grace has already had too much coffee. She knows she'll pay the price for it later, but she feels like she's on a treadmill, unable to get ahead as the day whirls away from her. The itineraries are printed, and during each class period she only has the groups sing their numbers once, then turns on the movie "A Christmas Carol" for the rest of the period.

Emails have gone out to parents telling them when and where to bring their children, but she's printed fliers for each of the students to bring home just in case. Though this might be blurring the lines between a school and community activity, at this point she doesn't care. She's more worried about families forgetting to come and the whole thing ending up a disaster.

After each class, she gathers up the fliers that were left behind or turned into paper airplanes. She grimaces as she picks up one with a soggy, chewed up edge and throws it away.

River hasn't come in. Grace told her not to bother since they're doing very little singing today. What she didn't say is how worried she is about River being able to hold it together for the concert. Nights are the worst. What if River dissociates in the middle of the performance?

During her lunch break, Grace grabs her purse. She only has a few minutes, but that should be enough to grab a sandwich from the bakery on Main.

When she sees the note on her windshield, she freezes and scans the street in front of the school. Parked cars line the sidewalk, and an old man crosses the street walking a little white dog. Pulse thumping in her ears, Grace slips the note from the wiper.

This time it's written on a page torn from a notebook, the edge ragged and frayed where it was ripped from the spiral binding. Again, two words are written in the same rough hand:

I SAW

Grace's heart crowds into her throat. Hands trembling, she unlocks her car, double checks that the backseat is empty, and almost throws herself into the driver's seat. She jams her key into the ignition with a panicked ferocity and backs out so fast she nearly hits the opposite curb.

Why is she being targeted with these mysterious notes? Who is leaving them and what do they expect her to do? More importantly, *what* did they see?

Evan calls just as she pulls up to the bakery. Grace hesitates, then silences the call. When her phone rings again a few minutes later, she ignores it. Guilt burns in her stomach. She's intentionally ignoring him, and he's going to figure it out sooner or later.

More than anything, she wishes that she didn't have to ignore him. That she could answer his call and flirt and make plans for another date.

Instead, she brings her sandwich back to the school and eats it at her desk. While she eats, she pulls up music teacher postings in other states. But that only makes her lose her appetite, so she closes the window. She's overreacting. It might not come to that.

Her phone buzzes again, but this time it isn't Evan.

Grace sips her water and answers it.

"Hello?"

"I caught you," Max says. "I worried you'd be in the middle of class."

"It's my lunch break. How are you?"

"Getting anxious to get back on my feet. Good thing you gave me something to keep busy or I'd be pulling my hair out by now. Wow, Grace, this guy is a piece of work."

"Yeah?"

"Auctioned off his own daughter's virginity at the age of eleven. What kind of sick pervert does something like that? The grandma's just as bad. She claimed not to be involved, but she paid the bills and took a cut of everything so she got ten years. Died three years into her sentence, though."

"She did?"

"Yeah. Heart trouble or something. So, Grace, you've gotta tell me. What happened to Elizabeth? You know her, right? That's your friend?"

Grace hesitates. "She's doing good. Married and expecting her first baby."

"Wow. That's incredible. You'd expect a survivor of that kind of abuse to be on the streets with a needle in her arm."

"She's pretty amazing. I mean, it hasn't been easy." That's an understatement of epic proportions. "But she's getting therapy, working on stuff, you know. Did you find out anything about her mom?"

"Not really. Sorry. Records that old aren't digitized, so it's tough. Last known address was in Tallahassee in 1990. I did find out her maiden name was Howard and she worked as a paralegal in Pensacola during the '80's, but that's the last record of any employment. She was an only child and her parents both died in the mid-90's. There's more info on Eugene, but that's from the early 2000's. Janice was out of the picture by then."

Grace is glad she didn't mention her search to River if it's not going to lead to anything. "Well, thanks for looking. I really appreciate it."

"Sorry I couldn't be more helpful. There was one other thing, but I don't want to read too much into it."

"What's that?"

"Janice Howard had a small 401(K) set up from that paralegal job in Pensacola. It wasn't much, because she only worked there for a couple of years. But in 2002 she withdrew all of it. Took the tax hit and everything."

Grace straightens. "She did? That would have been about three years after she left."

"Well, it might not have been her. The account that the money was transferred to was in both her name and

Eugene Ketchum's. So maybe he was short on cash and decided to stick it to her for leaving him."

"Hmm." Grace's flicker of hope snuffs out.

Max pauses. "Or…he knew she wasn't coming back. Maybe he knew she would never show up looking for that money."

Grace checks the time. Her next class will be coming in soon. "My friend has been remembering some things from her childhood. Disturbing things. If Eugene killed Janice, would there be any way to prove it after all this time?"

Max blows out a heavy breath. "Not without a body. She was never reported as a missing person, but that's not too surprising if they moved around a lot and she didn't work or have a lot of friends. Especially if Eugene intentionally kept her isolated. Social media wasn't a thing yet, so it would have been pretty easy to disappear."

"Question is, did she disappear willingly or did he kill her?"

"That's a question for the professionals. I'm out of my depth here, Grace."

"Well, thank you for looking. If you'd found her and she was living off a pension in Denver or something, then at least we would know."

"That would be nice and tidy. Sorry I can't wrap it up and stick a bow on it."

"So…what would you suggest we do now?"

"Your friend could go to the authorities and tell them her suspicions. Without any evidence it would be her word against his."

Grace shivers. "No, she'd never do that."

"Or she could contact a true crime journalist and ask them to take up the case. Shine a light on it and see what they dig up. It's a long shot, but you never know."

"She's trying to keep a low profile."

"So we'll probably never know then."

"And Janice won't get justice? That's wrong, Max."

"I know. But it's not up to us. And we could be totally wrong anyway. This is all conjecture."

The tell-tale sounds of an approaching class echo down the hallway. "I've gotta go," Grace says. "Thank you for your help. I really do appreciate it."

"Take care of yourself, Grace."

"You too." Grace shuts off the phone and sees two new texts from Evan. One is a photo of the decked out sanctuary.

> Your risers just got delivered. Looks great, right?

Before she can answer, the door opens and students file in in a loose line, saving her from thinking of a response.

RIVER

RIVER KNITS like her life depends on it. The blanket is halfway finished already, even though she's taken it out and restarted three times. She wishes she had a piano to work out the chaos in her mind. But she doesn't, so she's settled for putting in earbuds and picking up her knitting.

It isn't helping.

Bess is crying and screaming. Gene pushes her to the door and Bess hurts her hand falling against a piece of broken glass.

Knit. Purl. Knit. Purl. Four knit stitches at the end for the border.

There's blood on Bess's hand. Blood on the wall where she reached out to steady herself. Gene is tugging on her wrist, telling her to hurry.

River breathes deeply. She needs a break. But how can you take a break from your own head?

Last night after dinner, Todd suggested taking a trip to Rogue River for the holidays. Her first thought was wondering how they could afford it, but she tried to be excited for his sake. It was the happiest she's seen him in days. He's been so withdrawn lately, miserable even. She's been so caught up in her own problems she's barely noticed. He won't tell her what's wrong, but she's sure it's because of her.

Maybe this trip will be just what he needs. Maybe it will be good for them both.

Or maybe Libby and Bess will ruin it.

The weight of the blanket pulls on her knitting needles as it takes shape. She holds it in her lap, rubbing her hand over the soft yarn and trying to envision the finished product to make sure she got the size right. It's warm where it's been resting against her legs. Will it be too warm for the baby? Not warm enough?

She's been studying so much and plans on taking a class for new parents at the hospital after Christmas. But she still feels inadequate to be a mom. Libby and Bess know even less than she does. How will they treat the baby? What if they can't take care of him and something bad happens?

Knit. Knit. Knit. Knit. Turn the blanket to start on a new row.

Bess's blanket had a satin binding that was smooth to the touch and soothed her when she rubbed it at night in her bed. Even when it got so old that the threads were coming out and it was hard to find edges with the satin intact, Bess held it against her face and rubbed and rubbed and rubbed. Now River wonders what happened to it. She doesn't remember having it in the pink room in the basement, so it must have been gone by then.

River had counseling the day before, but she can't remember any of it now. She hates it when Bess or Libby take over in a session so River can't talk to Erica about what she needs to talk about. She wants to talk about her mom. She wants to tell Erica how Mama had planned on running away together. She wants to tell her what Bess remembers from the night Mama left.

Maybe Bess already did? River doesn't know.

But she remembers the way Mama looked wearing a purple t-shirt. Blood running down the front from where it's dripped down her face. Her face is almost as purple as her shirt, bruised and swollen to look like a stranger.

River gasps. Her hands tremble. The knitting lays forgotten in her lap.

She reaches for her phone, thinking of calling Grace. But she'll be in class now.

River is on her own. She'll just have to get through it.

DECEMBER 13

THURSDAY

DAY OF DISAPPEARANCE

GRACE

GRACE FELT the events of the previous night as a weight behind her temples, pressing and demanding. She didn't call River to see how she was doing, but she watched the clock, anxious for the time when River would come in. Would she remember what had happened at the Devil's Teeth overlook last night? Would she remember dissociating and turning into Bess?

Ten o'clock came and went, and River still didn't show. During lunch, Grace pulled out her phone and saw a missed call from River. She dialed right away.

"Hi." River's voice sounded tired.

"How are you feeling?"

"Not so great. I'm sorry I didn't make it in today."

"It's all right. Don't worry about it. Did you get any rest last night?"

River ignored the question. "Todd said I dissociated and you brought me home. I'm sorry."

"You don't have anything to apologize for," Grace said firmly. "It's not your fault. I'm glad I was there to help."

It was true. As the shock had worn off, it had been replaced by a resolve to do whatever she could to help River.

There was another long silence.

"Do you remember much about last night?" Grace asked.

Pause.

"I remember picking you up. I was going to drive you to the lighthouse."

"Yeah, we went there. But that's where you...dissociated, I guess."

"Bess?"

"Yeah."

"She's been showing up a lot lately."

Something about the way she said it gave Grace pause. "Is she...are there others?"

"There's Libby. She's...different than Bess."

"How's that?"

"Libby's older, a teenager. More...angry. She scares me sometimes. I'm glad you didn't meet Libby."

Then so am I. "Is there anything I can do? Do you need me to find someone else to play for the concert?"

A part of Grace hoped she'd refuse, knowing it would be really hard to find anyone who could fill in that close to the performance.

But River didn't even consider it. "No, I'll be fine. Playing the piano is good for me. I'm sorry I couldn't be there today, but you can count on me for the concert. What about this afternoon? You're decorating after school, right?"

"Don't worry about it. Seriously. You're welcome to come if you feel up to it. But the PTO is going to do the majority of it tomorrow. I just thought it would be fun to get the kids involved. I'm sure I'll have more help than I really need."

"Todd took the day off today. Maybe I'll have him bring me if I feel up to it."

"Okay, but only if you want to. Don't feel pressured."

In the silence that followed, Grace's mind went back to that moment when River had grabbed her arm in a panic.

"River, do you remember what you said last night? About your mom?"

River's phone crackled a little bit.

"I don't know what I said. But I remembered some things. What did I say?"

"It's...hard to explain. But it sounds like you were really afraid for her."

"I think he killed her." Her voice was flat.

The words settled over Grace. Ugly and hard. She didn't know what to say.

"Maybe he didn't," River continued. "Maybe she really did leave that night for good. But Bess thinks he killed her."

"So...what do you do now?"

River yawned on the other end of the line. "I'll talk to Erica next week. I don't know that there's anything to do."

"But...it's your mom."

"And a confused, repressed memory from a crazy woman isn't going to be very convincing."

"You're not crazy."

River laughed without humor. "I'm the very definition

of crazy. This is what people mean when they talk about locking people up."

"No. You're not like that. You're not a danger to anyone. I know you, River. Whatever you went through as a kid, whatever your brain is trying to process now, you don't deserve to be locked up."

"And what if I do something like that after the baby's born? What if I dissociate and Bess goes off and leaves the baby? I'm really worried about that."

"Yeah, I'll bet." Grace couldn't offer any reassurances. A nanny would be an obvious solution, except there was no way River and Todd could afford one.

The pressure behind her temples increased.

She had some money left over from her mom's estate. Not much, but it was a little. Could she use it to get River help taking care of the baby?

If she would accept it, that is. Grace would have to bring it up delicately.

She glanced at the clock. "Well, the choir will be here in a few minutes. Is there anything I can do for you today?"

"No, but thanks. Todd's here. He's taking care of me."

"All right, get some rest. Take care of yourself. And if you aren't up for it tomorrow, don't worry about coming in. We've got a whole week until the concert."

The concert seemed so silly to worry about when talking about a possible murder and River's mental health crisis. But Grace packed her unfinished lunch away and tried to give her full attention to the chamber choir. It was hard when she had to both play piano and lead at the same time. The choir felt off today, or maybe it was just Grace. She called the rehearsal early and held up a small stack of paper.

"Anyone who can meet at the First Hope Church to help decorate after school, I'll see you at four-thirty. If I don't already have your permission slip, bring it with you."

This caused a murmur of approval and lifted the spirits of the kids as they filed out the door to catch the last few minutes of lunch recess. Not for the first time that day, Grace was grateful that it was almost the weekend. And only one week of school left after that before the holidays. They all desperately needed a break.

DECEMBER 18

TUESDAY

5 DAYS AFTER DISAPPEARANCE

GRACE

WHEN GRACE EXITS THE SCHOOL, the energetic flow of children meeting buses and parents makes her smile. Seagulls circle overhead, their cries a shrill overtone to the boisterous conversations and laughter that surround her. The wind sweeps clouds briskly across the sky, their shadows passing below as the wintry sun fights for dominance.

As Grace moves toward her car, she notices a man sitting on the low wall near the parking lot. It's the backpacker, the one she assumes is homeless. What business does he have hanging out at the elementary school?

She turns on her heel and fights against the tide of children and staff to make her way toward Marilyn. She finds her signing a first grader's neon pink arm cast, adding her name to a growing collection. Marilyn looks up as Grace approaches.

"There you go, Soli. I hope it heals soon!"

Soli leaves, beaming as she examines the principal's signature.

Grace pitches her voice low and leans closer to Marilyn so she won't be overheard. "There's a man sitting over on the wall watching the kids. Do you want to send someone to ask him to leave? I don't think he has a reason to be here."

Marilyn follows her gaze and frowns. "I've seen him around town lately. He's not one of our parents."

Grace thinks about all she's learned from River and tries to check her prejudices. In River's experience, someone like Matthew Knight who has the trust of the school community is as likely to be a danger to kids as a transient stranger. Maybe even more likely, since many predators intentionally seek out professions where they have easy access to children. Is it fair to treat the homeless stranger as a threat because he doesn't fit into polite society? She now knows how unsafe polite society can be.

"I'm not trying to assume the worst," Grace says, conflicted. "I just thought you should know."

"Oh, look. He's leaving now." Marilyn sounds relieved.

Sure enough, the man is shuffling down the sidewalk, leaning forward to counter the weight on his back.

Grace relaxes, but she follows him with her eyes as she returns to her car. Why did he come to the school? What is his story that he chooses a transient life living on the fringes of community where he'll always be viewed with suspicion?

Something doesn't sit right about it and needles Grace's mind as she pulls out of the parking lot. Someone left a note on her car during school hours. Could it have been the stranger?

She stops for a crowd of children crossing with the crossing guard. The man has already turned the corner and is moving slowly down the hill toward the Shell station.

That could be River.

The thought comes out of nowhere and immediately fills her with shame. River spent time living on the streets when she had no other option. Nowhere safe to go. Had people looked at her and judged her? Thought their children and wallets weren't safe when she was around?

The hypocrisy tears at Grace like a pain in her chest and for a moment she can't breathe. River didn't deserve suspicion.

But Grace does.

She was charged with protecting the children. Advocating for those who couldn't advocate for themselves. But when it mattered most, she failed.

Grace takes a shuddering breath and tries to push away the feeling of self-loathing that grips her.

How long can she live like this?

The road clears ahead of her and she gently pushes on the gas.

However long it takes.

DECEMBER 13

THURSDAY

NIGHT OF DISAPPEARANCE

RIVER

THE TV BATHED Todd in a cool blue light. He'd fallen asleep watching the news and as night descended, River resisted turning on a lamp in case it woke him. She didn't know how long he'd been up the night before. She'd woken up in bed with her hair still damp from the storm and no memory of how she'd gotten there. No memory beyond going to pick up Grace earlier that evening.

She wished she could remember what happened so she could apologize to Todd. She'd tried, but he'd just shaken his head and left the room.

What good was an apology when she couldn't promise not to do it again?

And now, Grace knew. Nothing would be the same between them.

Would Grace distance herself from River? Would she see her as a psycho who couldn't be trusted? Would she think she was possessed?

This is why River was so careful not to let anyone know. But when they'd talked on the phone earlier that day, Grace hadn't sounded afraid. Worried, yes, but worried *for* River. Maybe she wouldn't be scared off that easily. It was too much to hope that their friendship would survive, but miracles were possible, right?

A light rainfall began, pattering on the trailer roof. Bess was always more afraid in the rain. Libby hated how scared Bess was all the time. Sometimes Libby would go out in the rain just because she knew Bess hated it.

River wasn't sure why Bess hated the rain so bad. Did it have something to do with that night? Or was it because of the time Grandma Billie had locked her out of the house overnight during a tropical storm? Bess had huddled against the back door all night, buffeted by wind and rain and shaking long after the storm calmed.

River shivered. Maybe she should go help at the church after all. Staying busy and being around people might keep Bess away. And then, if she had a minute alone with Grace, she might be able to apologize more fully about last night.

She grabbed her coat and purse.

It was raining harder now, sounding like gravel on the fiberglass roof of the carport. It fell in a sheet in the gap where the carport roof didn't quite meet the house. Already there was standing water in the street, reflecting the strand of Christmas lights hanging on the neighbor's cedar fence. River ducked and hurried to the car.

Rain made the streets midnight dark, even after River turned onto the main road where streetlamps cast pale halos of light. The wipers kept up their rhythmic march, and she turned the defrost on full blast to fight the clouding of the windshield. She stopped at a red light and watched as a kid crossed in front of her, a hoodie pulled up against the rain. Young teen, she guessed, though she couldn't see their face. Were they going home to a warm house and a fresh meal? Or were they wandering the streets because anywhere else was better than home?

A car honked and she started. The light had turned green without her realizing it. She eased forward and scanned the road. Where had the teen gone? How long had she been sitting there?

Maybe this was a bad idea. She wasn't in great shape to be out in public tonight. Fred Meyer was just ahead. She would stop and pick up a few groceries, then turn around and go home. Make dinner for Todd and show him how much she was trying.

Surely she could handle that much.

GRACE

THE RAIN BROUGHT AN EARLY DUSK, bringing a celebratory air to the lights inside the First Hope Church. Xander had forgotten his permission slip, so Grace sent him home with a fresh one to get signed. Some parents waited in the parking lot, and Savannah's mother stayed to help.

When Diana showed up without a permission slip, Grace faltered. If she sent her home to get one signed, Grace knew she wouldn't come back. So she didn't say anything about the stack of papers and put Diana to work helping Savannah tie garland to the adhesive hooks on the decorative wall at the front of the rostrum. The room buzzed cheerfully with the sounds of children working, while Grace's speaker played Christmas music from its perch on the top of the piano.

The ambiance was spoiled a little when Darren and Robert got into a farting contest.

"Gentlemen!" Grace said sharply. "Let's remember to show respect for this house of worship."

Robert muttered something about the house of gas and Darren laughed.

Grace was glad Evan wasn't there to hear their disrespect. Or maybe he would have known how to handle them. He worked with teenagers in the youth group, after all.

An hour and a half later, parents started arriving to pick up their kids.

"Are you sure you're okay if we leave?" Savannah's mother asked.

"Absolutely. Thank you so much."

"I don't want to leave you with all the clean-up," she said, eyeing the open boxes and bins spilling out in the back of the room.

"It's fine. I still have a few things to do tonight. You go ahead."

Laughter rose and fell as boys and girls left the church until Diana was the last to leave.

Grace was about to encourage her to go when a booming voice filled the foyer.

"Never fear, reinforcements are here!" Evan came through the doorway holding a large box taped together with duct tape.

"I've got a tree!" he announced. "Found it in the attic."

Before Grace could reply, Diana gasped. "Can I help set it up?"

"Of course!"

Grace should have sent her home. The other kids had all gone. But Diana seemed so excited that Grace wondered if her family even had a Christmas tree at their house. She hadn't noticed one two weeks ago when she was there.

The artificial tree was old and dusty and shed needles as freely as a live tree. They had to attach each branch separately in a certain order, and the attachment points were just as likely to bend the joint as accept it.

"Sorry," Evan apologized as they finished the first layer, all a little daunted at how much was left.

"It'll be lovely," Grace reassured him.

By the time they finished, it was close to seven, and Grace was feeling the effects of her interrupted lunch.

"Can we put lights on it, please?" Diana begged.

"You'd better head home," Grace said with a smile. "I wasn't supposed to keep you this long as it is."

Diana's face fell. It was subtle, just a lessening of the light in her eyes. Her childlike joy was instantly replaced with uncertainty. Self-consciousness even.

You can't solve her problems, Grace reminded herself. *There will always be one more child who needs more than you can give. You have to have boundaries.*

It was easy to say in the abstract. But it wasn't abstract when Diana was standing before her, freckles on her nose and crooked teeth she hadn't yet grown into.

"Tell you what. You go on home tonight, and I promise I'll save the star for you."

Pink rose in Diana's cheeks. "Really?"

"Absolutely."

Diana left the church with a spring in her step.

Evan watched her go. "That was nice of you. Everybody needs to feel special, and she needs it more than most."

"She's a sweetheart," Grace said honestly. "I wish I

could do more to help. But I don't know..." She paused and considered whether or not to go on. "How does it work for you? When you suspect abuse or neglect, but you don't have any hard evidence, how do you know when to report it?"

Evan's expression darkened and he pursed his lips in thought. "Honestly? It's hard. I always expected there would be clear signs, but more often than not it's putting two-and-two together. People tend to use code words instead of coming right out and calling it what it is. I try to err on the side of reporting."

Guilt made it hard for Grace to look him in the eyes. "That's probably best."

To her surprise, Evan grimaced. "I don't know. If a teenager spouts lies to their friends because they're in a bad mood, do their parents deserve to be dragged through the nightmare of being investigated by social services? It's hard to know what's best when innocent people's lives are turned upside down."

Grace thought back to the kind of teen her sister had been. Jess had manipulated their mother and treated her like dirt if she didn't get what she wanted. If Jess had made allegations of abuse out of spite, it would have destroyed their mom.

"You sound like you speak from experience," she said.

"I wish I could say I didn't. Let's just say there's more than one family who refuses to return to First Hope as long as I'm the pastor here."

"I'm sorry."

He breathed in deeply and let out a heavy sigh. "It's a risk I'm willing to take to protect kids. When all is said and done, I'm more worried about them than I am protecting the adults."

Is that what Grace was doing by not calling the hotline number to report her experience at Diana's house? Was she too worried about protecting the adults? Or about being believed?

Was she too worried about protecting herself?

Making a mental note to talk to Marilyn about it tomorrow, Grace turned away to clean up the overflowing bins.

"Ack!" Evan slapped himself in the forehead. "I forgot! I was so excited to show you the tree that I forgot I brought you dinner!"

"Dinner? But…I thought we were doing dinner tomorrow."

"I know, but I figured you'd be hungry and picked up some fish and chips. They're probably soggy now. Hold on."

He was back in under two minutes, holding a brown bag stained with grease.

Grace grinned. "You're a regular miracle worker. I'm starving."

"Well, they were fresh out of loaves, but I figured this would work in a pinch."

Grace raised an eyebrow. "Loaves and fishes? Your preacher puns need work."

Evan laughed. "I'll keep practicing. Come on, we can eat right here on the pew. Just don't tell anyone."

They spread out the baskets of fish and chips, Grace's mouth watering at the smell of fried food. The fries were indeed soggy, but the fish strips weren't too bad. Soon her fingers were wonderfully greasy and her stomach was content.

She eyed the artificial tree. "I think I'll go ahead and string those lights tonight."

"Let's do it," Evan said, and Grace was delighted that he included himself.

While he looked for another extension cord, Grace threw away their trash, then popped in a piece of gum for good measure. The minty flavor washed away the taste of fried fish, which she appreciated as Evan joined her. He stood close, maybe closer than he really needed to, as they threaded lights back and forth around the branches, knocking more plastic needles loose with every pass. Grace occasionally caught traces of his sweet woodsy scent, and it made her want to close her eyes and breathe it in.

"That's it! Let's get the full effect." Evan turned off the overhead lights and they basked in the tree's glow. The only sound was instrumental music drifting from the speaker. The tree may have been old and sparse, but the lights transformed it into something regal.

Until a middle strand winked out.

Grace burst out a laugh.

"Aw man!" Evan shook his head, grinning. "Were there any other strands left over?"

"I think so." Grace dug through a bag to find another strand of lights wrapped in a tight ball. "I can't promise they'll work any better. Can you find the ends?"

Evan was digging through the branches, trying to isolate the defunct strand. "Ow! I've got one but I can't find…what if we just plug in this strand and lay it over the top? No one will notice from far away."

Together they pushed the new lights deep into the branches, trying to fill in the darkened spot. Evan stood right behind her, working on the higher tier while she focused on the one below. His hand brushed hers, awakening every nerve to his touch. Her head swam with his nearness, and her giggle was tinged with hysteria when she dropped the strand and pulled half of it back out, requiring them to start over again.

At last they were finished and they stood back, admiring their work. Evan draped an arm over her shoulder and she leaned into him. It was getting late and she was exhausted, but she didn't want the evening to end.

"I have a question for you." Evan's voice was smooth and rich. "And it's okay if you say no."

"What is it?"

"Would you mind if I kissed you?" he asked.

Grace blinked. She'd never been asked before. She was grateful for the low light as her face flamed hot.

She turned to him, feeling a tingle of anticipation run down her spine. "I'd like that."

Evan's eyes reflected the bright lights of the tree, and she had only a moment to wonder how his full lips would feel on hers. He reached for her hands and lifted them to his lips. Goose bumps rose up to her elbows when his hot breath touched her skin.

She giggled. Is that all he'd meant? Or was he teasing her? She opened her mouth to clarify that she'd given permission for a *real* kiss, when he lowered her hands and pulled her toward him. His dark eyes seemed to see into her soul, and her heart raced as she rose up to meet his lips with hers.

Just before they touched, something buzzed between them followed by a digital chime. Startled, Grace pulled away.

"Sorry," Evan apologized, reaching for his pocket.

"It's okay. Always on duty, right?"

He nodded and answered the phone, turning away. The excitement of the moment ebbed away as the coolness of the room settled around her, calming her spinning head.

Not wanting to seem nosy, she busied herself cleaning up. But her real interest was on what would happen after he hung up. Could they pick up where they left off?

When she heard, "I'll be right over. Give me a few minutes," Grace knew that the moment was truly dead.

Evan hung up and looked at her apologetically through his long lashes. "I've gotta go. I'm so sorry, I feel like a complete tool."

Grace tucked her hair behind her ear and smiled to hide her disappointment. "Don't worry about it. I have a key. I'll lock up."

"Are you sure?"

"It's fine. We're still on for tomorrow, right?"

"Absolutely. I'll pick you up at six." Evan slipped on his gray puffy jacket and hesitated like he wasn't sure what to do next.

Grace imagined crossing the space between them, and giving him a farewell kiss full on the mouth. But just as she started to shuffle her feet, he turned and walked to the door.

"Good night, Grace," he said. "See you tomorrow."

"See you. And thanks for dinner." Her voice sounded far more calm than she felt.

He turned back and shot her one of his dazzling smiles. "Happy to provide a little miracle wherever I can."

When she heard the outer door close behind him, Grace let out a disappointed sigh. They'd only known each other a few weeks. Maybe it was too soon for kissing. Maybe in the light of day tomorrow, Evan would regret asking. But it felt like they'd known each other longer. The more she got to know him, the more she wanted his good favor. Would that pass if they took their friendship to the next level? Was it better to keep things where they were?

One thing was for sure, the kiss that almost happened made her know what she wanted. Friendship was nice, but it wouldn't satisfy her for long.

DECEMBER 18

TUESDAY

5 DAYS AFTER DISAPPEARANCE

GRACE

THE EVENING of the Christmas concert is blustery, but dry. Wind buffets the side of the house, shaking the windows as Grace dresses in her black pencil skirt paired with a red Angora sweater that is meltingly soft. She makes a special effort with her makeup, thinking of Evan with a kind of bittersweet longing. She can't help but smile as she applies a deep red lipstick. Even he should notice *that*. Then she pulls her hair back and spends nearly an hour curling it, pinning each ringlet delicately into a carefully cultivated mass of curls. It's a lot of effort for such an elaborate look, but most of the Ellis Cove community will be staring at the back of her head all night. She might as well give them something to look at.

She finishes the effect with red satin heels, an indulgence that rarely sees the light of day. Her feet will complain before the night is over, and it's not a very practical choice considering the puddle-pocked church parking lot. But the extra height gives her a boost in confidence, and she needs all the help she can get tonight.

Milton is sleeping on the back of the couch, and when she drops her heavy music bag on the cushion, he rouses. He stretches, long and sinuous, and bounds off the couch to the floor. Watching him reminds her of Max and their conversation earlier that day. Should she tell River what he learned about her mom? Or, more importantly, what he didn't learn? Would River be angry that Grace asked him to look into her past?

She goes through her concert binder to double check she has all the music in the right order, thinking through every aspect of the concert to make sure she hasn't forgotten any important details. In spite of the distractions of the past few weeks, she doesn't think she's neglected anything critical that will get in the way of the evening running smoothly. She knows from experience that there will always be little hiccups she didn't foresee, but if she's done her job right, the audience will never notice.

While she goes through these last motions, thoughts of River's mom encroach on her mind. It seems wrong to keep the information to herself, but she doesn't want to overstep her bounds. And she really doesn't want to trigger River to dissociate tonight, of all nights. Still, her mind won't settle. Something like guilt pulls at her, telling her that she shouldn't keep information from River that concerns her.

Finally, she texts River.

I've got your candy canes to give to the kids. Thanks again for thinking of it! They'll be thrilled.

She waits, but River doesn't respond. So she adds,

Tomorrow we should celebrate, just you and me. We've earned it. Want to come over for dinner?

Without the stress of the concert hanging over them, that could be a good time to tell River about Max's research. She types *I have something I want to talk to you about,* but then she pauses. Erases. River's text comes a moment later.

Sure.

It isn't much, and Grace can't guess from it what River's mental state is. But it's enough that she's made firm plans to talk to River about her mom. She can put her conversation with Max out of her mind for now. There will be time for that later.

An hour before the concert, with a flutter in her stomach, Grace checks her bag for the last time and heads to her car.

DECEMBER 13

THURSDAY

NIGHT OF DISAPPEARANCE

GRACE

AFTER EVAN LEFT, Grace basked in the warmth of the lights and the heady smell of cinnamon pine cones wafting from baskets near the entrance. She didn't feel tired anymore. Not now. She felt alive in a way she hadn't felt since before her mom died. Maybe longer.

She wanted to hold on to that feeling, so she lingered, adding some finishing touches just in case Evan returned and they could pick up where they'd left off. And if he didn't—she thought with a thrill—there was always their date tomorrow.

She pulled open another bin and discovered a set of miniature trees that would work well as tabletop decorations in the foyer. By the time she'd finished assembling them, she was yawning and Evan still hadn't returned. She checked her phone. It was past ten, and she had work tomorrow. The other decorations would have to wait.

She hoped to have everything set up before Sunday so the First Hope congregation could enjoy it during their

Sunday service. But there was still plenty of time. And the more excuses she had to come to the church, the more opportunities to see Evan.

Smiling to herself, she put on her coat and grabbed her purse, then shut off all the power strips before leaving the sanctuary. The darkness made the space feel empty and forlorn, so she walked quickly to the exit. When she pushed open the outer door, a blast of rain greeted her. She made a run for her car, tossing her bag in the back and wiping the rain from her face.

As she reversed out of the parking spot, her headlights swung over the gravel pile and caught the reflective bumper of another car. Wondering who was leaving their car at the church overnight, she drove slowly toward it and stopped when she recognized the gray Taurus with one blue rear door.

River's car.

It was parked on the far side of the gravel pile, almost hidden in the shadows of the nearby woods.

Had River changed her mind and decided to come to the church after all?

Had she dissociated again?

Feeling a sense of dread settling into her stomach, Grace pulled alongside the Taurus and tried to see if anyone was in the car. Rain streamed down her passenger window, making it hard to see. She put her car in park and reached for an umbrella. Leaving her car running, she jumped out and ran to the Taurus.

The driver's seat was dark and empty.

Rain beat on her umbrella as she turned around, her unease increasing. No lamp posts illuminated the parking lot this close to the woods, but her headlights streamed mournfully on the distant trees. Where was River?

Then, over the sound of her own breathing and the rain drumming on her umbrella, she heard it. A scraping sound.

The gravel pile.

Grace reached for her phone and turned on the flashlight. It wasn't much, but it was better than nothing. She moved around the Taurus, the wind lifting the ends of her hair and sending a chill down her neck.

Rock crunched under her feet as she stepped closer to the gravel pile.

The scraping sound stopped.

Grace's heart thudded against her chest.

"River?" she called uncertainly.

She rounded the gravel pile and stopped, freezing in place as her brain tried to take in what she saw.

Todd stood over a shallow hole with a shovel in hand. Rain soaked his clothes and hair. He squinted and raised a hand to shield his eyes from her light.

At his feet lay Diana, a blanket loosely draped over her. She looked…wrong. Her hair was matted black on one side. Dark lines ran across her cheek.

Todd grabbed the edge of the blanket and covered Diana's face, but Grace had seen enough.

"What happened?" It came out as a strangled shriek as she tore her eyes away from the body up to Todd's face.

He was trembling and could barely get out the words. Snatches came in bits over the rain. "Accident…I didn't know…River…I couldn't…what to do..."

Grace's stomach plunged inside out. "What. Happened." She stepped closer, panic making her want to scream.

He wiped at his face with a sleeve. "River hit her with the car." His voice cracked with anguish. "It was an accident. She didn't see the girl until it was too late. She didn't mean to. It was an accident," he repeated.

"Where is River now?" Grace demanded.

"She's home. She's sleeping. I told her I'd take care of it."

Grace swore under her breath and looked over her shoulder at the empty parking lot.

"Why didn't you call an ambulance?"

Todd's face was washed out in the light of her phone, his eyes wide. He spoke in a rush, like these thoughts had been running on a loop. "She's dead. An ambulance won't fix that. And if police get involved, they'll take River away. Maybe send her to jail. I can't do that to her. It would kill her. And what about the baby?"

"So you're not going to tell the police?" Grace tightened her grip on her phone. She thumbed it to unlock it.

Todd stepped toward her and she stepped back. Instinctively, she planted her feet and raised her hands like she'd practiced in Jiu-Jitsu class.

Todd raised his hands in supplication. "I'm not going to stop you. If you want to call the police, go ahead. But think about what this would do to River. Even if she doesn't go to jail, she'll never be able to live with herself knowing she killed this girl. She wasn't herself; I doubt she'll even remember. Finding out would push her over the edge. I can't lose her, Grace. Would *you* do that to her?"

Grace faltered. She remembered River standing on the edge of the cliff. If Grace hadn't been there, would River have made it home that night? If River thought her life was hell now, how would she live with herself after learning she'd killed Diana? Could Grace risk it?

"What about Diana's parents?" she countered. "They deserve to know what happened to their daughter." But even as she said it, Grace doubted her own words. Did people like that deserve the same courtesies due to loving parents? If anyone deserved to be in jail, it was Diana's parents. Not River.

"I have to think about River and the baby," Todd said firmly. "I can't worry about the girl's parents."

Grace noticed vaguely that she was shaking.

This was wrong. She should call the police. But River...

"Well, get it over with. What do you need?"

Todd's shoulders shrank with relief. "Just keep an eye out for me. It won't take too much longer now that I've cleared the gravel away."

Grace felt sick and icy cold. She moved back to the other side of the gravel pile. Suddenly she felt so exposed. Her car was still running, tail lights glowing, headlights shining into the woods, announcing to anyone passing by that she was there. She reached in and switched off the ignition, praying that Evan wouldn't return.

For the next thirty minutes, she stood vigil in the shadows near Todd's car, her stomach roiling as she listened to Todd digging. What was she doing? Was she insane? It wasn't too late, she could still call the police.

She could tell them what had happened and explain why River wasn't to blame.

But she couldn't bring herself to do it. It wasn't River's fault she dissociated. It was Grandma Billie's. It was Gene's. They were the ones responsible for Diana's death. And in a way, so were Nora and Leo who never cared for Diana the way they should have. Who only gave her fear when she needed safety.

Grace kept her phone tucked in her pocket.

The sound of digging stopped. She heard grunting and the dragging of a heavy weight. She wanted to vomit. A set of headlights approached from down the street and Grace gasped.

"Someone's coming," she whispered loudly.

All was silent behind the gravel pile. Grace heard nothing but the rain and the pounding of her own heart.

The car turned before it reached the church, and the street was empty again.

"It's fine. They're gone."

The sound of shoveling returned, and soon shifted to the high brash sound of gravel on steel. Each shovelful scraped against her nerves and made her want to scream. But in a few minutes, that was over too.

Todd emerged from the far end of the gravel pile. He looked like a specter, with the pale orange light from the parking lot lamp posts accentuating dark pouches under his eyes.

"You're a good friend, Grace. I...I really don't think River will remember this in the morning. Probably best not to talk to her about it."

Grace nodded. She couldn't speak. What could she say?

He popped the trunk of his car, but paused before placing the shovel inside. "Thank you." he said soberly.

"Don't thank me," Grace whispered fiercely. She turned and walked toward her own waiting car, leaving Diana behind.

DECEMBER 18

TUESDAY

5 DAYS AFTER DISAPPEARANCE

GRACE

GRACE DRAWS in a sharp breath as she pulls into the First Hope Church parking lot.

The gravel pile is gone.

Fresh gravel now lays several inches thick over the whole lot. She feels a sickening sense of both fear and hope. They've buried the evidence. They've buried Diana. And they didn't discover the truth. There's no police tape or any indication that they found anything. Only cars lined in rows over the place where the pile once sat.

The relief she feels is immediately overpowered by self-loathing. Her stomach squeezes painfully and Grace is glad she didn't eat.

Evan meets her at the door, looking stunning in a black fair isle sweater. His smile loses some of its luster when he sees her expression.

"You okay?"

Grace manages a weak smile. "Doing great. I'll be even better after tonight."

"You nervous?"

She shrugs. "In all the right ways."

The foyer to the church glows with a comforting warmth. *Come in from the dark.*

But what about when the darkness is in you?

Grace searches in her bag for the shiny programs she picked up from the printer after school. "These can go on the table near the entrance."

"Ah, these look great." His enthusiasm makes her want to shrink away.

She leaves the programs with Evan and heads toward the sanctuary. The smell of cinnamon and pine greet her with a burst of holiday scent. Artificial, she knows, but still triggering the intended response. Cozy.

But Grace only feels hollow inside. Will she always feel this way? Will it ever get better? How long can she carry this secret without it ruining her life?

Will her own life be the cost of trying to save River's?

Grace sits on the front pew to sort her music one final time. She's checked and double-checked, but she can't be too careful.

When Evan comes and sits next to her, he smells woodsy and warm, and it stirs an ache deep within her. Her body wants to respond to him, to relax into his warmth, but she keeps her spine rigid.

"I got tickets for Carmina Burana," he says. "You still able to go?"

"Oh, right. When is it again?"

"January tenth."

So soon.

"Let me check." As she thumbs through her phone calendar, she tries desperately to think of an excuse that will sound legitimate. *Just tell him yes.* But it's dangerous to spend time with Evan now after what she did. He deserves so much better.

Grasping at nothing she says, "I have an appointment sometime that week after school but it looks like I forgot to write it down. I'll call tomorrow when they're open and see what day it is."

She inwardly grimaces. What a sorry excuse. If she really wanted to go, she would have said, "I'll call to reschedule."

Evan knows it too. He pulls back almost imperceptibly.

"How did your sermon go on Sunday?" she asks, desperate to show him she cares.

"It went well."

"Tell me about it."

He gives a little sigh. "Well, it was about the daughter of Jairus and how Jesus delayed coming to her, but how the miracle was that much greater because of their pain."

"Oh? How do you mean?"

"If he'd come earlier and healed her before she died, that would have been a blessing for the girl and her family, sure. And that's as far as it would have gone. But raising her from the dead changed everyone's lives who witnessed it in a profound way. My point was that in those moments when he does the same to us, waiting to ease our pain, that he has something so much greater planned. Basically."

"I wish I'd heard it. It sounds lovely."

Evan's expression darkens. "Nora didn't think so. I wasn't trying to be insensitive. I wrote the sermon weeks ago, and it applies to us all because everyone feels forsaken sometimes, right? But she was spitting mad and said I shouldn't have been talking about girls being raised from the dead with Diana still missing."

Grace's breath hitches. "I'm sorry. I guess there's no way you can be all things to all people, can you?"

Evan frowns, and Grace worries she said something wrong.

"This sort of thing can destroy a person," he says solemnly. "She needs God more than ever but she's angry and won't let him into her heart. If I can't help her now in her greatest suffering, then what does it matter if I spend the rest of my life trying to do good for anyone else? I might as well quit and find a regular day job."

"Stop it," Grace says firmly. "You can't be responsible for whether or not she accepts your help. Just because she doesn't like it doesn't mean you should stop offering."

"The truth will set us free," Evan says with a sad smile. "But that doesn't mean it's easy to hear."

Grace grimaces and turns back to her music so he can't read her face.

After a minute, Evan asks tentatively, "You and River are good friends, right? Do you think she and Todd are doing okay?"

Grace looks up at the large cross hanging on the wall and considers how to respond. "Under the circumstances, I think they're doing as well as can be expected. I don't know how much you know about River, but she's got some unique challenges. It's hard on Todd, but he tries."

Evan nods thoughtfully. "I hope they know they can come to me if they need more support."

"I think they do. It's great that you've put together

that men's group. Todd probably needs it now more than ever."

"That's what I think, if we could only get him to come."

"What do you mean? River says he goes every month."

"No, he doesn't. I always invite him. I think he could really connect with some of the other men there."

Grace frowns. "Then maybe they aren't doing as well as I thought. River thinks he joined the group. He must be lying to her about it."

Evan sighs. "I had a feeling things weren't right between them."

"Careful. I hear pastor-pressure settling in."

He gives her a half smile and again she feels drawn to move closer.

"I just wish people would realize that keeping secrets from each other only drives you away from the people you love. I see it all the time in my work. When people can be open and honest with those they love, then real healing begins."

Grace's smile dies so quickly she nearly chokes on it.

"What if..." she begins.

What if I told you something that made you hate me? What if I told you the truth? What if I went to jail for it? What if River got locked up? What if River learned the truth and the shame of it killed her?

Evan looks at her expectantly.

"What if he's just trying to protect her?" Grace says. "I'm not sure River can handle the truth about a lot of things in her life right now."

Evan nods. "It's a fair point. Sometimes the timing

has to be right, especially if you're still building trust. But sometimes those are the excuses we use to avoid doing the hard thing and then it just festers inside us."

Festering. Grace knows what that feels like.

When River and Todd show up at the church together, Grace watches them a little differently. If what Evan said was true, Todd is keeping something from River. But can Grace really blame him? She knows what his life is like and isn't about to judge how he handles it.

He still seems solicitous to River, taking her coat and hanging it up. Carrying her bag for her. But there isn't any real warmth. He's probably thinking of that night, just as Grace did when she pulled up and saw the gravel had been spread.

She avoids catching his eye because she doesn't want to see. She doesn't want to know if he's thinking of it too.

"You look lovely," Grace says to River. She's wearing a red knit top with a long white sweater draped over it.

"Thanks. I'm outgrowing everything at this point. I'm trying to make it all fit so that I don't have to buy new clothes. I've only got eight weeks left."

"So exciting!"

River's smile looks tired. "Exciting…nerve-wracking…I can't tell the difference anymore. I worked on a blanket today." She pulls out her phone and shows Grace a picture. The teal yarn looks so soft that Grace's fingers itch to touch it.

"It's beautiful!"

River won't meet her eyes, and Grace realizes that if River was knitting that much, she must have been having a tough day. She thinks again about what she learned from Max and is glad she hasn't told River yet. It can wait.

The first of the teachers and volunteer parents arrive, and Grace is quickly caught up in reviewing assignments and itineraries. River warms up at the piano, playing seasonal melodies as more people trickle in.

Thirty minutes before the concert begins, families start arriving. The children are ushered off to the classroom wing while parents and guests are welcomed to the sanctuary by two sixth graders dressed in their holiday best.

The noise in the sanctuary increases by degrees as neighbors greet each other, with the thread of River's background music weaving through it all. It's a scene that should be infused with Christmas spirit, but Grace just wants it to be over.

Every time she passes the outer door and sees the parking lot filling with cars, she thinks of the gravel pile that is no more. Thinks of all the weight of those cars compacting the earth. Thinks of being buried beneath all that pressure. Finds she has a hard time breathing.

It's a relief when the top of the hour comes and Evan nods to her. She gives a little nod back.

The lights in the sanctuary dim, all but the floodlights above the risers.

River finishes the last chord of *O Little Town of Bethlehem* and the audience quiets as Evan steps to the microphone.

Grace doesn't listen to Evan's welcome. Instead, she gestures to the teacher waiting in the shadows to escort the first group—third graders—onto the stage. Their freshly scrubbed faces are bright under the lights. One little girl is wearing a bow so large that it waves into the face of the boy behind her. The audience chuckles their delight as he bats it out of the way.

Grace takes her place before the risers, the air thick with anticipation. Fifty pairs of eyes watch her from the risers. Hundreds more behind her. And River, waiting for that first signal to begin. She raises her arms and waits for the expectant silence to swell until it almost drives the sound forward.

She begins.

EVAN

THE THIRD GRADERS are timid at first, their voices lost in the high arching ceiling overhead in spite of River's energetic introduction to *Ding Dong Merrily on High*. But it's a song that demands enthusiasm, and soon they rouse with the spirit of it.

Evan stands in the back of the sanctuary to help latecomers quietly find seats. There are rows of folding chairs set up in the overflow area, allowing close to two hundred extra people to attend. The sanctuary and attached hall are full, and the temperature of the room is rising with so many warm bodies packed in the space. As near as he can tell, most of the town has come out for the concert. He's not sure what attendance was like when the concert was held at the school, but if he were to guess he'd say attendance hasn't suffered even though it was held at the church.

That gratifies him immensely. More than it probably should, he realizes. But for Grace's sake, he's glad the night has been a success. He hopes in a few days, when the pressure of the concert is gone, that she won't carry such a weight about her. That she'll be able to relax and find some time to unwind. Even better if she'll let him join her.

Each class sings two numbers—one more subdued and another full of energy—providing a mix of the traditional and the unfamiliar. Grace leads them fluidly, and Evan enjoys watching snatches of her expressions as she turns to one side or the other. Always encouraging. Always positive. The kids respond in kind, with beaming smiles and an occasional wave to a parent in the audience.

The second graders have just finished *Petit Papa Noel* and are filing off the stage when Evan notices a shadow of someone lurking in the doorway. He steps over to welcome them and is surprised to see Jim, the man he met in the woods with Diana. He's seen him around town but hasn't spoken to him since Jim rebuffed his offer of help.

The last place Evan expected to find him was in the church at the Christmas concert.

"Welcome Jim," he says in a low voice. Jim looks like he's ready to bolt and Evan holds out his hand as if greeting a friend. "Would you like me to find you a seat?"

"No." Jim ducks his head. "I'm not here for the concert. I need to talk to you, Father."

"I'd be happy to chat. Can we make an appointment for tomorrow?"

"It needs to be now." Jim glances at the front of the sanctuary where the chamber choir is taking the stage. He seems twitchy and Evan suspects that if he leaves, he won't come back.

But Evan doesn't want to miss the chamber choir. This is the final performance of the night, and Evan knows how much Grace has poured her heart and soul into these kids. It feels like a final benediction, even more poignant with Diana missing.

"I'd like to help you, Jim. But just now we're in the middle of a concert. If you want to wait and watch, I'd be happy to visit with you after it's over."

Jim shuffles his feet and glances toward the exit. When he looks back at Evan, a fire burns in his gray eyes. He steps aside for a mom taking her young daughter out to the restroom.

After they pass, he leans in and whispers fiercely. "I got something to tell you about that missing girl."

DECEMBER 13

THURSDAY

NIGHT OF DISAPPEARANCE

GRACE

GRACE HUNCHED over the steering wheel, trying not to think about Diana's pale face under the harsh glow of the cell phone flashlight. By the time she made it home to her driveway, she was shivering uncontrollably.

She turned off the engine and was so desperate to get inside that she almost left her keys and purse in the car, barely remembering to grab them at the last minute. She stumbled into the house and kicked off her shoes, peeling off her coat and discarding clothing as she made her way down the hall to the bathroom. She turned the water to full hot and sat in the shower, letting the water beat down on her back, running down her head. But still she shook.

Still she couldn't get warm.

Diana had looked so much smaller in death. Her lifeless eyes accused Grace. Grace who should have taken care of her. Grace who Diana trusted. Were the black shadows in her hair blood or dirt? Grace didn't know for sure. She should have taken a closer look.

She wished she'd never seen it.

What had she done? Hidden the death of a child? What was she thinking? She could still go to the police. It wasn't too late. Surely they would understand it was an accident. Surely they would have mercy on River.

River hated the police. She was terrified of them. What would it do to her to be arrested? What if the authorities didn't understand? They had failed to protect her when she was a child. What if they turned on the one person who deserved mercy?

Grace closed her eyes and willed herself to cry. To release the horrible tension building inside her chest. But she couldn't. She felt dried out inside. She felt pulled tight like a piano string.

When the water started to cool, she shut it off. Stumbled into pajamas. Laid on her bed without sleeping. Maybe if she could sleep, it wouldn't be real.

But every time she closed her eyes, she saw Diana lying there in the dirt, her hair tangled and limp. Grace grabbed a blanket and went to the living room. She needed light. She needed people. She turned on the TV, searching for something to distract her. Something to drown out the memory of the sound of the shovel digging into gravel.

It wasn't too late.

If only she knew what would happen to River. If she could be certain that River would be treated with kindness and respect. If she could be guaranteed that she wouldn't be held responsible for Diana's death, then she would make the call. But there were no guarantees.

To turn River in would be the worst betrayal of all. Grace couldn't do it. She *wouldn't* do it.

After a while she dozed but immediately jolted awake again, the horror of the night crashing down on her. She shifted on the couch, trying to get comfortable. Trying to calm her racing heart.

It was hours later that a single thought occurred to her.

Tell Evan.

He was compassionate and kind. He knew how to carry other people's crosses, didn't he?

No.

Like her, Evan was a mandatory reporter. There was no way that he would keep the truth from the police. But maybe Grace could talk to him about it without giving anything away.

She almost got up to look for her phone. She almost dialed his number. But she stayed rooted in place as if the couch held claim over her. If she moved, she might crack.

She couldn't crack. River needed her more now than ever.

DECEMBER 18

TUESDAY

5 DAYS AFTER DISAPPEARANCE

GRACE

FOCUSING her full attention on nothing but the music and the performers, Grace's anxious stress melts away. She knows the vaulted ceiling swallows the sound and makes it hard for the children to hear themselves. But the lights, the audience, and the warm applause between numbers feeds their energy and compensates for the unfamiliar acoustics. It's deeply satisfying, and Grace feels more like herself than she has all week.

Then the chamber choir takes the stage to end the program and Grace feels a jolt pulling her back to reality as she spies the gap between Josie and Savannah. The memory of that night rushes back with a vengeance. A dark creeping sensation curls from her back around her middle. Steeling herself, Grace affects an encouraging smile and avoids looking directly at the spot where Diana should have been.

The risers creak underfoot as the chamber choir settles into position.

They begin with *In Dulci Jubilo*. Layla performs the solo

well, but Grace can't help but think about Diana's audition. She'll never have her moment to shine now.

The audience claps appreciatively and Grace steps to the side to allow the choir to enjoy the applause. She looks toward the back of the room where Evan has been standing all night. He isn't there. She hasn't realized how much she counted on him being there until now that he's gone and she feels his absence as a tangible loss.

The applause quiets and Grace resumes her position in front of the choir. She stands still, waiting until the stirring crowd settles into hushed expectation.

A child in the back squawks and is quieted by his mother.

River plays a single, solitary note. It fades into silence and Grace signals the choir to begin *Lux Arumque*, the number they sang at the candlelight vigil. A challenging number during the best of times, the children watch her face in earnest as she leads them through it. The haunting melody echoes through the hall, the dissonant tones reverberating then resolving in a breath-taking conclusion.

The crowd is so rapt with attention that as the final note dwindles into silence, no one moves. No one dares to break the spell. At last, a few tentative claps are joined by others and swell into an appreciative wave that washes over the choir, bringing a heightened color to the children's cheeks.

The crowd comes haltingly to their feet in a standing ovation. Grace smiles indulgently. It doesn't take much to bring a small town audience to their feet, but this group earned it.

Grace gestures to River and the applause increases in

acknowledgment. River stands and bows her head graciously. Grace feels a surge of gratitude. River hasn't missed a beat all night. She couldn't have asked for a better evening.

Now that it's over, she feels almost debilitatingly weary. She's given everything she has and all that's left is a hollow shell.

The overhead lights come on and parents gather at the front of the sanctuary to greet her with hugs and handshakes, commenting on the beauty of the music and the lovely room. Grace's cheeks ache from forcing a smile. The room is warm and her movements are sluggish. A headache radiates from the base of her skull.

Grace scans the crowd, looking for Evan. He should be hard to miss, but she can't see his prominent figure above the crowd.

River appears at her side and Grace embraces her awkwardly, trying not to squish her belly.

"You were wonderful," Grace murmurs. "I can't thank you enough."

River lets out a long breath. "It went well, didn't it?"

"Fantastic. I hope you'll sleep long and hard tonight. You've earned it."

Something like amusement flickers in River's eyes and Grace feels foolish for suggesting it. As if River could do something as common as get a good night's sleep.

Then Nora Beck is there, pushing Danny forward. Danny's hair hangs long on his brow, brushing almost to the freckles on his nose, and Grace fights the urge to lift it out of the way so she can better see his eyes.

"Miss Miller, I wanted to give you something."

Grace's dull headache intensifies as she strains to hear his words.

Looking over Nora's shoulder, she sees Evan standing with Todd. He catches her eye but doesn't smile. He looks serious. Troubled even. His expression sparks a feeling of alarm in her chest, and her smile to Danny feels thin.

"I found this in Diana's room and thought you might need to have it back."

Danny holds up a few sheets of salmon-colored paper stapled together in the corner. Grace recognizes the sheet music she'd given Diana to preview the song they'd be learning in January. For a moment she can't breathe, as if she's fallen from a great height and landed hard.

"I saw that ding on your car." Evan's voice carries over the din of conversation. "What happened?"

Grace stills, her hands on the sheet music.

"Not a big deal. Just a minor fender bender," Todd replies.

"You need any help getting the light fixed?" Evan continues. "I changed mine out over the summer. I can help if you need it."

Grace has a hard time focusing on Danny, she's so distracted by Evan's question. She knows how their car was damaged. Does River? Will Evan's questions trigger River's memory? She doesn't dare turn and look.

Todd's voice is disinterested. "It's all right. I'll take care of it. Just haven't had time."

With effort, Grace drags her attention back to Danny. She doesn't care about the music. It's a photocopy and easily replaced. But Danny is a different matter. Danny, with his pants that hang too short and his t-shirt with a hole worn through the sleeve. Danny, whom Diana always tried to protect. Who already had so much working against him and now will have his life forever changed by not having his big sister there to look out for him.

Grace tucks the music under her arm and reaches for his hands. They are cold in spite of the warm, crowded room. "Thank you for returning it, Daniel. You're a good brother and I know how much Diana meant to you. We're all praying for you and your family."

A shadow passes across his face and she realizes her mistake. He pulls away and turns his back. This won't be the last time people refer to Diana in the past tense, but Grace is horrified to think she is the first.

"Excuse me, Mrs. Vincent?"

Xander Robinson approaches River with his mother and a teenage boy wearing a sherpa-lined denim jacket at his side.

Mrs. Robinson wears an apologetic expression, but she speaks in a businesslike way as if she's planned out what to say. "Micah told us about what happened the other day. I want to apologize for his behavior."

River can't seem to meet her gaze. "I'm sorry if he was scared. I didn't mean to make him feel threatened."

What did River do now? Grace's gaze slides to Todd and —as if reading her thoughts—he glances at her. In that brief moment she reads all the dread and guilt he shoulders. It's tearing him apart. Grace moves to intervene but doesn't know what to do.

"Well, just so you know," Mrs. Robinson says firmly, "he's been grounded from his skateboard until he pays for the damages."

Evan is watching the interaction with a frown. Grace has never noticed how stern his jaw can look without his ever-present smile.

Someone bumps into Grace and she turns in time to catch a laughing toddler before he falls.

"Sorry about that!" his mother says, grabbing him by the arm and pulling him away. "Stop running in the church. You just hit that nice lady."

When Grace turns back, Todd has wrapped one arm protectively around River and is leading her toward the outer door. What was that all about? Did River nearly cause another accident? Almost hit another child? After what happened with Diana, why is Todd letting her drive at all?

Evan watches them go with a troubled expression. The room is clearing and Grace edges over to him. It isn't so loud now, and she no longer has to raise her voice to be heard.

"How was it?" she asks. "Could you hear them all the way in the back?"

Evan's eyes soften as he turns his attention to her. "They sounded great. You've really brought this community together. I can't imagine a more perfect way to celebrate the holiday season. "

His praise falls flat in her ears, though. He seems distracted and distant. Maybe he's just tired. She wants to ask what's wrong, but doesn't want to be nosy. And she doesn't like the way he was watching River.

"Thank you," she replies. "And thanks again for letting us perform here tonight."

"It was my pleasure." But he doesn't look pleased.

Instead, he says, "I'd better help clean up the rest of the chairs. Excuse me."

Grace watches him leave and buries her disappointment. She's been avoiding him all week. Is it any surprise he's finally getting the message?

RIVER

THE NIGHT AIR is cool and moist. River tucks her chin into her scarf for warmth. She did it. She made it through the concert. She stayed River the whole time. But it was hard. She was struggling to keep her grip by the end. She needs to get home where it's safe.

Todd starts the engine, and River realizes she's still standing by the passenger door. Usually he would open it for her, but he's already in the driver's seat.

"Let's go," he says impatiently, his voice muffled through the door.

River obeys, opening the door and settling into the seat with its familiar scent of dust and age.

"Come on, shut the door," he complains as she tucks her skirt to make sure it doesn't get caught in the door.

The parking lot with its one entrance is backed up with cars.

"We can't go anywhere anyway," River points out. Or was it Libby who spoke? Libby has some choice words she wants to say to Todd.

"We could have if we hadn't been the last ones to leave."

Libby wants to point out that they are hardly the last ones to leave, and in fact, it's rude that they aren't staying to make sure Grace isn't stuck cleaning everything up by herself.

River stays quiet.

After a few minutes, Todd sighs. He turns to River and squeezes her knee.

"How are you feeling? Must be exhausted after that. Glad it's over?"

Is she glad it's over? Certainly there's a feeling of relief. Pride in a job well done. But also a sense of disappointment. With the concert behind her now, she'll have less to keep her busy. The days home alone will be longer. All sorts of time for Libby to get into trouble.

River nods. "The kids did a good job."

Todd snorts. "Did you see the one who flipped off the audience? It was hilarious."

River didn't, but she remembers the crowd laughing unexpectedly in the middle of the fourth grade performance. "I wondered what was going on."

They creep forward a little closer to the exit. River finds herself watching out the window where the gravel pile used to be. It was there so long she isn't used to having such a clear view of the woods. The trees look sinister in the dark, like they could be hiding anything or anyone.

Watching.

EVAN

EVAN PLACES the last of the folding chairs on the rack and pushes it to the storage room. He nods and smiles as the last few people who stayed to help clean up—some he recognizes and others he doesn't—put on their coats and head toward the door. He can't shake the darkness that's settled into his heart since he talked with Jim.

"I know what I saw," Jim insisted. "I couldn't tell what it was they were burying, but it was a man and a woman and whatever it was they were hiding was the right size for that little girl."

"You're sure it was a man and woman?"

"Pretty sure. Two people, and one of them was tall like a man. He's the one who dug the hole. I didn't want them to see me, so I stayed in the trees. The next day I saw the girl's picture all over town. She was a sweet kid. Still hasn't turned up, right?"

Evan nodded, his mind racing, trying to figure out what to do. "And you didn't tell the police?"

A line of sweat formed on Jim's brow where his

stocking cap rested, and the scent of him filled the small office.

"What would you think if you were a cop and someone like me came to you and said I knew where the missing girl was buried? I'm no idiot."

And how do I know you're telling the truth now? Evan wanted to ask. But he didn't challenge him. Jim didn't seem the kind of man who trusted easily, and he didn't want to scare him off.

"I'll have to tell the police. They're going to want to question you."

"No, see, I thought this through. You go to the police and tell them you got an anonymous tip about suspicious activity the night she disappeared. If they find her body where I think, then they can start their investigation from there. The car I saw was dark. Black, with one of those Crater Lake license plates. I saw it later at the school and left a note to try and scare them into going to the police."

Evan rubbed a hand along his chin, scratching at the stubble. "You probably oughta leave it alone. No more notes. I'll talk to the police, but I won't give your name unless I think I have no other choice. Deal?"

"They'll have a hard time finding me even if you do."

Now Evan flips off the lights to the overflow hall and works his way around the sanctuary, unplugging or turning off the decorations. He doesn't want to be mixed up in this, and he wishes Jim had gone straight to the police. But if Jim is telling the truth and whatever he saw happened on the church's property, Evan is going to be involved whether he likes it or not.

When he gets to the foyer, only Grace is there, gathering up the remaining programs and sliding them into her bag. Beyond the outer door, the parking lot is empty.

Grace looks beautiful tonight with her hair pulled up and wearing a sweater that looks as soft as spun sugar. She's been hard to reach the past few days and he almost wondered if she was intentionally avoiding him. But now she lingers with a weary smile, her eyes catching the lights from the garland strewn over the sanctuary entrance.

He tries to smile in return, but the weight of Jim's story drags at him. He's seized with an urge to tell Grace what he heard, but knows it would be wildly inappropriate. It's the burden of being a clergyman—carrying the secrets of others without being crushed by them.

"You must be exhausted," he observes.

"It's a good tired," she says. "Only one more day until break."

He picks up her jacket and slips it onto her shoulders. A tendril of hair has loosened and fallen on her neck, and he brushes it out of the way so it won't get caught under her collar. He stands close enough to catch the sweet undertones of something fruity on her hair or skin.

Close enough to wrap an arm around her waist and pull her close.

But the moment doesn't feel right. Not distracted as he is with the question of whether Diana is buried in the parking lot near the woods. It might be nothing. Jim might have been confused at what he saw. But until Evan knows for sure, he won't be able to think of anything else.

GRACE

GRACE FEELS exhaustion deep in her bones pulling her to the earth. She yawns involuntarily as Evan helps her with her jacket. Maybe tonight she'll finally sleep. Really sleep, the way she hasn't in days. No lights on to drive away the nightmares. No steady noise to keep the memories away.

Her heart skips as Evan gently brushes a lock of hair from her neck. She tries to make herself relax, to enjoy the moment. To lean into him. *Don't think about it now. Just be present.* If she turns around, she knows his warm lips will be waiting for hers. There, in the darkened foyer with only the lights of a Christmas tree casting a warm glow, anything is possible.

But she can't fall for him now. Just outside the door, the empty parking lot stretches to the woods and her eye is drawn to the corner near the tall cedars. A skin-crawling sensation creeps up her arms, and she steps away.

Cool air fills the space between them and Grace almost hurts with it.

Tell him. Tell him what you did. It's better that he hates you for the right reason than to think you don't care.

In the dim light, it would be so much easier. They're all alone. She could explain why River isn't to blame. Why Grace has to protect her. Why she did such a horrible thing.

But she can't find the words. Instead, she turns around and faces Evan with enough space between them that she can keep her eyes from lingering on his lips.

"Thank you. Thank you for everything," she says. Then, before she knows what she's doing, she leans toward him and kisses him on the cheek briefly. Just a peck. Then she turns and leaves the church before she can change her mind.

RIVER

THE CAR ENGINE shudders to a stop and River realizes they're home. She can't remember the drive back from the church. Who took over? She glances at Todd to try to gauge whether it was Bess or Libby.

Or worse, someone new.

Todd doesn't look at her.

It's long since passed the time when apologies would do any good.

The baby rolls over, giving her that same stomach-sinking feeling that she feels when driving too fast over the railroad tracks. She grabs the bulge instinctively.

"You okay?" Todd asks.

"Yeah. Baby's just waking up. The baby who still doesn't have a name."

Todd leans over and places his warm hand on her stomach protectively. "How about Sam?"

River mulls it over. Sam. Sammy. Samuel. "It's nice."

"Or Christian."

River shakes her head. "I knew a Christian when I was a kid. He made fun of my teeth."

Todd reaches for the door handle. "It's getting late. You don't have work tomorrow, right? But I do."

It's the last day before the holiday break and Grace doesn't need River at the school. The students will spend all their time watching movies and having Christmas parties. River doesn't know how she'll fill her time at home alone. The baby blanket isn't taking as long as she'd hoped.

She follows Todd up the steep steps to the back door and into the house. Libby wants to poke Todd on the butt, but River's hands are full carrying her bag and water bottle.

"I wish you hadn't rushed out of there," River says. "I wanted to help Grace clean up. It would have gone faster if we'd stayed."

Todd jiggles the doorknob to get the key to turn. "She'll manage."

She'll have to now, won't she? Libby huffs in annoyance.

River shakes her head, trying to quiet her.

Libby is close. So close. Just waiting to seize control. River drops her purse on the table and heads to the bedroom, the trailer vibrating as she walks. She takes off her coat, switches on the bedside lamp, and goes to the bathroom to wash her face. It's going to be a rough night; she can already tell. She's so tired. She just wants to sleep.

Can't you wait? Can't you skip it tonight?

She looks at her reflection and wishes for daylight.

She changes into a pair of Todd's old sweat pants that she's using for pajamas these days. One of his t-shirts stretches across her belly, the sleeves hanging down past her elbows.

A creak sounds near the door and Todd leans into the room, both hands braced against either side of the jamb. "I've gotta go see Jerry about that car he's trying to sell."

"Right now?" River glances at the clock.

"He's working swing shift this week and I need to catch him before he leaves for work."

"I thought we couldn't afford another car."

"We can if we sell the Taurus. That would help with the payments."

"But then we'll still only have one car."

"But it'll be a nicer, newer car that will last us longer than that piece of junk."

River is too tired to argue. "Whatever you think. I'm going to bed."

"I'll try not to wake you."

Libby doesn't say goodbye.

GRACE

GRACE DOESN'T BOTHER to turn on her Christmas lights when she walks in the house. The tree looms like an intruder in the corner, only vaguely visible in the light from the streetlamp outside. She drops her choir bag next to the couch and heaves a sigh.

What if she had invited Evan over? She wouldn't be alone now, wrinkling her nose at the dirty dishes piled in the sink. She wouldn't be heating a solitary cup of water for chamomile tea. Instead, she would prepare drinks for the two of them, turn on some mood music, kick off her satin heels, and snuggle next to him on the couch with a soft throw over her knees.

When she's with Evan, all Grace wants to do is forget about River, forget about Diana. Just pretend that she didn't see what she saw and do what she did.

She could have told him tonight. She finally could have shared her secret. But the way he looked at her…it's like he knows her heart and believes it's good.

He believes a lie.

She can't look into his eyes and pretend everything is okay. Pretend she didn't do something so horrible she deserves to be locked up for it. But to tell Evan the truth is to betray River. She won't.

Just as the microwave chimes, she pads into the kitchen in her pajamas and slippers. She drops in the tea bag, watching the water bubble up as she weighs it down with a spoon. While she waits for the tea to steep, she picks up her phone.

A text message waits from River.

I'm having a hard time. Can you meet me at DT?

Adrenalin surges and chases away Grace's exhaustion. She thumbs a quick reply as she heads to her room to change her clothes. Why is River at the overlook in the middle of the night?

She'd better bring a flashlight.

LIBBY

AS SOON AS the door shuts behind Todd, Libby grabs her coat, searching for River's phone. The pockets are empty. What did River do with it? If Todd is going to be gone for a while, she might have time to slip out and score some weed.

But she needs a phone.

River's purse is on the table in the kitchen, sagging like a marshmallow. But when Libby checks, the phone isn't there. She scans the room, puzzled.

There. Sitting on the floor by the couch.

That's strange. River went straight to the bedroom after they got home. Why is her phone on the floor? And sitting tossed aside as if whoever used it doesn't realize they dropped it.

Libby picks it up and turns it on. There's a text from Grace.

Give me a few minutes. But I promise I'm coming. Don't do anything until I get there.

Libby frowns. Did River text Grace? Not that Libby can remember.

She opens the conversation. Sure enough, River sent a text about twenty minutes earlier asking Grace to meet her.

I'm having a hard time. Can you meet me at DT?

So sorry. Of course.

Libby frowns.

River didn't send the text.

GRACE

RIVER'S gray Taurus is parked near the stairs that lead from the Devil's Teeth overlook to the beach. The bumper shines in Grace's headlights as she pulls into a nearby spot. The driver's seat is empty.

Grace's heart races. She asked River to wait in her text, but there's no sign of her.

Grace grabs her flashlight. Wind strokes the sea grass edging the cliff as she makes her way to the wooden staircase.

That's where Bess went. But Grace found Libby on the unprotected shelf overlooking Devil's Teeth, outside the safety of the guardrail. Libby is more bold. And reckless. Question is, who is River tonight?

She pulls her jacket tighter against the wind and crosses the parking lot to the viewpoint side. The lighthouse lens cycles rhythmically, lighting the tops of trees on the headland before sweeping out over the dark expanse of ocean.

Grace scans the slope beyond the low guard rail, but

there is no sign of River. The ledge where she found Libby isn't visible from the parking lot. Acting on a hunch, she climbs over the guard rail and starts down the narrow path.

The pounding waves seem louder in the darkness. Louder even than at Shore Acres. Blood pulses through her temples. It's hard to sense where the edge is and she keeps her gaze fixed on the ground to keep vertigo at bay.

She makes it to the shelf, but River isn't there. She must have gone to the beach after all.

Relieved, Grace turns.

A shape looms out of the darkness.

Grace's breath catches. She shines her light into Todd's face.

"Todd! You scared me. I got River's text. Where is she? Is everything okay?"

"River's fine," he says. He steps down to the ledge, close to Grace. Too close. She reflexively takes a small step back.

"Where is she? I was worried—"

Todd grabs her wrist so fast the flashlight drops to the ground. Grace reacts instinctively, bending her elbow and pulling her wrist free in the first move she ever learned in Jiu-Jitsu. But Todd moves fast, grabbing her with both arms.

Grace struggles but Todd is bigger and she can't break his grip. He pulls her toward the edge and she trips. His hand clamps over her mouth, muffling her cries.

Terror—blazing, maddening terror—floods her limbs. A fine spray washes over her from the waves crashing in the chasm below. The fallen flashlight beam shoots out into open air and blinding dark.

Think. Use your training.

She kicks out and hits something soft with her heel. Todd grunts and his grip loosens. Spit collects under his hand, making her mouth wet and slippery. With a wrenching effort, she tears herself out of his arms and lunges away.

She stumbles and falls, her chest heaving for air, trying to get back to the parking lot.

Without a flashlight, she struggles to keep her feet and falls again, grass and grit biting into her hands. Her knee hits a sharp rock, but she ignores the pain and scrambles to her feet.

Todd lunges into her from behind, knocking her to the earth.

His breath is stale in her face and one hand claws at the scarf around her neck, trying to find a point to squeeze.

She is going to die. If her body doesn't fall to the sharp rocks at the bottom of the cliff, he is going to kill her with his bare hands.

She kicks her legs uselessly against his heavy weight. She moans in fear and pain. Her right arm is pinned beneath her, but her left is free and she gropes for something to poke or pinch or scratch. His breath is hot against her cheek.

"I'm sorry, Grace. This wasn't supposed to happen. But River can't find out the truth. She can't find out what I did. You're the only one who knows and I knew you'd figure it out after tonight."

What was she supposed to figure out? Grace can't think. What is he talking about?

I don't know what you're talking about, she wants to say,

but she can't speak with one hand crushing her mouth against the earth.

Above her head, a beam of twin headlights cuts the air.

Todd ducks into the grass and Grace tries to scream, but she breathes in dirt and her voice is lost on the wind.

His weight shifts to avoid the lights overhead. Grace tucks her knees in, rounding her back to shake him loose. His hold slips and she crawls forward, gaining her feet.

The path is lost in the darkness and the hill is steep. Her blood pounds in her head, terror tasting like iron in her throat.

"Help! Please!" she calls again, praying that whoever is up there will hear.

Hands grab her from behind and drag her away, pulling her back down the slope. She grunts as she hits the ground, her elbow erupting in pain. Todd's bulk weighs her down and she fights in frenzied desperation, shaking her head, but thick hands cover her mouth and nose, grinding the back of her head into the ground.

She tears at his hands, unable to breathe. Panic floods her brain as she fights for air. She scratches at his face and, in a flash of luck, feels an ear, grabs it, and pulls as hard as she can.

Todd rears back and swats at her hand, knocking it away. But it's enough. She twists and rolls, wriggling out from under him.

In the darkness she can't see where to strike, but she kicks out fiercely anyway. Her boot connects with something hard and Todd grunts in pain. Seizing the chance, she lunges up the hill toward the parking lot. This time she doesn't yell for help, not wanting to give her location away if Todd is chasing after her.

Heart pounding in her throat, she expects to feel his hands at any second. Is that ragged breathing her own? Or his just over her shoulder?

As she nears the top, a beam of light swings her direction.

"Grace?"

The light blinds her and she shields her eyes. Someone is there. Someone knows her.

"Help me!" Her voice sounds weak as she grabs the guardrail and climbs over, panting with the effort.

The light drops and someone runs toward her, silhouetted against the headlights on the opposite side of the parking lot.

"Grace! Are you hurt?" It's Evan. He catches her and pain flares again in her arm.

"Careful! My elbow."

River follows close behind. "Where is he?" she demands, her voice strong and sharp even against the wind. She swings the flashlight down the slope, but the beam is lost in the darkness.

No sign of Todd.

"He's down there somewhere. He tried to…he was going to kill me." Grace hears a note of hysteria in her voice. She's trembling slightly but not from the cold.

Evan grips her tighter and pulls out his phone.

River steps closer to the edge, flashlight pointed down the trail to the ledge.

"Don't! He's still out there!"

"I'm not afraid of him," River says, and her voice is hard.

Not River.

Libby.

Grace reaches for her but Libby shrugs her off.

"Libby, please. Stay with us where it's safe."

"I just want to watch where he goes. Make sure he doesn't get away." She climbs awkwardly over the fence, pregnant belly brushing the top as she straddles it.

Evan is speaking to a 911 dispatcher, sheltering his phone against the wind. The phone light barely illuminates his profile.

Grace's shirt clings to her with a layer of sweat, cooling now that she's still. She shivers and pulls her jacket tighter. Across the way, the lighthouse shines steady and sure. Oblivious to the pounding in her heart.

Evan hangs up and turns his worried frown on her. "What's wrong with your arm? Can you move it? Are you hurt anywhere else?"

"I…I don't know." The skin of her face and arms burns, and her knee aches where she landed on the rock. But she's alive. "Get Libby. I mean, River. Don't let her go down there."

"She's okay, I see her light."

Grace leans into him gratefully. He steers her toward the car. Its engine is still running, the headlights shining toward the sea.

"How did you know to come?"

"River called me. She said Todd sent you a message pretending to be her. She needed a ride because he'd taken the car. But I don't understand what's going on. Why would Todd do that?"

"I don't know. I promised not to tell…"

"Tell what?" Evan's voice is firm. Filled with urgency to understand.

"Todd told me River killed Diana. Not on purpose. It was an accident. That's how her car got damaged."

"No...no, it wasn't that." Evan sounds agitated. "Micah Robinson said she almost ran into him in the parking lot of Fred Meyer. He hit back with his skateboard, taking out a light and leaving that big scratch."

Understanding dawns. Micah wasn't another accident. His was the *only* accident. And with that realization, Todd's words finally make sense.

"Oh, so that's why..." Grace groans. "I didn't realize...but Todd must have thought I did. He must have thought I knew the truth, but I didn't. I believed him." She feels such a surge of anger she wants to spit.

Evan's patience is fading. "What are you saying, Grace? What happened?"

Grace pulls away. She can't raise her eyes to his.

"I saw where he buried her. Todd must have killed her himself. And...I helped him hide the body." Unshed tears burn the back of her throat.

Evan's hands drop to his side.

"It was you? *You* were the one there that night?"

Grace doesn't know how he knows. It doesn't matter. Now he'll know everything.

"I didn't know what to do. He told me River did it on accident. That she wouldn't remember. I've seen her that way; it could have been true. I couldn't go to the police. And with the baby coming and things already being so hard for her, I knew it wasn't her fault and telling the police wouldn't bring Diana back. But it would destroy River."

"But, Diana's family…This whole time they've been suffering—"

"You think I don't know that?" Grace's voice rises in anguish. "I've been so sick about it. I didn't know what to do. But he lied to me. It wasn't her. It was him."

"I can't believe it," Evan says. The whites of his eyes are wide in the reflected light of the flashlight. "I never would have…River told me she found child porn on his phone. I've never heard her that angry before. She sounded like she hates him."

"It's not River. It's Libby. She's never liked him. She must have suspected the truth."

Evan pauses. "Who's Libby?"

Grace shakes her head. She looks back toward the cliff but the light is gone. "Where is she? I don't see her flashlight."

A siren sounds in the distance.

"Stay here, I'll go check."

Grace leans against the car, feeling limp. Drained from the pressure that has been building for the past week. Ever since she found Todd in the parking lot with Diana at his feet. Ever since she agreed not to call the police.

Her pulse picks up as flashing red and blue lights appear around the bend of Oceanview Drive. She doesn't know what will happen now. But at least River will be safe. She won't go to jail. She'll be able to raise her baby. Alone, yes. But at least the baby will have a mother.

A light bobs up the slope. Libby is returning. Evan stands against the guardrail, silhouetted against her light and the steady beam of the lighthouse in the distance. Grace can't hear their conversation, and she watches with trepidation as Libby approaches. Will she be angry? Will she hate her as much as Grace hates herself?

Libby opens her arms and throws them around Grace. "That's the stupidest thing I've ever heard. Why did you protect that bastard?" She squeezes her tightly.

Grace feels a sob rising in her throat and chokes it back down. "I thought I was protecting you. I didn't want you to go to jail for something you didn't mean to do. And your broken headlight, I thought..."

"Why didn't you ask me? I could have told you what that punk did to the car."

"I'm sorry. I thought I was doing the right thing. I was just trying to protect you."

Libby releases her and steps away, shaking her head. "It wasn't your job, Grace. Haven't you learned? I protect myself."

Grace wilts. A single police car pulls into the parking lot, cutting the siren but leaving the lights flashing.

"Did you see him?" Grace asks Libby as the officer gets out of the cruiser.

Libby shakes her head. "Couldn't find him."

Grace feels a flash of fear. If Todd is still out there, will he go after her? Or does he know it's too late? That she's already shared his secret.

Evan approaches the officer first and Grace can't meet his eyes as he passes. One nightmare is over. But another is about to begin.

CHRISTMAS EVE

RIVER

RIVER FACES THE POLICE ALONE. The uniformed officer stands at the top of the stairs that lead to the beach.

"I'm afraid you can't come here, Mrs. Vincent."

Of course he knows her name. Surely they all know her name by now.

"Someone told me you found a body on the beach. Is it my husband?" River is surprised at the coolness in her own voice. It matches the dead feeling inside.

The officer's stiff expression doesn't soften. "I can't answer that." He glares at a couple who are approaching the stairs, a blanket on the man's arm. "I'm afraid the beach is currently closed to the public."

"What?" The woman cranes her neck to look over the edge of the cliff. "Why?"

The man looks down the stretch of pale sand almost gray under the cover of clouds. "How about the jetty access? Is that open?"

"As far as I know. But you won't be allowed this far north."

"But this is the best view of the lighthouse," the woman complains.

"I'm sorry, ma'am. There's nothing I can do."

Grumbling, the couple turns away. River watches them go but doesn't make a move to follow.

A gust of wind makes her wish she'd worn a warm hat over her exposed ears. There are drawbacks to keeping her hair so short.

"It really is for the best that you go home, ma'am. Sergeant Polaski will be in touch if there's anything that concerns you."

River doesn't want to be there anymore than he wants her there. Just the sight of his badge makes her throat constrict. "I deserve to know if it's my—if it's Todd." She doesn't like to call him her husband, not now after Diana's body has been found.

Signs of sexual abuse and asphyxiation, Sergeant Polaski said. But River knows what those words really mean. She can envision all too well Diana's fear as Todd lured her into the house and invited her to the nursery. That horror is all too familiar.

The fresh one—the shame and disgust that define her days lately—is that she didn't see the signs herself.

Libby knew. She suspected something.

River wishes she'd paid closer attention. She could have saved Diana if she'd realized what Todd was capable of.

Libby is close. River senses her curiosity and anger crackling in the back of her mind, pushing to get to the front. It was probably Libby's idea that she come here, she realizes. She didn't even tell Evan she was coming.

He would have talked her out of it, or at least insisted on joining her. But she doesn't want an audience.

The officer's radio murmurs with instructions River can't quite make out and he lifts it to his mouth.

"Mrs. Vincent is here," he says. "She's asking about her husband."

There's a pause and the radio crackles again. "It's gonna be a long wait," a tinny voice says. The rest of the response is unintelligible.

River wanders over to the edge of the cliff that looks out over Devil's Teeth and the lighthouse standing guard above. On the other side of the headland, the sheltered harbor is wide and calm. But on this side, the lighthouse stands as a beacon warning of danger and treachery.

A flash of yellow off to the left draws her attention. She follows the makeshift trail down to the ledge. There, far below where the low tide has left the beach naked and exposed, people in uniform move among the rocks. Her eyes track the scene quickly, zeroing in on the one body that isn't moving. From this distance it could be a sea lion or tangle of seaweed, a shapeless mass laying on the rocks. But she knows it's neither of those things.

River releases a heavy sigh. She hugs her hands to her belly protectively. Todd is gone.

But River isn't alone. She has someone who needs her. And she'll do whatever it takes to be there for her baby.

GRACE

GRACE PICKS UP THE PHONE, unsure who's on the other end of the line. Hoping and dreading at the same time. She doesn't blame Evan for not calling her. He hasn't spoken to her since that night at Devil's Teeth, and she understands why he's keeping his distance. But every time she gets notified that she has a phone call, she hopes it's him.

She'll never forget the expression on his face when he learned the truth. Anger, grief, betrayal. Everything she had feared. Everything that kept her silent. Everything that keeps him silent now.

But still, as she picks up the receiver, she feels a flutter in her chest, hoping to hear his warm voice on the other end.

"Hello?"

"Gracie, is that you?"

Jess. Grace's throat tightens.

"Hi, Jess. It's me."

She's sitting at a table with a plexiglass partition on

either side giving her the illusion of privacy. Sherrie, a woman in her forties who only has a month left on her sentence, is bent over her own receiver in the other cubby.

Jess sounds on the verge of tears. “I just heard from Greg about what happened. Do you need anything? You’ve got a lawyer?”

“Yeah, I do. Thanks, I’m fine.” It’s a strange thing to say while sitting in an orange jumpsuit in the county jail. Grace isn’t fine. Far from it. But she’s starting to sleep at night. And some of the women she’s met are nice enough.

“Greg says he talked to your lawyer. Is it true that they’re dropping the charges? They’re going to let you out of jail?”

“Yep, that’s what she says. In exchange for my full cooperation and testifying against Todd Vincent, which of course I’ll do. They just have to find him first.”

“What a miracle!”

Jess is winding up for another question, and Grace stops her before she can ask it. She really doesn’t want to talk about the case.

“How are you doing, Jess? I haven’t heard from you in ages.”

“Oh, I’m good. Really good. Things got a little crazy for a while, but I got out of L.A. and things are starting to look up. I’m in Michigan now.”

“Michigan! Wow.”

Jess laughs self-consciously. “Yeah. It’s a change. The winter is fierce! But it’s good. I’m staying with a friend and looking for work.”

Grace doesn’t know whether or not she’s telling the

truth. She feels that same old skepticism rising until she realizes it doesn't matter now. Grace can't do anything about it either way. So she decides to believe her sister.

"That sounds great. What sort of work are you looking for?"

Jess chats on about her rudimentary job prospects, and Grace tries not to think about her own career. Someday, when all this is behind her, she fears there are things she'll never get back.

"I'm going to have to go soon," Grace says when Jess's monologue runs dry and she can't think of anything more to say. "I'm so glad you called, Jess. It's so good to hear your voice." She means it, too.

"I'm sorry I've been AWOL. I want you to know you can count on me. You've always been there for me, Grace, and I want to be there for you."

Grace's throat tightens again. She rests her forehead against her fist. She's never been able to count on Jess. Not once. But it means a lot for her to offer. And maybe Jess can understand a little about what Grace is going through. When this is all over, Grace will be looking for a fresh start too.

"Thank you, Jess. Merry Christmas."

EVAN

RED and white lights brighten the roofline of Evan's parents' home. The windows of the modern colonial home are flanked by dark gray shutters and bedecked in evergreen wreaths that emphasize the structure's architectural symmetry. Indoor lights glow behind closed blinds, except in the family room where the large bay windows are uncovered. There, a flocked Christmas tree stands in grandeur, looking out over the street like Good King Wenceslas himself surveying his kingdom. Only with green grass instead of snow and bitter chill.

Everything about it seems warm and welcoming.

Exactly the opposite of how Evan feels.

He scrubs his palms over his eyes and sighs. Gathering on Christmas Eve is a tradition for those who live close to his folks. Normally the family time would be a balm for his soul, but lately he doesn't feel comfortable in his own skin. He doubts they can help with that.

Digging deep for courage, he grabs the wrapped gifts for his nieces and makes his way to the door. When he rings the doorbell, Acacia opens it. She breaks into a grin and hugs him tight around the neck.

"Uncle Evan's here!" she calls over her shoulder. Then, taking the presents from his arms, she flashes him a saucy smile. "Are these all for me? You shouldn't have!" She laughs over her shoulder as she disappears into the family room.

His mom appears around the corner from the kitchen, her smile strained.

"Oh, Evan." She envelops him in a soft hug. "How are you holding up?"

Evan is at a loss for words. Five days ago he stood on the sidewalk of First Hope Church and watched Diana's remains get pulled out of the ground. He spent hours at the police station answering questions about Todd and River and Grace. He was questioned by the board and wondered if his employment was at risk. He stood in front of his congregation on Sunday and shared a Christmas message of hope even though his own heart felt like it was full of poison.

The Becks hadn't been there.

Through it all, he's been checking on River daily to see what she needs and if the church can help.

But here, with his mom, he can finally set aside the pastor.

"I almost didn't come, but I really needed to get out of town."

"Of course you did. This is right where you need to be. You come on in and take off your coat. You've missed dinner but there's plenty of food. We're just cutting into the pies now." She tugs at his sleeve to pull him toward the kitchen where the smells of warm home cooking awaken his empty stomach.

Evan holds back. "First, can I ask that we not talk about it? It's all I've been able to think about, and for tonight I'd just like to forget."

"Of course." But there's a flicker in her eyes that hints at dozens of unasked questions. "I have to know, though, was it that woman with you at Shore Acres? The teacher they arrested?"

Evan feels the poison spreading and clenches his jaw. "That was her."

His mom presses her lips together in disapproval.

"But the newspapers didn't get the story right," Evan hurries to explain. "They made it sound a lot worse."

She raises an eyebrow. "Are you defending her now, child?"

Is he? Or is he defending the truth?

"I don't know. But there's lots of people hurting right now and spreading rumors won't help."

She nods. "All right, I hear you. Now come in and see if some eggnog can give you a little spark of Christmas cheer."

Evan follows her toward the kitchen and his waiting family, but as he does, he thinks of those who are alone that night. River, struggling with demons Evan still doesn't understand. The Becks, grieving a wrong so deep and ugly that no recompense will be possible in this life. And Grace, sitting alone in a cell at the county jail.

Thinking of Grace makes his own personal poison taste the most bitter. A part of him wants to talk to her, to hear for himself why she did it. But another part wants to believe the version of Grace the media is portraying, feeding his pain by turning her into the villain.

The more he hears of River's story, though, the more he understands Grace's choice. And he knows Grace isn't a villain. He just can't seem to get his heart to agree.

CHRISTMAS DAY

RIVER

THE COUNTY JAIL is a squat building that looks more like a warehouse than a jail, except for the slit windows high on each floor. River shows her ID at the door.

"How many weeks now, sweetie?" The middle-aged woman at the security desk knows her by name now.

"About seven."

"Bless your heart. Your friend will be right out. They're just finishing up the paperwork."

River stands aside to allow an older couple to pass through security, holding hands as they walk down the hallway toward the visitation room.

When Grace finally appears, River feels a lift in her spirits at seeing her friend in regular clothes again. The first time River visited Grace at the jail, she almost didn't recognize the woman who came into the room on the opposite side of the glass. It wasn't just the orange jumpsuit or the lack of make-up. Grace had lost something. Confidence. Hope. Self-respect.

Shame had stolen so much.

Now, Grace smiles and greets River with a hug. River leans awkwardly to accommodate the baby, but she holds on until Grace is ready to let go.

The woman at the desk waves them out and wishes them a Merry Christmas as they step into the brisk seaside air with a light mist falling.

Grace sighs as River leads her to the car.

“Thanks for coming to get me.”

“Of course. Thanks for letting me stay at your house so I didn’t have to go back to the trailer. Milton’s my buddy now.”

“Oh good. I’m glad you didn’t have to be alone for Christmas.”

“Did you do anything to celebrate?”

Grace snorts and shakes her head. “No. Every day is pretty much the same here.”

“I’m sorry.”

“Don’t be. I’m ready for Christmas to be over.”

When they get to the car, River hands off Grace’s keys and goes to the passenger side.

Grace settles into the driver’s seat and hunches over the steering wheel, her head resting on her forearms.

In prayer or relief or sorrow, River can’t tell. Maybe all three.

After a long silence, Grace lifts her head and starts the engine.

“Sorry. I just needed a moment.”

“It’s fine. Take your time.”

Grace glances at River. “How about you? How are you doing?”

River sighs. “Oh, you know me. I’m bumbling along.”

“What does your therapist say?”

"We haven't talked about things yet, but I gave the police her name so she might already know what happened. I have an appointment next week but that might be it for a while. My insurance was through Todd's work."

Grace makes a sound of sympathy. "I'm sure you could get help from the state. Maybe even through the office of disabilities. It's not like you can support yourself right now. I'll bet you could—"

"Grace," River interrupts. "It's okay. I'll handle it."

Grace looks abashed. "Of course. Sorry."

"You worry too much about me. That's what got you into this mess." River softens her accusation with a smile.

Grace falls silent until they reach Highway 101.

"I'm sorry about Todd," she says at last. "I can only imagine how hard that must be for you."

River waits for the pain, but instead she feels only numb. It's like that sometimes, like she's dead inside. And then it comes roaring back with a fierceness that steals the breath from her lungs.

"He wasn't the man I thought he was," she says. "I wish I never let Diana anywhere near us. I still don't understand…I should have known what he was capable of, but I guess I was too wrapped up in my own problems to see it."

"Monsters come in different varieties," Grace says darkly. "You can't blame yourself. I'm really sorry it ended the way it did, though. I know you must be angry with him, but he was still your husband. If I'd gone to the police in the first place, he would still be alive."

"Todd's choices were his own. Whether he jumped or

fell from that cliff, he had no one else to blame but himself."

River knows it sounds cold. The thing is, she doesn't fully believe it. There are plenty of nights she cries for missing him and then hates herself for it the next morning.

But the one person she doesn't blame is Grace.

"Is your immunity still good even though he won't be facing trial?"

"Yeah. The DA was pretty sympathetic. I'm just sorry you had to get dragged into it all."

"Don't be. I'm the reason you're here, remember?"

Grace's smile is strained. "Like you said, my choices were my own. Do I wish I'd done things differently? Absolutely. Everything I did just made it worse."

"But you meant well by it. That's gotta count for something."

"I don't know. I'm glad the DA thought so. And, on the plus side, now I get to be the prodigal one in the family instead of my baby sister. She called me yesterday and it's the best she's sounded in years."

River snorts. "Way to take one for the team."

Grace chuckles. After a pause, she asks, "Do you know what really happened that night?"

River shifts in her seat to relieve pressure on her tailbone.

"All I remember is that I was going to come to the church and help you. But I was...struggling. I decided to pick up groceries for dinner, but it was raining so hard and I was already having a hard time as it was. I almost hit that kid in the parking lot, and he hit me back with his skateboard. So I went home and told Todd and he sent me to bed. If Diana came to see me after she left the church, I don't remember."

Grace nods. River doesn't have to explain about the blank spots, the missing pieces of time that she never gets back. Whatever police reconstructed from that night, they weren't considering River a suspect.

The road follows tight curves along the coastline, opening to a view of heavy clouds hanging low over a brooding gray ocean.

Grace turns on music as if to lighten the mood. "So, have you decided on a baby name yet?"

"Not quite. But I'm narrowing it down. I've thrown out the list and started fresh. Your friend—Max?—he and I have been in touch. He sent me some information about my mom's parents. They seemed like decent people. I might use something from their side of the family."

"That's cool. And...have you decided whether to talk to the police about your mom?"

"Not yet. There's no rush. Gene isn't going anywhere for a while yet, so I've got time." River runs a hand along the back of her neck where her hair is in need of a trim. A trim she can't afford now.

Grace glances her direction and gasps. "What happened?"

River's sleeve has slipped past her elbow. She hastily pulls it to her wrist.

"What is that?" Grace asks, her tone sharp. "Show me."

"It's nothing."

"That doesn't look like nothing."

"I got my arm caught in a dresser when cleaning up

after the police searched the house. I've always bruised easily. But it's fine."

She keeps her tone light, but Grace frowns.

"It looks pretty bad."

"It's nothing, really."

Grace glares at the road ahead and River can practically hear her mind churning. Her voice grows deadly still. "It was Libby there that night when Todd fell."

"Yeah. So?"

"How do you know she didn't...?"

"You told me that Libby couldn't find him."

"I know, but..."

"What are you saying, she fought with him and pushed him off the cliff? Look at me, Grace." River gestures to her pregnant belly. "Do you think I could have overpowered a man twice my size?"

"No, of course not."

"I'm pretty sure I would remember something like that, and I know how I got that bruise."

"Bruises." Grace emphasizes the plural.

"Just being a klutz."

"It looks like it hurts."

"It's fine."

Their conversation dies until they reach Ellis Cove. There is a profound sleepiness over the town with businesses closed for Christmas Day. They only see one other car out on the street.

Grace avoids the route that would take them past First Hope Church. River is glad. She avoids it these days too. Set against the backdrop of the thick forest, it looks sinister in a way it never did before.

She hasn't been back to church since the night of the

concert. She can't face all those eyes. Curious. Judging. Pitying. It feels like being fifteen again when Gene was arrested.

A part of her wants to move away. She and Evan have talked about it more than once. After the police finished tearing apart her house looking for evidence to piece together what happened to Diana. After they found Todd's body washed up on the beach near Devil's Teeth.

She hates the little trailer now. But she won't move away from Ellis Cove. Not yet.

Not while Grace needs her.

"Do you see Evan much?" Grace asks shyly.

"Sure. We talk almost every day. He's been really great at helping me sort through things with the police. The church is helping me out with food and bills right now, and he's even talking about raising money to help me get a car."

Investigators took hers as evidence, and she doesn't know when she'll get it back. She doesn't want it anyway.

"Wow. That's amazing."

"Yeah, I suppose." River grimaces. Relying on others doesn't come easily.

"Does he...do you know if he's still mad at me?" Grace keeps her eyes fixed forward.

River tries to find a way to answer honestly without hurting Grace's feelings. "I think he just needs time. He's a good man. He'll come around."

"I wish I could explain to him. But how do you explain something like that? I can't see how he'll ever trust me again, and I don't blame him."

"I don't know about that. Give him some credit. He's all about changed hearts and new beginnings, remember?

If he doesn't believe it can apply to you, then his whole life's work is a lie."

"Hmm." Grace's shoulders slump a little. "Speaking of work, that's first on my to-do list tomorrow. I've got to talk to Marilyn about tendering my resignation."

"You think? Even though the charges were dropped?"

"How could I go back to teaching those kids after this? How could I face them or their parents?" Grace shakes her head. "No, I've thought about this all week. There are other music jobs out there. My sister is in Michigan, so maybe I'll look out there."

"Wow. That's really far away." River leans back against the seat, taking it in.

"It doesn't have to be Michigan. I don't have to decide anything right now. The middle of the school year isn't a great time for looking anyway, and I still have a little money left from my mom to get by for a while. But I can't just go back after the holidays like nothing ever happened. I won't do that to them." She gives River a sad smile. "Besides, then I could help you with the baby."

"Hey, don't worry about me. I've got Libby to take care of me."

Grace snickers as River knew she would. She doesn't tell Grace about the new addition to their group. She's still trying to figure her out for herself.

They pull into Grace's driveway and River reaches for the door. It's a long drive from Coos Bay and she needs to use the bathroom.

But when she starts to walk away from the car, the hum of the driver's side window rolling down makes her pause.

Grace is still sitting inside.

"I hurt him, River," she says quietly.

River leans closer to hear her better.

"At the end," Grace says. "I think I hurt Todd and that's why I was able to get away."

"It's okay. You did what you had to do."

"But, if he was injured bad enough, maybe it wouldn't have been that hard to push him off the cliff." Grace's eyes are sharp and probing.

River holds her gaze without flinching.

"Merry Christmas, Grace. Welcome home."

AUTHOR'S NOTE

Dissociative Identity Disorder is a grossly misunderstood mental illness that frequently crops up in media in sensational ways. It's used as a gimmick, a surprising twist, or to reveal an unsuspecting villain. I believe that fiction has the power to shape our understanding of the world and—more importantly—the people we share it with. Perpetuating these harmful stereotypes only makes it more difficult for those who suffer from serious mental illness to be treated with respect.

Instead, I've learned—as Grace does in this story—that supporting someone with DID can be a place of privilege. I'll be gratified if even a few readers come away from this story enlightened about the wonderful, good people who suffer from this condition. My experiences make me especially sensitive about portraying it authentically and compassionately, and while River's experience doesn't represent all people with DID, they do constitute the most true-to-life parts of this story.

THANK YOU FOR READING!

I hope you've enjoyed your time in Ellis Cove. If so, please consider leaving a review on Amazon, Goodreads, or BookBub. (Or all three for you overachievers!) Thanks for helping get my work into the hands of other readers like you.

As a special thank you, I want to share a bonus epilogue that takes place two months after the events in *This Side of Dark*. This exclusive epilogue is available to download when you sign up for my newsletter. If you're aching for reconciliation between Grace and Evan, you won't want to miss this scene. As a special perk, you'll also be the first to know about upcoming projects and new releases.

Here's an excerpt to give you a taste:

Grace retreats to a pair of chairs placed in a little alcove by a window overlooking the parking lot of the hospital. The lactation specialist came to teach River how to help the baby nurse, so Grace left the room to give them privacy. She sinks into the chair and looks out at the advancing twilight. She's exhausted, but it's a better kind of exhaustion than just lack of sleep. This is something different.

Witnessing the birth of River's son was both primal and sacred at once. The intensity of watching River push until she trembled from the effort, the anxiety of not being able to do more than cheer her on, the stench of the blood and the amniotic fluid and then a wrinkly little purple alien creature that somehow was a perfect human with the tiniest fingers and toes and a pointy head with a squishy face and that moment when he cried for the first time and her heart both swelled and broke at once.

She feels like she's been wrung out emotionally so that all that's left is a feeling of awe.

It's been a long day but she isn't eager to go home. It's a long drive back to Ellis Cove, and she won't come back until morning, so she wants to make sure River is in good hands before she leaves. The nurses' station is around the corner and the sounds of cheerful chatter and beeping phones become a backdrop to her empty thoughts.

Until she hears a deep voice that she knows so well her whole body becomes alert at the sound.

Suddenly Grace is aware of her unwashed hair pulled back into a ponytail and the baggy sweatshirt she's been wearing all day. She dressed in a hurry when River woke her up this morning and chose comfort over style. Now she feels a coating of the day's grime settled into her pores. Of course this would be how she looks when she finally sees Evan after almost two months of avoiding him.

She's barely gotten to her feet when he comes around the corner and sees her. He pauses, one hand clutching a pastel gift bag with white tissue paper rasping against his knuckles.

Want more? Download the full scene at carenhahn.com/darkbonus (or use the QR code below).

Small town. Dark secrets.
Whose lies are worth killing for?

"Suspense, romance and it'll keep you wanting more"

"Nonstop suspense with shocking twists I never saw coming!"

"...from start to finish I could hardly put it down!"

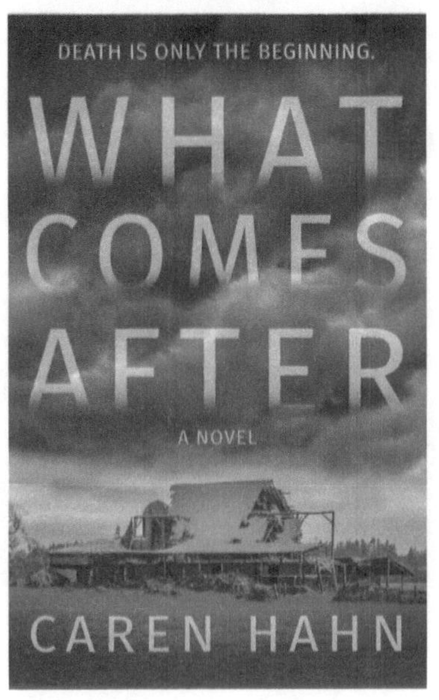

CAN JUSTICE BE SERVED FROM BEYOND THE GRAVE?

"deliciously suspenseful"

"had me hooked from the beginning"

"a few twists to keep the reader on their toes and a final chapter that brought me to tears"

What do a high-octane mommy blogger, a Wild West romance, and a [possibly] possessed antique doll have in common?

You can find them all in my FREE collection of short stories. Visit carenhahn.com to download your copy!

ACKNOWLEDGMENTS

Many creative types found that 2020 was a challenging year, where stress and uncertainty drained their ability to produce new art with typical vitality. Personally, I found it extremely challenging to find time to write with all six kids home from school for a solid year, and my husband facing a bout of pandemic-related unemployment. This is the only manuscript that I completed during that time, and in many ways it echoes the extreme contrasts we lived through in those days.

Light and dark, misery and joy, a victim of abuse preparing to welcome her own child into a loving family, Christmas celebrations tainted by an unthinkable crime, the juxtapositions go on and on, each highlighting the extreme of the other. Even the characters in this novel constitute both the best and worst of humanity, sometimes within a single person.

But the influence of COVID-19 didn't stop there. The performing arts have always been important to me, and they were one of the first casualties of the global pandemic. Maybe that's why it seemed fitting to feature choral music so prominently in this story. I never felt the absence as much as I did during the Christmas of 2020. No amount of playing holiday music in private made up for not being able to enjoy it as communities and congregations. So in those months of November and December 2020, when I was first drafting this story, it was a bit of an indulgence to escape into a world where communities could celebrate the season by gathering to enjoy live musical performances.

I have to give a mention to Carol Hall, the standard by which all music teachers will forever be measured in my mind. For decades, the elementary school Christmas concert in my hometown was a holiday staple, thanks to her dedication and countless hours of work to bring it to life every year. Many aspects of Grace's music program are patterned after the program Carol built, and from which so many children, like myself, benefitted.

Most of the locations in This Side of Dark are fictional, with select few exceptions. If you ever happen to be visiting the southern Oregon coast between Thanksgiving and New Year's, do yourself a favor and visit the holiday lights at Shore Acres. It's a magical experience inside the gardens and a tumultuous experience standing at the edge of the headland in the dark as the waves pound the cliffs.

Both snug and unsettling? Sounds about right.

I decided to lean into the religious themes in this story because I find that belief systems make up a critical part of so many people's life experience, but tend to be either absent or vilified in so much of storytelling today. Writing about small town Oregon life means there's something disingenuous about separating characters from their faith as if it doesn't impact their lives at all, so all three characters in this story have a strong religious belief. Does it spare them from the crises in their lives? No. Does it inform how they move through the world?

Absolutely. My goal isn't to make a case for or against religious belief. It's simply to create realistic characters who look like the people who would make up a community like Ellis Cove. And it's to respect that religious faith is an important part of how people experience life, especially when facing the darkest evils this life has to offer.

I appreciate my beta readers for this project, who included Crystal Brinkerhoff, Cori Hatch, Jenny Hahn, Andrew Hahn, and Cindy Schofield. It was a mess when you saw it, but improved thanks to your feedback. For sensitivity reasons, not all beta readers on this project can be publicly recognized, so to those important readers whose names will go unacknowledged, please know how much I appreciate you from the bottom of my heart. I hope I've honored the trust you've placed in me by sharing your stories. You know who you are.

I appreciate Rachel Pickett of Polished Copy Editing Service for cleaning it up and making it ready to put into your hands. Editors are essential to a great finished product. But when you have an editor who really gets your writing and is invested in your story, that's priceless.

Lastly, I want to mention that no book I've written is possible without the support of my husband, Andrew. And not just because he does most of my covers (though this one is shatteringly gorgeous and has quickly become one of my favorites.) More importantly, he believes in me and my work in a way that keeps me going in my darkest moments.

ABOUT THE AUTHOR

CAREN HAHN is a Mystery and Fantasy author of relationship-driven stories featuring empathetic characters who are exquisitely flawed. She grew up in a tiny logging community with more than its fair share of tragedy and violent crime, giving her early exposure to the dark side of life.

Caren graduated from Brigham Young University where—between courses on Humanities, English Lit, and Biblical Hebrew—she squeezed in as many Creative Writing classes as she could. She lives in the Pacific Northwest with her family.

Receive a free collection of short stories when you sign up to get updates at carenhahn.com.

Follow Caren on Amazon or BookBub to learn about new releases, and connect with her on social media to learn about all the bits that come in between.

www.ingramcontent.com/pod-product-compliance
Lightning Source LLC
Chambersburg PA
CBHW020522310726
48979CB00014B/2177/J